MOTHERS IN LOVE

THE GOOD, THE BAD, AND THE UNBELIEVABLE

Edited by Ron Hogan

Other books in this collection:

When Love Goes Bad
Falling In Love…Again
Forbidden Love
Losing It For Love
When Love Sizzles
Love In Strange Places
Bedroom Roulette
Women Undone

Second Acts Series– by Julia Dumont
Sleeping with Dogs and Other Lovers
Starstruck Romance and Other Hollywood Tails
Hearts Unleashed

Infinity Diaries – by Devin Morgan
Aris Returns, A Vampire Love Story
Aris Rising, The Court Of Vampires

Age of Eve: Return of the Nephilim – by D.M. Pratt

Mothers in Love

The Good, The Bad, and the Unbelievable

By Anonymous*

*The stories presented here were first published as "true stories"... at a time when it was necessary to hide the true identities of the women associated with these tales to avoid scandal. We have chosen to maintain the veil of the authors' anonymity to protect the innocent... and the not so innocent.

The timeless love stories from
True Romance and True Love live on.

Edited by Ron Hogan

A BROADLIT BOOK

BroadLit

April 2013

Published by

BroadLit ®
14011 Ventura Blvd.
Suite 206 E
Sherman Oaks, CA 91423

ISBN 978-0-9887627-9-4

Produced in the United States of America.

Visit us online at www.TruLOVEstories.com

This collection is dedicated to all of you who are looking for true love or have already found it.

TABLE OF CONTENTS

Introduction

While the most important relationship in the majority of *True Love* or *True Romance* stories is between a man and a woman, no couple is an island, and the people around them can exert influences in all sorts of different ways. Over the decades, motherhood has been a powerful theme in both magazines, one that can be used in different ways to address a variety of women's experiences. There are so many stories we could have chosen for this anthology; these fourteen offer a representative—and, I hope, very entertaining—sample.

The first batch of stories focuses on women who've become single moms through abandonment or widowhood. While these two magazines were ultimately promoting an ideal of marriage and family, as the divorce rate went up one-parent households became increasingly common, and it made less and less sense to potentially offend readers who were trying to raise children on their own by suggesting there was something shameful about being a single mom. There were limits, of course; having a baby out of wedlock, especially if you were a teenager, was still strongly discouraged. Overall, though, you'll see a solid respect for single mothers and the work they do, even if it's linked to a desire to see them married again at the first best opportunity.

It wasn't always the woman who brought children into a relationship, though, so we'll take a look at a young stepmother's dilemma—trying to establish a healthy marriage while negotiating a new relationship with a reluctant child.

After a brief detour into domestic hardship, we'll consider how a struggling marriage can be tested by a handsome stranger—and how children can force us to remember our priorities. Then we'll meet a group of women for whom motherhood is a source of emotional turbulence. Some of them made the painful decision to abandon their first children because they were afraid they couldn't provide them with a good home; some of them are so fixated on the idea of being a mom that it drives them to desperate acts.

So far, the mothers have also been the stars of the story—but what happens when they become the antagonists? As I was putting this collection together, I kept an eye out for stories about women who have to deal with mothers trying to "fix" their lives for them. Sometimes their moms have good intentions, but often it's a case of selfish interference. Either way, it's up to the young women to (respectfully) stand up to their mothers and make their own relationship choices.

As you read these stories, you may notice a few common elements. Many times, if the women narrating the stories talk about their own childhoods, you'll learn about how difficult things were for them growing up, and how they're determined life will be better for their own children. It's an aspirational theme that extends beyond motherhood into much of *True Love* and *True Romance*; heroines frequently pull themselves up from the edge of poverty into relatively more stable working class or even middle class lives. (I say "relatively" because economic downturns are a regularly occurring threat; their domestic happiness depends on their ability to make it through the hard times.)

You might also notice how young many of the mothers in these stories are; it's not unusual for them to have their first children soon after graduating college or even high school. As with the aspirational messages, this tells us something about the audience that the two magazines were trying to reach—how they worked to create stories that both resonated with their readers' experiences and gave them hope for greater happiness. That hope was never an idle fantasy, though. Think about how many stories end with women realizing they've learned a valuable lesson about coping with adversity, and how they'll need to find the strength to apply that lesson over and over again in order for their marriages, and their families, to flourish. That message comes through over and over, whether it's about a woman trying to raise a child on her own or a woman who's desperate to have a child, a woman who's afraid the spark has gone out of her marriage or a woman who's still struggling to get out from under her mother's thumb.

Our own lives may not be as extravagantly melodramatic as the stories in this collection—with some of them, I would definitely hope they aren't! But I suspect many of us will be able to see something like our experiences in their broader emotional outlines.

SNAKES, RATS, AND LITTLE BOYS—OH, MY!

It's all in a day's work for this harried-but-coping single mom!

Meet Jan Halpern, a young single mother who's just bought her first home; it's a bit of a fixer-upper, and she doesn't have a lot to spend, so she's doing it all on her own—all part of the effort to make a good life for her son, Theo. "My childhood was awful and so I really have no idea how a good mother is supposed to act," Jan confesses. That's actually a huge understatement. It turns out she grew up in homeless shelters and the run-down apartments of her alcoholic mother's "boyfriends," and she's fought hard to achieve her success, even overcoming her ex-husband's walking out on her shortly after Theo's birth.

There's one thing that's carried over from her childhood suffering, though, and that's a deep fear of rats. So when she hears scratching noises in the walls of her home, she calls on Theo's teacher Mr. Anderson for help.... and of course he turns out to be as patient and helpful as he is handsome. And great with children—watch how quickly he establishes himself as the best father figure Theo's ever had.

As the realtor handed me the keys to my new, little house, I was definitely beaming with pride. In my entire life, I'd never lived in an actual *house*. And the fact that I'd earned the money to buy this one made myself, made the moment even sweeter.

Though I sometimes wished I had a man to share times like that with, I'd learned to savor my independence.

"This is the key to our new life," I told my young son, Theo. Taking his hand, I left the realtor's office and walked to the do-it-yourself moving shop a few doors down to rent a truck for the move from our apartment into our house. A neighbor's teenage sons had already agreed to help me move what little furniture and belongings we had for some spending money and pizza and soda for lunch.

Everything was boxed and ready to go and things went smoothly from there. Theo played in our new backyard on the swing set while the teenagers and I hauled the boxes and furniture from the truck into the house. When we were done, I returned the truck and Theo and I went home to start unpacking the boxes and get settled. This little house was a dream come true and living there was going to be like living in a mansion compared to the places I'd lived before.

But I soon learned that home ownership has its downside as well as its upside. I expected to do the yard work and bought the previous owner's lawnmower and gardening tools since they were moving to a condo. I was smart enough to know that things would occasionally break, but since the house wasn't new, this seemed to happen regularly. The previous owners were old and must've let things slide since they planned to move. At times, like when the pipe under the kitchen sink burst, I wished I had a man to help out around the house. But since I didn't, and my budget didn't allow me to hire professionals, I had to learn how to do things by myself. Thankfully, there was a do-it-yourself plumbing supply store nearby and the people there would explain things to me when they sold me the parts I needed.

In September, Theo enrolled in the local public elementary school that was only a few blocks from the house. He'd already met some of the neighborhood children before he got there, so he felt very comfortable on the first day of school. There was even an after-school program right at the school, so childcare was easier than before. Everything finally seemed to be going smoothly until the night before Back-to-School Night, which was to take place shortly before Theo's birthday.

"Mom, can I have a snake for my birthday?" Theo asked as he did his homework at the kitchen table while I made dinner.

"May I please have a snake?" I corrected, stalling. One of my teachers was a stickler for good grammar and I'd picked up the habit of saying things properly. I knew I'd gotten as far as I had partly because I can communicate well.

A snake, I thought. I'm definitely not thrilled with the idea. As a single mother, snakes are things I don't want to have to deal with. Yet my son is so sweet and good and never really asks for anything. I hated to turn him down. "I don't know, honey," I said. "Snakes are just so slimy." I continued to cut up the vegetables for the stew I was preparing as we talked. Theo normally doesn't like vegetables, but he really loves my stew. The good thing about it is that we can have the leftovers for another night and that means I have more time to spend with him instead of having to cook again.

"Snakes aren't slimy, Mom. I already told you we have ten of them in terrariums in our classroom. If we earn bonus points for being good or doing good work, Mr. Anderson lets us take them out and play with them. I'm sure he'll let me take one out so you can feel it during Back-to-School Night. Then you can see for yourself."

"All right, honey. I'll do it," I reluctantly agreed.

My childhood was awful and so I really have no idea how a good mother is supposed to act. Still, I try as hard as I can to be a good mother to Theo by spending time with him, taking him to museums, helping him with his homework, and even doing things I don't particularly want to do. I was certain that the mere thought of a snake in my house would probably give me nightmares.

A few nights later, we went to Back-to-School Night. My mother never participated in any of my school activities. Actually, when I was little, I sometimes didn't even get enrolled in school if she couldn't pull it together. That would never happen to Theo.

Theo's teacher, Mr. Anderson, welcomed us and told us his plans for the school year. When he was finished, Theo gave me the "grand tour" of his classroom. He was so proud and excited as he showed me all of his work and introduced me to his new friends. It was nice to meet the other parents, as well. Many of Theo's papers and drawings were hung up on the bulletin boards with big A's written on them. I was very proud of him.

Since there were so many terrariums in the room, it would've been hard to miss Theo's beloved snakes. He asked permission and was allowed to take one out to let me touch it. Unfortunately for me, Theo was right. I timidly touched one and learned that snakes are indeed smooth and dry--not slimy at all. Still, those tongues darting in and out of their mouths made me uncomfortable, and I wasn't exactly thrilled with the idea of one living in my house. While Theo was happily occupied with his friends, I spoke to his handsome, charismatic teacher, Mr. Anderson.

"I'm Jan Halpern, Theo's mother. Theo absolutely loves your class." "Thank you. I love having him in the class," he said, smiling. His white teeth flashed brightly against his dark skin. I couldn't help but notice his kind, brown eyes. "He's a great kid, and as you can see from his work, he's doing very well. He even likes to help his classmates when they don't understand something. He's earned more bonus points than anyone else so far this year."

"That's so he can play with your snakes! He's a good boy, anyway, but he'd really like a snake. From what he's told me, I know that snakes eat rats and I've been afraid of rats since I was a little girl," I admitted, shivering a bit. "Even if I were going to feed it to a snake, I couldn't bring myself to buy a rat, much less actually bring it into my house. Isn't there some sort of prepackaged, dried snake food you can buy? You know, snake kibble or something like that?"

His eyes twinkled mischievously and he said, "Snakes are carnivores, my dear Ms. Halpern. Even sushi is much too well-done for them. They prefer their food alive, whole, and moving."

"That's unbelievably gross and exactly what I was afraid of."

"It's not gross, it's just one of nature's little variations," he said. "Some of my students' parents have actually found the process of snakes eating to be very interesting. Actually, snakes probably think it's weird that we cook our food."

The thought of snakes thinking anything made me laugh. "They probably do, but I still think I'm going to have to disappoint Theo on this."

"You might not have to; there's another possibility. Some of the water snakes you can buy eat live goldfish. You haven't been afraid of goldfish since you were little, have you?" he teased.

"No, I haven't. I wouldn't mind having a bowl of goldfish in the house. And I'm pretty sure I could deal with sacrificing the occasional goldfish."

"That's great. See, if you look hard enough, most problems have reasonable solutions." He smiled.

I smiled back at Mr. Anderson, impressed with his positive attitude. I couldn't help but look at his bare ring finger as he handed me a folder from a stack on his desk. "So many of my students end up convincing their parents to let them get snakes that I've written an informational packet. This will help explain the art and science of raising happy, healthy pet snakes."

"Thank you, I think," I said, still not sure that I wanted to be getting into what I was thinking about getting into. "Even though I'm a major sissy, I don't want Theo to be one, too."

He laughed. "We're all sissies about something. For me, it's roller coasters."

"Really?"

"Absolutely. You're not too much of a sissy if you're even considering buying him a snake. Don't worry; snakes really are low-maintenance pets. They don't eat very often and they don't shed hair all over the house! If you have any problems with Theo or the new snake, call me. I'd be happy to help."

"Thank you," I said, shaking his hand. He had a nice, warm hand-shake and a warm smile. *Theo is lucky to have such a caring teacher,* I thought. I had a teacher like him in high school who was a mentor to me. Without that teacher's help and encouragement, I would never have even *thought* about college and I wouldn't have known how to get the scholarship that made it all possible for me. I didn't even want to imagine what would've become of me.

But Theo's Mr. Anderson is a lot better looking than my teacher was, I thought.

That Saturday morning, I took Theo to a pet store that specialized in reptiles and fish. I bought him a water snake and a small terrarium with gravel, a small bowl for water, a small, hollow log for the snake to hide in, and a warming rock. I also bought a bowl with a few goldfish and some goldfish food. We named the snake Sammy. Theo was absolutely thrilled; I was guardedly tolerant.

Later in the afternoon, Theo had a cake-and-ice cream birthday party with a few friends. The children played simple games and had a good time together. For favors, we gave out bags of plastic bugs, snakes, and lizards which were a big hit.

After the other children left, we had a simple supper of canned soup and grilled cheese sandwiches. At bedtime, Sammy was in the terrarium on Theo's bureau, and Theo was one tired, happy little boy. "This was absolutely positively the best day of my life, Mom," he said drowsily.

"I'm glad. Happy birthday, Theo."

By the time I kissed him good night, he was already asleep.

I was tired, too, but not quite ready to go to sleep. The day had been fun for the children, but it amounted to another workday for me and I was still wired up. I made myself a cup of herbal tea and carried it and a magazine to the comfy, floral-print living room sofa.

I loved how quiet it was in my little house. There was no noise from the neighbors to keep us awake—only the sounds of birds in the morning and crickets at night got my attention on our tranquil, little cul-de-sac.

Theo's birthday, combined with an article in the magazine entitled "Men Who Leave," made me think of my ex-husband, Mark. Now he was a fine looking man: tall and broad shouldered like Mr. Anderson. But that was about where the similarities between the two men ended.

We met in college. Jan and Mark. To us, our names sounded so cute together. We got married after college and waited for a few years to start our family. Soon after Theo was born, though, Mark left for work one day and never returned. "I won't be coming back," Mark's deep, bass voice said on our answering machine. "I just wasn't cut out to be a husband and father. Good-bye, baby. Love you."

I didn't erase the message for a year. There was another message after it, so I couldn't instantly redial to see where he'd called from. I couldn't understand how he could love me and then leave me. But then again, I should've been able to since that's the story of my life.

It's impossible to describe how horrible receiving that message was for me, but thank goodness he was considerate enough to have left it. I was still absolutely devastated by the fact that he'd deserted us, but that message had saved me from tormenting myself and wondering if he'd been in an accident, had amnesia, or was dead.

Even so, I tried to find him. I hoped to convince him that we could work things out. I even hired a private investigator who I couldn't afford. But Mark had completely vanished, leaving no forwarding address or phone number. It's amazing how someone can for all intents and purposes disappear from the face of the earth without too much trouble if they really want to.

My mother died during my first year in college and I never knew my father. After the grandmother who raised him died, Mark was shuffled around to different foster homes. He'd lost all contact with his abusive biological parents years before I met him. When we met and began talking about our pasts, I thought he was a kindred soul—alone like I was. I wanted to finally be connected to someone I loved and to be part of a real family. Evidently, Mark didn't feel the same way or simply didn't know how to do that, so he ran. Fortunately, he left me with Theo, the best gift I've ever received. So with Theo as my family, I got on with my life.

By the time I'd read as far as the love story in the magazine, my eyes began to close. Finally exhausted from my busy work week and the preparation for the day's festivities, I washed up and got into bed. I'd just fallen into a deep sleep when an annoying scratching noise that I recognized from long ago woke me with a start. My heart pounded and my throat tightened. I pulled my covers tightly around me, trying to protect myself.

Our house is pretty isolated. Our street was named Town's End Drive because at the time it contained the last group of houses on the outskirts of town. Nearly twenty years after our house was built, though, the community outgrew its boundaries. Houses have since been built in other areas of town and excavations had recently started on a new subdivision near ours. Our street name wouldn't change, but we'd no longer be at the end of the town. Fortunately, due to local ordinances, the construction began after I was awake and ended before I got home from work. Other than more dust in the house, it hadn't been a problem.

At Back-to-School Night I'd told Mr. Anderson that I'm a sissy, but since Theo's birth, I'd been stronger than I ever imagined I could be. I had to be; I had no choice in the matter. Therefore, I tried to convince myself that the annoying scratching noise that had woken me up was a tree branch brushing up against my window. When I looked out, though, everything was perfectly still. There was no wind moving any of the branches. Taking my trusty, old baseball bat out from under my bed, I turned on the front porch light and peered out the window, hoping to see an opossum or a raccoon, but no person or creature appeared to be out there. I repeated the procedure as I looked into the backyard. Nothing was moving out there, either. Satisfied that there was no prowler, I checked the locks on the doors and windows again and got back into bed.

Just as I was dozing off I heard that awful scratching sound again. It wasn't a loud sound. Actually, it was a relatively soft sound, like the annoying drip of a faucet. While wishing it were only that, I heard the unmistakable and dreaded sound of tiny feet up in the attic running across my bedroom ceiling. My nightmarish, impoverished childhood flashed through my mind, and I was horrified.

When we weren't living on the streets, my mother, a rarely employed alcoholic, usually housed us in infested tenement rooms or her "boyfriend's" apartments when we couldn't stay in some sort of shelter... She did her best to take care of me, but she could barely take care of herself. Growing up with her for a mother was a nightmare. I lived in dread of the rats and roaches and parasites and the people who made my childhood so miserable. I thought I'd moved far away from my frightening past, but I shuddered with the realization that my cozy, little, safe home had been invaded by rats—horrible, disgusting, biting, germ-carrying rats!

I turned on the lights and didn't sleep for the rest of the night.

With the help of the *Happy Homeowner Handbook*, I'd taught myself how to mow a lawn, put in sprinklers, paint rooms, hang curtains, and fix broken pipes. I could probably spray for bugs myself, but I simply couldn't deal with this on my own. Because of my fear of rats, I needed professional help for this problem. I'd somehow have to stretch my budget to pay whatever it cost.

At daybreak I searched the phone-book for an exterminator. I just had to find one. I called every name in the book. Since it was Sunday, no one answered. Some had answering machines, though, and I began to panic as I left message after message on each company's machine.

I tried to convince myself that I was a self-reliant, grown-up person. Even though I'd be extremely embarrassed to admit my problem, I knew I could simply go to the hardware store and buy traps or poison. I could ask someone there what to do. Heck, there might even be a chapter in my book. But I couldn't make myself look up "rats" in the index. And after what I'd heard the night before, I knew there was no way I could make myself open the attic door to set the traps. Still, I absolutely couldn't spend another sleepless night and still be able to function at work and take care of my son.

Theo must've been pretty tired from the day before because he slept later than usual that morning. "Good morning, Theo," I said to him, smiling, as he came in already dressed.

Unaware of my distress, Theo came over to me, handed me Mr. Anderson's snake information packet, and asked, "When are we supposed to feed Sammy again, Mom?"

"Not for a while," I said, trying to sound calmer than I felt. "The man in the pet store said that he fed him before we bought him. Remember?"

"Yeah. I know snakes don't eat as often as people do, but I thought if I was hungry for breakfast, he would be, too."

Smiling, I ruffled Theo's dark, curly hair. "Why don't we have a picnic this morning?" I said.

"That sounds like fun."

I poured him a glass of juice and gave him some cereal and milk outside on the picnic table. I was definitely glad that I keep the cereal in plastic containers instead of their original boxes. It meant I didn't have to worry about what might have gotten into it.

I didn't get anything for me to eat because I was simply too nervous to be hungry. I kept hoping the phone would ring and one of the exterminators would come to save me. As Theo ate, I glanced at the packet and noticed Mr. Anderson's name and home phone number on the cover.

Snakes eat rats, I thought. *Mr. Anderson could feed mine to his snakes. And he told me to call if I have a problem. Get a grip, Jan; you're extremely sleep-deprived. The man wasn't talking about personal problems when he said that to you. You absolutely cannot call him. You're a big girl; you can deal with this yourself. Besides, he's not an exterminator—he's a teacher.*

Too panicked to heed my better judgment, I said, "Theo, let's call Mr. Anderson and double-check how we'll know when Sammy is hungry."

"That's a great idea, Mom!"

I picked up the phone and dialed the number on the packet. Mr. Anderson hadn't been wearing a wedding ring, but many men don't. I couldn't help wondering if there was a Mrs. Anderson who'd answer and be annoyed to have her weekend interrupted early in the morning by a hysterical parent. I was having second thoughts and was about to hang up when Mr. Anderson cheerfully answered.

"Hello."

"Hi, this is Jan Halpern, Theo's mom. Sorry to call so early on a Sunday morning," I said hesitantly. Looking at my watch, I realized how extremely inconsiderate I was being.

"No problem. Did you end up buying Theo a snake for his birthday? He was pretty excited about it on Friday." Mr. Anderson sounded genuinely interested and excited about it.

"Yes, I bought him a water snake. Thank you for the suggestion. We named it Sammy."

"That's great. Theo must be thrilled."

"He is. Can you hold on a minute?"

"Sure."

"Theo, stay out and finish your breakfast. I'll be right back out."

"Okay, Mom. Say hi to Mr. Anderson."

Carrying the phone into the house, my eyes darted around the room, searching for possible vermin. I spoke softly. "Look, I'm sorry to bother you on the weekend, but something terrible has happened. I can usually take care of my problems myself, but I just don't know what to do this time." I was rambling and my voice was high-pitched and nervous.

"You sound panicked. What's the problem? Are you having trouble with the snake in the house?"

"Everything's okay with the snake. He's actually kind of pretty. We got a terrarium and a warming rock and goldfish to feed him. But the problem is . . . well. . . ." I lowered my voice even more, not wanting to even say it out loud. "I think I have rats in my house."

His voice was compassionate and not teasing at all. "And you've been afraid of rats since you were a little girl."

"Yes. Yes I have. I just don't know what to do. I called every single exterminator in the telephone book. They're all closed. I left messages on their machines, but nobody's called me back. When Theo asked me about feeding Sammy and showed me the snake packet with your name on it, I called. I really shouldn't have. It's totally inappropriate. I'm sorry I even bothered you about this."

"It's okay, calm down. I'd be happy to come over and help you out."

"I couldn't ask you to do that. I shouldn't have called. I really don't want to impose."

"Please, stop worrying so much about it. You have no way of knowing this, but I'm an Eagle Scout. It's my sworn duty to do good deeds and I'm way below my quota for this month. Tell me where you live and I'll come over."

"Bless you. You're a wonderful person. We live on Town's End Drive. Number 1023."

"Oh, you're out near that new housing development they're building," he surmised. "Poor little rats. The excavations for the new houses must've destroyed their habitat. They're probably just as unhappy as you are and looking for somewhere new to live. I'll stop at the hardware store for supplies and be right over."

"How can I ever thank you? I'll pay for whatever you buy. I'll even make you lunch."

"I'd trap mountain lions for you for a good, home-cooked meal. Hold on tight. I'll be right there."

Finished with his breakfast, Theo brought his bowl and cups in and I washed them immediately. I. hadn't heard the scratching sounds since the sun came up. The rats must've tired themselves out by keeping me up all night. My eyes still darted around, though, just in case.

Then I thought about what to cook for Mr. Anderson. My mother hadn't cared much for food, preferring to drink her meals. Out of necessity, I'd taught myself how to cook and I'm pretty good at it.

Happy to have something to occupy myself with, I took the chicken I'd been planning to cook for dinner out of the fridge. I started to open a cabinet door to get a pan out when I heard a soft, squeaking noise coming from somewhere in the kitchen cabinets. I bit my lip and tried not to scream or frighten Theo. Practically throwing the chicken back into the fridge, I quickly went outside with him to wait for Mr. Anderson. Having no choice, I explained the problem to Theo, who was much more interested than alarmed.

"Ratman at your service, ma'am!" Mr. Anderson said cheerfully as he unloaded a toolbox, a ladder, traps, and wire mesh from his shiny, brown pick-up truck.

"Hi, Mr. Anderson," Theo said, smiling. "What's all this stuff? I want to help catch the rats! Are you gonna shoot them?"

"Slow down, Theo. First of all, I don't have a gun. Second of all, that's not how you solve this or any other problem. Give me a minute to get organized here and I'll explain it all to you."

"Okay."

"Thank you so much for coming," I said.

While keeping his distance, Theo continued to inspect what Mr. Anderson had brought. Once he'd finished unloading everything from the truck, Mr. Anderson explained, "We'll trap the ones already in the house and put mesh over any openings near the eaves and crawl spaces to keep any others from coming in here in the future."

"That sounds like a good plan," I said. "I had no idea what to do. Look, I'm going to have to apologize to you right now. I was going to start cooking lunch, but I thought I heard some rats in the kitchen cabinets somewhere."

"Oh, well, so much for my home-cooked meal! Where did the noise seem to be coming from?"

"It sounded like the drawers under the cutting board."

"That's a good place to start, then," he said, pulling on some thick work gloves. "I'll go take a look."

"May I come, too?" Theo asked.

Seeing my panicked expression, he said, "Why don't you stay out here and keep your mom company for now? That would be a big help."

"All right."

Mr. Anderson was in the house for just a few minutes, but it seemed like hours to me. Finally, he called out. "If it's okay with your mom, Theo, would you please come in and bring me the cage and the towel I left out there?"

I nodded my approval; sure his teacher would keep him safe. "Sure, Mr. Anderson," Theo said, happily joining him in the house.

They were in there for a while longer. When they came back out, Mr. Anderson took the cage, which he'd covered with a beach towel so I couldn't see what was inside, out to his truck.

Running over to me, Theo said excitedly, "Mom, it's so cool! A mama mouse had babies in that big drawer in the bottom of the cabinet where you keep the grocery bags. She was smart. She made a nest out of ripped up grocery bags. We think we got all of the mice out and Mr. Anderson said he's going to keep them, if it's all right with you."

"That's fine with me," I said, sighing in relief.

"They're just field mice looking for food and shelter," Mr. Anderson explained. "They're not dirty, diseased city rats. They're country mice—clean and perfectly harmless."

"If you say so," I said, relieved that he'd solved my problem. "I still have a problem accepting that any rat or mouse is clean and harmless."

"Trust me," Mr. Anderson said. "You changed your mind about snakes, didn't you?"

"Yes, but old fears are hard to get over. How would you like to go on a roller coaster?"

"With the right person to hold my hand, I could probably get used to it."

Suddenly feeling shy from the flirty direction the conversation was taking, I looked away. Joining in the conversation, Theo said, "I'd go on a roller coaster with you."

Looking over his head at each other, we began to laugh.

"Thanks. Theo," he said. "Maybe one day you, your mother, and I will do that. But today, we have a job to do. Let's get working."

"Okay."

"I'll go wash everything in the cabinets while you do that," I said, not caring how clean Mr. Anderson claimed mice are. I washed as they put traps in the attic just in case and hammered wire screens around any possible entrances around the foundation of the house. Before he started securing the upper part of the house, the two of them came in.

"I'd like you to be out there to help hold the ladder," Mr. Anderson said.

"No problem. Is height the aspect of roller coaster rides that you really don't like?"

"And falling from heights," he said, grinning.

"Got it. I could go up there while you hold the ladder," I offered.

"I'll be fine."

Theo's stomach rumbled. "Theo, are you hungry?" I asked him.

"Yes."

"That boy must be having a growth spurt," I said. "He always seems to be hungry. Would pizza do instead of a homemade lunch?"

"Of course. I'll finish up when we get back."

We ate at the local pizza parlor. I had a discount coupon. I felt very comfortable sharing a meal with Mr. Anderson and Theo. I couldn't believe that I had an appetite after what had happened.

While Theo played a few video games, I began to relax. Then I couldn't seem to stop talking. I told Mr. Anderson—Miles—about the rats in the tenements, about Mark leaving when Theo was born, and about how hard it was for me to leave Theo with a babysitter when I went to work.

"You've come a long way since then. Jan; you're successful, you've raised a wonderful boy, and you've made a lovely home for the both of you."

"Thank you." I picked up the check. Miles put his hand over mine; his teasing expression at Back-to-School Night had been replaced by a look of frank, masculine interest.

Theo must've run out of change, because he suddenly sat back down at the table. I couldn't decide if it was good or bad timing on his part.

"I'm treating today," Miles said. Before I could protest, he asked, "May I please have a rain check for that home-cooked meal?"

"Yes, you may," I answered. "As far as I'm concerned, you may have as many rain checks as you want for helping me out today."

"I'd like that," he replied.

As Miles and I gazed into each other's eyes, Theo grinned and said, "Mr. Anderson sure knows the right way to ask a question, doesn't he, Mommy?"

"Yes, he does, honey."

As we headed home together, I suspected that he had all the right answers, too. THE END

Since Her Hubby Left Her, She's Been-
DOWN AT THE END OF LONELY STREET

In the previous story, Jan's failed marriage was safely back in the dim past, but Genie's relationship is just now coming apart—even as she informs her husband that she's pregnant with their second child. Luckily, she lives in an apartment building full of sympathetic neighbors who are eager to help her with her four-year-old son.

How is it that abandoned wives in pulp romance stories almost always manage to find the most perfect men—handsome, attentive, great with kids—the second time around? The one to keep an eye on here is James, a widowed veterinarian with "twinkling blue eyes" who lives next door and is always on hand to smooth over one of her son's anxious outbursts or to deliver some extra groceries when Genie's paycheck is stretched too thin.

Genie's plight in this story, at least, feels a bit more realistic. Jan's miserable background is almost like the dark half of a distant fairy tale; she keeps telling us about what a horrible childhood she had, but she's doing pretty well now, and with very little explanation of how she turned things around. When Genie's husband walks out, though, it's only a few months before her savings evaporate, and though she's pulling her life back together, she's still "earning just enough for rent and groceries" for herself and two small children. Although she doesn't lay it out explicitly, the arrival of James could ultimately mean a lot more than just a loving partner for her and a strong male role model for her kids.

"Having a second child won't make any of our problems go away, Genie. Don't forget, you thought you could change me with the first one."

I bit my lower lip, willing myself to endure in silence, to not lose my composure while our son, Jonathan, could hear us.

Another surge of anger welled up inside of me. Was it just out of spite toward me that Patrick had never been the kind of father our son deserved?

My husband let his cutting words hang in the air. As I wordlessly studied his face—the defiance in the thrust of his chin, the challenge in his cold gray eyes—I couldn't help but be reminded of our son, Jonathan, when he was being disobedient. Patrick was daring me to react. What did he want from, me? Hot anger? Tearful pleas? I wouldn't give him the satisfaction.

To my relief, my determination prevailed. My face remained impassive, ultimately forcing him to speak first.

"You wouldn't want to hold together our marriage just because you're expecting?"

I clenched my fists, my short nails digging painfully into my palms. But my tone was flat.

"Of course not."

No, I didn't want Patrick to stay with me only because of the baby. Or because of Jonathan. I wanted him to do it for us, for all we had once meant to one another, and could mean again. But I knew that I couldn't bear to single-handedly patch our relationship back together again another time, only to watch it come apart at the seams all over again. The words to hold him back, to keep him tied to us, would no longer come to my lips.

Patrick waited in vain for me to beg, plead, rant, and rave. Finally, his expression softened. I stiffened as he leaned over to brush his lips against my forehead.

He is really going to leave us.

Only when the door shut behind him did I spot our four-year-old son huddled behind the couch, silent tears staining his flushed cheeks.

"Oh, Jonathan," I murmured, crouching down to embrace him.

But he wanted nothing of me. His sobs finally broke free as he pushed me away and fled to the privacy of his bedroom.

As if the gesture could ease his suffering, I stood with my palm pressed against his closed door, feeling his pain sear through my heart.

Patrick had always hated our apartment. While I found our sunny little place cozy, he found it claustrophobic. But what he hated most of all about it was the lack of privacy. Admittedly, the walls were woefully thin and, with our shared entrance, our comings and goings were always observed. And the building primarily housed retirees with a lot of time on their hands to devote to keeping tabs on us. But, particularly after Patrick started spending fewer hours at home, I privately found it reassuring knowing that I could always count on one of our neighbors being within hearing range should Jonathan or I ever need anything. Although we all remained just polite acquaintances, I sensed that they cared about me and Jonathan, and their presence made me feel more secure.

And they didn't let me down. Patrick moving out couldn't have gone unobserved in our intimate apartment building. Nor, no doubt, could my puffy red eyes, or Jonathan's' uncharacteristically sober demeanor, have escaped their notice. They let me know, in their silently supportive way, that they were there for us both.

A week after Patrick left, I was forced to go back to working full-time at the bank, as I had before my son was born. Jonathan is a social child and had always enjoyed going to day care in the afternoons; but that first morning, he threw himself onto the floor in the hallway outside our door and had a tantrum, refusing to go.

With all of the disruption that our lives had gone through in recent days, I didn't want him to have to adjust to a full day of day care any more than he did. But what choice did I have? I had to put food on our table. My eyes stinging with unshed tears, I spoke to him gently, trying to keep my tone light and remind him of all his friends, of all the fun things he would be doing while I worked at the bank.

He started to cry. Not loud, insistent wails, but low, half-resigned sobs. I wavered, against all logic, my heart breaking. Just then Chrissie, a friendly redhead next door with a five-year-old, stuck her head out of her door and asked, out of the blue, if Jonathan would enjoy spending the morning with her son. She insisted that I would be the one doing *her* a favor, since my son was such a good influence on C.J., her little boy.

Jonathan's face immediately brightened, this time with a child's hope and infectious enthusiasm. I could have cried with gratitude.

Particularly in those first months after Patrick left, it seemed to me, that my friends and family were always coming through just as the enormous reality of responsibility threatened to overwhelm me.

One unlikely lifesaver turned out to be Dr. James Burnett; a veterinarian who had his practice downstairs and apartment next door. Everyone referred to him respectfully as "Doc Burnett." With his graying temples, neatly trimmed beard, and wire-rimmed glasses, he didn't look like a "Jim," and certainly not a "Jimmy." Actually, he reminded me of Sigmund Freud, although I didn't think that the famous psychoanalyst had been over six feet tall, or blessed with such twinkling blue eyes.

The doctor had always been friendly in a quiet, but genuine way, even during the eight months he'd spent nursing his wife.

The illness had reduced her from a vibrant, gregarious woman to a frail, yellowed skeleton, finally taking her life two years ago. Yet even as he mourned, he had never ceased to be a thoughtful neighbor to all of us.

One day, when I had gone to pick Jonathan up from day care, I found my son distraught on the front steps, sobbing so hard that he had to gulp for air. An older boy had told him that divorced daddies always stopped visiting their children. Six weeks had passed since Patrick had last come to see Jonathan, and I privately feared that he might stop visiting altogether.

"Is Daddy ever coming back to live with us?" His big, brown eyes looked pleadingly up to mine. I sat down and slipped my arm around his small shoulders.

"I don't think so, pumpkin," I murmured with a weak smile.

The force of Jonathan propelling his little body into my arms almost knocked me over. For some time we just held each other as we cried, gently rocking back and forth.

As if by telepathy, Doc Burnett was there to meet us on the front walkway as we returned to the apartment. The friendly giant of a man kneeled down to the level of my son.

"Jonathan, I'm afraid that I need your help. There are far too many animals down in my office to tend to. I just can't pet them properly all by myself."

"Mommy, can I? Can I go with the doc?" His eyelashes were still wet from tears, but his face was aglow.

Doc Burnett stood up and turned to me, the light in his blue eyes dancing. "Could you possibly spare your boy for an hour or two to help me out with this emergency?"

I beamed back at him, but feigned reluctance with my voice. "Well. Dr. Burnett, if it's *truly* an emergency."

Within three months after Patrick's departure, the little money I had salted away had been depleted. My next paycheck wasn't coming for another two weeks. With the growing baby's appetite raging inside of me, I had managed to eat our kitchen cabinets bare, except for a jar of mustard and four potatoes sprouting scary-looking roots.

Jonathan and I were staring at them, and I was wondering what I could do with potatoes that I hadn't already done in the last four weeks, when we heard a knock at the door. Doc Burnett stood in the doorway, his generous arms so loaded with groceries that they almost obscured his face.

He set the bags down on the counter. "I must be experiencing the first stage of Alzheimer's. I forgot that I did all my grocery shopping two days ago. I bought everything on the list twice. Now the food will all spoil—unless you can make use of it."

I immediately saw through his pretense, but we were too hungry—and too sick of potatoes—to play proud. My son jumped up and down as I unloaded the groceries, mentally identifying each item as I did so.

Grape jelly . . . hot dogs . . alphabet soup . . . macaroni and cheese . . . sugared cereal. . .

"Is this the way you normally eat, Dr. Burnett?" I couldn't suppress a smile.

"You know what they say. Eat young, stay young," he said, making a face at Jonathan.

"Oh, is that what they say?" I teased. And, despite my empty bank account, despite the electricity bill that needed to be paid and the muffler that needed to be repaired, despite the fact that I felt like I had a blue-ribbon watermelon bursting out of my belly—I laughed. I laughed for the first time since Patrick had left. Jonathan, without needing to understand why, began giggling himself in his endearingly hysterical way. And soon Doc Burnett joined us in his heartwarming baritone.

In the last couple months before my daughter was born, things started to fall into place. I found a job conducting telephone surveys out of the apartment, so that I would be able to spend more time with Jonathan and stay home with the baby once it came. With that modest income and the occasional child support payment from Patrick, I was earning just enough for rent and groceries. I crossed my fingers, allowed myself a sigh of relief, and finally started to look forward to the birth of my daughter.

Ruth took after her daddy—the curly hair, the full mouth, the large eyes I knew would turn into a rich brown, and, unfortunately, the chronically unhappy expression. Jonathan had been an easy baby; raising him had done nothing to prepare me for his colicky sister. Ruth's cries kept me pacing the apartment day and night, bouncing her on my shoulder and humming lullabies. It was the most difficult period of my life.

But it seemed that whenever I started to feel as if I couldn't take a second more of Ruth's howling, Doc Burnett would appear at the door and beg to take his "precious angel" out in her stroller. He silenced my protests by insisting that his motive was purely selfish: Pretty women found inept men with babies irresistible.

I laughed. And agreed. Most gratefully.

Finally, precisely one day after Ruth turned six months old, I woke up and looked at my bedside clock in shock. It was eight o'clock in the morning. My daughter was still sleeping after ten hours! I bounded out of bed, almost giddy with excitement. After reassuring myself that the baby was indeed fine, I made Jonathan a quick breakfast and headed for the shower. I lingered long under the pounding spray, luxuriating in a long-needed shower massage. Having the time to apply makeup for the first time since Ruth was born, I gave in to the impulse, pausing to study the thirty-one-year-old face in the mirror. The reflection looked much younger than I had been feeling. And prettier.

I realized that the day Patrick left, I had stopped caring about whether or not I looked attractive. All that had mattered to me had been taking care of the kids, so I let all other sides of myself that weren't bound directly with my role as mother go into hibernation.

But my old, baggy sweats wouldn't do today. Instead, I selected a slim denim jumper and soft peach blouse. As my hands absentmindedly smoothed down the skirt before the full-length mirror, a sudden flash of Doc Burnett's disarming smile popped into my mind. But Ruth's morning howl promptly distracted me from any further thoughts of my neighbor.

That evening I unpacked groceries in the kitchen while Ruth slept in her crib and Jonathan arranged plastic and wooden clothespins on opposite ends of the dresser in the bedroom. Clothespin soldiers, complete with toothpick weapons stuck through their centers. A soft knock at the door echoed through the apartment. I felt an expectant constriction in my chest as I went to answer the door.

Doc Burnett filled the doorway, flashing a shy smile. "Good evening, Genie."

"Hello."

"What's Jonathan up to?"

All of a sudden I felt awkward in his presence. I welcomed the chance to divert his, attention to my son. I nodded toward the open bedroom. "He's in the midst of battle . . . the wood against the plastic."

Jonathan's version of gunfire filtered out to us. I smiled up at our visitor. "See what happens when you refuse to buy violent toys?"

Doc Burnett poked his head into the war room. "Who's winning, champ?"

"Plastics," Jonathan replied impatiently, as if the answer were obvious.

He smiled indulgently. "You wouldn't feel like visiting with the animals today, would you?"

Jonathan just shook his head silently, continuing to play soldiers with one hand and rub his eyes with the other.

Afraid of stirring my son's ire, I whispered, "I think that he needs to go to bed."

"Ruth's already sleeping?"

I held my crossed fingers up in the air. "It looks like the colic might finally be over. She slept over ten hours straight last night. Even I slept for eight." As I spoke, I suddenly realized that I still felt as if I could use eight more hours—if not a full twenty-four.

A peculiar expression flickered over Doc Burnett's face. His gaze traveled around the room.

"So, what excuse am I going to use now?"

He flushed crimson.

My heart began to hammer almost painfully against my ribs. Instinctively, I averted my gaze to the floor, seeking safety in the swirling pattern in our faded carpet.

At first, I thought that he had unintentionally spoken his private thoughts; but when I dared to lift my head, I found his eyes looking directly into mine, sparkling that brilliant blue.

"You don't need one . . . James."

His expression softened when he heard his name from my lips for the first time. Glimpsing the tenderness in his eyes sent a sudden wave of panic through me.

"But you have to remember that Patrick only just left us. . . ."

"It's been a year now, Genie," he reminded me gently.

"I have two children. . . .

"Two beautiful children."

"And they're my first priority."

"I wouldn't want it any other way."

To prove his point, he then started opening the cabinets in the kitchen, finding by instinct all that he needed to make our dinner.

I hesitated only briefly, letting him shoo me away without a struggle. Sinking into the couch felt so good that an involuntary moan escaped my lips.

I heard my self-appointed chef whispering to my son in his bedroom.

"Champ, the United Nations is calling a temporary cease-fire so that their generals can get some much needed rest"

I had never tried that tactic before. But it must have succeeded, for the next thing I perceived from the land of slumber was the smell of garlic, onions, and tomatoes wafting into the living room, and the sound of James puttering around in the kitchen, humming an up-tempo lullaby.

He's a good man. I thought. And even as I drifted back to sleep, I was aware of the sensation of perfect bliss. THE END

A BOY'S WAY

**It was quite a problem for a boy to find
a new husband for his mother and a new dad for
himself all wrapped up in one package. But a
small boy has ways of working things out which
you and I would never think of.**

*Here's another "single mom" story, but this one has a twist: It's narrated
by her eleven-year-old son. Boy's father—who gave him the unusual name
because it was "the most beautiful word in the world"—has been dead for a
few years, and his mother is desperate to find him a new dad. None of the
men she dates would make suitable parents, though; they're all just trying to
make time with her and see Boy as an annoying obstacle, trying to buy him
off with presents. Dan Masters, a counselor at Boy's summer camp, isn't
going to be like those chumps.*

*Dan does his best to draw a depressed Boy out of his shell, encouraging
him to become an "all-around camper," against his mom's attempts to simply
buy him popularity with the other boys by throwing them a party. It's clear
from the beginning that Boy sees Dan as a father figure, and their relationship
reads as much more authentic than the rapid crush Dan develops on Boy's
mom—even if she is a famous model!—and the way she quickly decides this
man she's met a handful of times should be her second husband. Even by pulp
romance standards, it seems a little fanciful... but awfully sweet.*

Though I was only eleven, I remember it all as if it were just today;
maybe because, in a way, it is today . . .

Usually, my mother's voice reminded me of swift, full notes from
a little bell. Now her words were thin and tight as if squeezed out
between her fine, long fingers that pressed into my shoulder.

"You *must* make him happy," she told Dan Masters.

"We only can give him the freedom to let himself be happy, Mrs. Hadley." Dan Masters was leaning back against the train coach, watching us both, a friendly but puzzled smile curving away from the bit of his pipe. His clothes were tweed and big and loose, and he was made for them. My hand, from shaking his, was still tingling, but it felt stronger, too, as if something vital and alive from his hand had passed into mine. He was chief counselor at the summer camp I was leaving for.

"I feel like it's Boy's last chance," my mother said. Then, sort of wistfully, "And maybe mine, too."

"Maybe it's only your first real chance, Mrs. Hadley," Dan Masters said, gently, but as if he knew what he was talking about.

It wasn't time for the train to pull out, but Dan Masters must have wanted the good-by over with. He straightened up in one smooth motion, all ready to boost me onto the train, waiting while my mother kissed me.

Her soft mouth took a warm little tuck in one corner of mine. "Please have fun, Boy," she whispered, almost begging me. Her eyes were on Dan, though, with the same expression in them that I could feel in her whisper to me. Then she was hurrying away, a gold-tasseled spear against the gray of the train shed.

When we were settled in the seat Dan found for us, he said, "Boy Hadley, hmm? Your real name—Boy?"

I nodded slowly, swallowing hard, because I was afraid he'd laugh now, at my name, like others usually did. "A good sound name," he told me. "Common word, but as a name it's as different as an old pocket knife with a good blade. I've got one, incidentally, Boy."

At the look I gave him, he grinned. "Oh, a skeptic!" and he began feeling through his pockets, while asking me about my father.

I never knew how to talk about my father, and every time I said what I usually did, nobody understood, but I said it anyway: "I remember my father alive, but I can't remember his dying."

"I see," was all Dan said, and for a minute I was thinking freely and gladly of my father; it was just as if Dan had told me to go ahead—not to mind him. I couldn't remember when he named me Boy. That had been at the very first. My mother had told me about that, his being so glad I was a boy, the way they had prayed, and saying, "What to name him? Why name him Boy, of course—the most beautiful word in the world!"

I could remember a lot of other things myself, though: like his showing me, how to break a shotgun and thrust the shells home. Getting me used to a bicycle by riding me on his handlebars awhile. Racing me to see who could take a clock apart faster. Teaching me to throw a curve till he couldn't hit homers off me any more—

Just when he died, I didn't know. Everything'd been hazy and hidden away, with no one telling me anything, and I believing my father was on a long business trip. Till one day I just knew that he wouldn't ever be back and that now I had to go on living all the old good times over and over without ever any new ones.

"Here's that knife," Dan Masters was saying. "Try it, Boy."

I took it eagerly and opened it up to test it, the shiny blade *sending* a keen little line of shock along the ball of my, thumb "Golly," I said, "is that ever a swell knife!"

Then the train was starting to move, and out the window I saw my mother watching for me. I sidled up to the edge of the seat, all ready to wave. Till I saw the man with her.

I didn't know who the man was, because they all got to looking alike to me. But he took my mother's hand and even though she slipped it away, everything went out of me. All the excitement over going to camp and taking a train ride and Dan Masters having this swell knife flattened out like a bright colored tomato can under your stamping heel.

Now I could think only of the man out there and of all the others like him, and the way things had been, because of them.

My Mother was a model; and in a magazine here or a magazine there you could see her hair flowing soft and loose in the ads for open cars, or her teeth white and even in the toothpaste ads, or her figure slim and strong in sports dresses and evening gowns. I guess a lot of people all over the country thought they knew all about Anne Hadley, how she dressed and looked, talked and ate. But they never knew the expression on her face that was sometimes loneliness, sometimes all worry and hurt for me.

They never heard her say, with a voice as if the words were torn loose from her heart, "Boy, I want terribly for you to have a father. You need one so."

"I'm all right," I would say, anxious because I knew *it* was only for me she wanted that father, not for herself. "Honest, I'm all right." And I *would* be all right, I'd think—if they'd just let me go on remembering the fun with my father: his white shirt billowing out against my face in the stern of an outboard, or his brown hand guiding mine to bait a hook, or his head thrown back laughing with me at circus clowns.

"You've got to have a father, Boy," my mother would keep saying. "I'll try so hard to find a good one for you."

"All right," I said, smiling finally like that was a fine idea. Because that was the easiest, and because she was so young compared to other mothers that I was afraid I'd hurt her with the wrong answer.

There'd been so many men. It was like a parade. All of them wearing good clothes and smelling of high-priced barbers, and pulling out fat wallets to give me money. They brought my mother flowers. They brought presents for me, too and they'd laugh at me, saying, "Well, well, what a husky curly-head we are." Till they saw I couldn't laugh and would turn away, shrugging and muttering about such a kid being an old sober-sides.

Sometimes one of them might give me a football, and I'd be happy about it just then, I'd even say, "That's a swell football, sir. Would you like to come out and throw some passes with me?"

But he'd say, "No, you run along and play, sonny," and move closer to my mother, maybe starting to put an arm around her.

She'd shift away from that arm quick enough, but all the fun of getting the football would go out of me just the same. I'd forget all about it, not even taking it outside with me. Because this man was back there, trying to put an arm around my mother or hold her hand. And I wouldn't want to see anyone or talk to anyone, only be by myself, thinking about my father. Thinking so hard it was almost real again. That was why I didn't mind eating lunches alone, because my father would seem to be there, chuckling at me when I got the sugar and salt mixed. It would have been all right if my mother'd gone out to dinners too, instead of staying home till we'd eaten together.

There was one part of thinking about my father that got too real: remembering him whirling my mother around the room to phonograph music, picking her up and kissing her and telling me I had a long way to go before I could handle women like that, all three of us laughing without knowing exactly why, except that everything was warm and good and together. When I remembered that, I always stopped thinking of anything more, except the fear that maybe the new, man up there in our apartment now, maybe he'd be the one who finally stayed and every day could tell me to run along and play, and try to kiss my mother. Kiss her even against the look in her eyes that said she wanted him to keep away.

It had been like that again and again, and every time I thought this one might be the man, and it scared me. I'd even be afraid to talk and play with the fellows the way I used to. Because they'd have to mention their own fathers sometimes, and that would start them asking me if I was going to get another father, and I knew if I stayed around them I'd get sick inside or else fight.

So that's how it had been for a long time: a lot of presents from men telling me to take the new ball or top or erector set and run along and play, or take the money and go to a movie. Then, before I was even out the door, that little movement toward my mother and her edging away, looking as if she just didn't know what to think or do, and in .my own stomach sudden ice.

Even the laughter I heard at our apartment door, late at night when my mother had been out dancing or to a show, well, that was like really seeing it all, because I knew she'd be getting out of some man's reach even while she laughed. One of those nights, it was just a week before, she'd shut the door quietly but quickly, then tiptoed into my room, the hall light behind her haloing her hair but keeping her face shadowed.

She hesitated in the doorway, and for a second I was going to pretend being asleep, because my throat was filled up and hurting worse than the day I swallowed a too-big bite of apple. For I was remembering how once she'd come every night to the doorway like that, only not alone: my father had always been there too, tall and broad shouldered, and soft-laughing behind her. And they would peer in, my mother would whisper back over her shoulder, "He's all right, Jim," and he would nod with great emphasis: "Our Boy? Of course he's all right, right as rain every time!" And then his arms would draw her back out of the doorway and tighten around her, and the door would close. But I could hear her own laughter suddenly muffled.

But now she was always alone, looking in on me, and my throat always hurt. But suddenly this one night I'd wanted her in there so badly, feeling the silk of her dress cool to my hot cheek and smelling her .perfume, while her soft fingers laced in and out between mine.

"I'm awake," I called, and with an unsteady little laugh she came on in and sat on the edge of my bed. She was so light she hardly pressed the bed down at all.

"At this hour!" She clucked her tongue but her fingers were beginning their caress. "You know, you're a worse night owl than I am!"

"I'm sorry," I said. "But I've been trying to sleep."

"Of course, darling," she said quickly. "But you're excited about school ending, aren't you, and being promoted to the seventh grade." All at once her voice sounded very tired. "I mean, I wish that were what kept you awake. You're always awake, Boy. Worrying and wondering about me and—my gentlemen friends."

"It's all right," I said. "Golly, you've got to go out and have fun once in awhile." And I meant that, I really did, because to keep my mother cooped up would be like caging a beautiful, wild bird. She was something like a bird anyway; my father used to say that when they danced her feet never touched the floor.

"But, Boy," she was saying, "I don't have that fun. I'm unhappy because you're unhappy. You need a father so, and I can't seem to find one who suits you. Why not, Boy? They give you presents, they're nice to you."

"They're fine," .I said, but I knew she didn't think so either.

"If only you liked one of them enough, I could stand him, Boy, whoever he was. That wouldn't matter so much."

"I'll try," I promised. "I'll try to like one of them."

"Yes, you'll try," she said with a little sigh. "You always try, and it hurts you; I can see it. I—oh, we miss him so, don't we? Need him—" She was quiet then, her hands closed tight over one of mine as if warming it. Finally she went on, "You don't even play with your friends anymore, do you Boy? Maybe you need a summer away from me, at some camp."

I didn't want to be away from her, but I was certainly thinking about a camp, all right. Where everything and everyone would be new, where nobody'd be telling me to run along so they could try putting an arm around my mother.

"I'd like going to camp," I said. "I'd like it fine." And she hugged me, hugged me so fiercely that I felt in her all the loneliness and hunger for something gone that I'd ever felt in me—and something else, a sort of desperation . . .

So now I was going away to camp, but it wasn't helping much, after all. I felt a package in my pocket my mother had said was a going-away present from a new friend, and I knew it was from the man at the station with her. It was like saying, *Here you are, now run along and play*, run clear off to a camp. And the fun and excitement were just about all over.

"Listen, Boy Hadley," Dan Masters was saying, with a gruffness that didn't fool me a bit, "if you're not going to give that knife some attention, hand it back. I've got some carving to do."

"Carving?" I said. "Can you carve, Dan?" Calling him Dan was easy and natural; I hadn't even thought about calling him Mister.

"Can I carve? Ho—listen to him!" Dan took a piece of wood from his pocket. The hull of a ship already was shaped into the wood. "Want to work with me, on this, Boy?"

"I'll say!" And for awhile I wasn't worrying about anything except how to get streamline into a smokestack. "That's some knife, all right," I said after a half hour or so. "I'd like to have it."

Dan looked at me sideways. "Sort of used to presents, are you, Boy?"

"Sure, Dan. I get a lot of presents. From my mother's friends."

"A lot of friends, too, I suppose," he said very quietly as if he hadn't meant to speak aloud. "Well, you can't have this particular knife, Boy. But I'll tell you how to get one exactly like it." His brown, big-knuckled fingers moved over the knife like he was petting a good dog. "We always give one as a prize at the end of the summer to the best all-round camper. Can you win it?"

"Maybe." But I didn't know; I didn't feel like an all-round camper. I way feeling again just like someone who's been sent along to play and be out of the way.

My mother came to visit me after two weeks. It was Sunday, and they told me right after church in the forest clearing. I ran all the way in to the camp store, where we met our visitors, ran as fast as if my father were racing along with me again, chuckling and goading me on.

My mother kissed me and laughed with me, -but her eyes were watching me carefully, looking for something. "You're happy here, Boy?" she asked finally.

"Why, sure." My voice was too loud. "Everything's swell."

"I wondered—your letters are so short. Well . . ." Then she was putting out a hand to Dan Masters, who had come up to us. While they said hello and things like that, I thought of how good they looked together. My mother, slim and so young in a summer dress with big red flowers all over it, her head tilted back to smile at Dan. And Dan, taller than ever beside her, his skin almost black against hers when he took her hand, his shirt open at the neck and his teeth a clenched whiteness on the pipe he never lit.

For a moment I could remember my mother and father together, remember for once without having to blink very fast.

"A mother must check up on her son once in awhile," my mother was saying.

Dan grinned at her. "Detailed report forthcoming, Mrs. Hadley." So now it comes, I thought, from him, too: Run along and play.

But he was saying, "I'm going to give Boy and some of the others a canoeing lesson right now, Mrs. Hadley. I'll send one of the counselors to see you and tell all about Boy."

I'd have felt pretty good, trotting over to the boathouse with Dan, if I hadn't known what that counselor would tell my mother. He would say I kept to myself and didn't make friends or join in any of the activities. He would say I was too quiet and that for all they talked to me, everyone except Dan, who only watched me as if he were doing a lot of thinking, they still couldn't make me into a good camper.

Because I'd found that maybe everyone here was new, but that in one way they were just like the fellows at home. They'd talk about their fathers and the things they did with their fathers, and before I could help it I'd be thinking that' all the good times with my father were over and could never be again except through remembering them. And that one of these days my mother was going to find a father for me who would give me presents so I'd run along and play; and there would be the arm around my mother, making me feel sick and afraid for her and for me.

Then I thought of how, after all, she'd come here alone today, and that was *something*. When Dan and I got to the boathouse, where some of the fellows were pushing a canoe into the water, I felt so much better that I hurried to put one shoulder in with theirs and help shove. They all looked at me for a quiet second, not understanding my wanting to help for a change. Till finally Joe Patterson said, "Well, thanks, Boy," and I was suddenly embarrassed and didn't say anything back.

After the canoe lesson, Dan Masters and I went back to where my mother sat on a stone bench by the lake. Her eyes were shining, but I guess only because of the sun glancing off the water; I could see little clouds of worry in her eyes, too. She didn't say anything important to me, just asked about the camp and did I like sleeping in a tent and was I as good a swimmer as my father always said I'd be. She told Dan she had talked to the camp cook, and found out our calorie count was perfect.

He laughed at that. "The most popular girl on the magazine covers, poking around our soup kettles!"

"And who *should* know more about calories, Mr. Masters, than a model?"

"Ah," Dan said with a twinkle, "but where you fight calories off, we fight to get them down these stubborn young throats."

My mother gave a little *Pooh*. "Yes, they look *so* underfed!" But there was something unsteady there under her laughter, and she and Dan kept gazing straight at each other, their eyes not casual at all. And for some reason I felt sort of warm and happy all through me. It was too soon when my mother said, "It's lovely here. I wish could stay longer, but I've a dinner date in town."

"Oh," was all Dan said, but he didn't seem so pleased, and I wasn't so happy more myself. Whoever that date was, I thought, he sure ought to be glad I wasn't around, so he wouldn't have to give me a present and tell me to run along.

After my mother kissed me, bending close to give my arm a warm squeeze and tell me to please, *please* have fun with everyone, she went off to where her car was parked, Dan slowing his long stride to keep very near her. So I turned around and started for my tent. On the way, some fellows playing catch let the ball get by and roll up to my feet. I threw it back to one of them and he waited to see if I was joining them, but I simply went on to my tent and was glad the other three fellows I lived with weren't there, just then. Because sitting there on my cot, wondering whom my mother's dinner date was with and if he was maybe going to be the new father I'd always been afraid of—well, I guess I cried a little.

At nine o'clock the camp bugler blew Taps. Everything was quiet, everyone was tired and would sleep quickly and deep, but I knew I wasn't going to sleep. The counselor who came into the tent after awhile didn't have to shake me, but he did and whispered, "Dan Masters wants to see you, Hadley."

I got into shorts and sneakers and felt along through the dark to Dan's tent about fifty yards away. He stayed there alone, and he was lying on his cot, reading by the electricity from the camp generator. He sat up, running his fingers through his short black hair and grinning.

"Didn't expect you so soon, Boy. You healthy youngsters are hard to wake usually."

"I wasn't asleep," I said; sitting down on the stool he pushed at me.

He gave me a sharp look. "Well, let me get to the point, so you can go back and try to get some sleep anyway. Boy," he said, "your mother said that she wants to give me some money to throw a big ice cream and hot dog party for the camp in your name."

"Say," I exclaimed, "that's a swell idea!"

"You think so, Boy?" He was smiling, but his eyes were trying to see inside me. And I guess they did.

"Why sure, Dan," I said. "The fellows'll like that."

"So would I, Boy," he said. "I'm crazy about hot dogs and ice cream. But just the same, I want you to write your mother and say you don't want to give that party. Don't say I told you, say you simply do not want to give that party."

I just looked at him, wondering.

"If it were anyone else than you and your mother, Boy," he went on, "I'd think it was a swell idea, too. But your mother doesn't understand that you can't buy the kind of popularity I want the fellows to have at this camp."

"Buy it, Dan?" I said, puzzled.

"Boy," he said, "your mother knows you don't get along here and she thinks a party, like a present, is all that matters to fellows. It isn't, lad. The campers themselves vote on the best camper of the summer, the fellow who wins the knife, and half the time it's somebody here at a sacrifice, whose folks can't afford to give away chewing gum, much less big parties."

"Well," I said, not very eagerly, "I guess you know what's right. I guess you know all about fellows, Dan."

He grinned. "I match wits with 'em enough all summer, and all winter too, in my academy chemistry classes. But listen to me, Boy, writing that letter isn't enough. I want you to let yourself become well liked here. Notice I don't say, make an effort--I say, *let* yourself. Every fellow here wants to like you. Whatever's bothering you, on your mind all the time, try to forget it for the summer. Whatever mistake has happened at home, I'll bet my outboard motor it wasn't meant to be. Your mother, Boy, is—" And suddenly he got the strangest expression, like he was looking way off at something that he liked very much even though it sort of amused him.

"Your mother," he went on, "is—young, Boy. She doesn't understand a lot of things, about fellows, the way your father did. It's up to you to work on yourself, make yourself happy so she won't be worrying about it and sometimes trying too hard along the wrong lines. You see?"

I didn't exactly, but I said, "I think I see, Dan."

"I guess you don't, not quite, but you will some day. Boy," he said, "suppose you enter one of the swimming events for the Blues next Sunday. Will you do that for me?"

For some reason I felt right then that I'd do anything for him, so I nodded.

"Good." He reached out and his fingers came hard and friendly into my shoulder. "Boy," he said quietly, "don't think you're peculiar because you get lonely. Everybody gets lonely."

"Even you, Dan?" I said, amazed.

He gave me a sad sort of smile. "Especially me, Boy."

I don't know why, but I *had* to do what I did; something made me dig into my pocket and pull out my little wallet where I carried a Confederate dollar and my membership card in the Roving Rangers, and two pictures of my mother. I handed Dan one of the pictures.

"Well, thanks, Boy," he said. "I like to have pictures of very pretty girls." He said it very lightly, but I noticed that he put it in the left breast pocket of his shirt and buttoned the flap so carefully you'd think the picture was going to stay right there forever.

"And just to make us even," he said, "here—" and he threw me his knife.

I caught it with a gasp. "Hey! For keeps, Dan?"

"No, Boy, not for keeps." Then he was grinning wide again. "But try it out for a few days, see if it isn't worth trying to earn."

I slept pretty well, after all. I'll bet I slept better than Dan . . .

The camp was divided into the Reds and Blues for all our athletic meets. I was a Blue, because every boy had to be something, but I hadn't been in any meets. So it wasn't easy to go up to Joe Patterson, who was captain 'of the Blues swimming team, and say, "Joe, I'd sure like to do something in the swim next Sunday." But right afterward I knew there wasn't any reason to be embarrassed. Because Joe acted like I'd been one of them all along.

"What do you do best, Boy?" he asked, taking out a notebook.

"I swim a hundred yards pretty fast," I told him.

"That's swell, Boy." He wrote my name down. "That's my event, too. We'll take 'em together!" Joe clapped my shoulder and the sting of it was good and warm.

I still didn't get into many games that week, because. I was practicing hard at my swimming till I felt I had a good race in me. "We'll take 'em, Boy," Joe said every time he saw me, and the other Blues would stop by to ask how my crawl stroke was coming, and say they were glad to have me on the team. It was a good week; by Sunday I was feeling something inside me besides a good race.

Before my event, Dan Masters told me my Mother was at the other end of the course, waiting to see me win, and that was all I needed. I felt wonderful, I knew I'd win, just like everyone had been telling me.

I don't know why it happened. Maybe it was our event being the one deciding the meet, maybe I'd have been too nervous, anyway. But I didn't win. I came second after Joe Patterson.

When we all waded up on shore, tired and panting, the fellows were watching to see how I would take it. I took it the only way I could, the only way I felt: I grinned over at Joe and I yelled, "You won the meet for us, Joe! You won the meet! What a swimmer!" Then everyone was yelling, especially the Blues, who were telling the Reds already how they were going to take the big basketball game too, with Boy Hadley playing for them.

Oh, I felt great, my heart beating, fast and high to be one of the fellows like this. And then—well, first I saw my mother, slim and touched by sunlight, waiting on the bank, one hand up in a little wave. Her mouth was happy and her eyes proud the way mine must have looked to her. Which was swell, till I saw the man with her, his hand on her arm, and suddenly I was so tired I didn't think I could even climb that bank.

I had to climb it, though, and my mother hugged me, dripping wet as I was, and said, "Your father would be proud of that race, Boy." But I looked at the man with her and wondered what else my father would think—did think, because hadn't he been swimming right along with me, egging me on, giving me his big friendly laugh through the splashes?

This man was a heavy man with a handsome red face, and he kept chuckling at me, though his eyes didn't smile at all, while my mother said, "This is Mr. Gropher, Boy." Mr. Gropher said that even with a funny name like that, he guessed I ought to have a prize, and he took out his silver pencil and gave it to me. After thanking him, I said I'd be down to the camp store as soon as I dressed. Then I ran along before Mr. Gropher had to tell me to.

I took a long time dressing. On the way to the camp store, I met Dan Masters and asked him if he'd seen my mother yet.

"I saw her," he said, but there were tight little lines penning in his smile. I guessed that he hadn't talked to her and wasn't going to this time. He was disappointed.

Somehow, I couldn't make myself even look at Mr. Gropher when I reached the store. He didn't say anything to me, either, just stood there shifting from one foot to the other, and after awhile he went away to his car, telling my mother she'd better hurry if they were going to get back to town in time for dinner.

"Look, dear," my mother said in a worried voice. "you liked the silver pencil, didn't you?"

"It's okay," I said. "It writes."

"And you like Mr. Gropher?"

"Well," I said awkwardly, "do you?"

Her eyes were suddenly all a-swim and she turned away with a little trembling going all through her; I could see it and I swallowed hard, wondering what I'd said. But she turned back to me again and she was even a little severe—for her. "The point is, Boy, you like presents from my generous friends, don't you?"

A BOY'S WAY 53

I nodded.

"Then why," she asked, "did you write that letter saying you don't want to give a party for the other fellows? They'd enjoy it. Boy, they'll like you even more than they do, and I want you to be liked and happy. You know that, dear."

"All right," I said, without really knowing how I felt—tired or just mad or just not caring about anything. I did know I felt older than my mother right then, because she seemed anxious and mixed up and not understanding anything the way Dan Masters understood. I'd known it was right to tell her not to send the party money, if only because Dan had said it was right, but it hadn't been easy to write the letter, and now she was making things tough. But I said again, "All right, you can send Dan the money," because I couldn't say no to my mother or hurt her.

And when she went away with Mr. Gropher, I was sorry she left, but glad too, because I didn't want anyone around me for awhile.

When Dan Masters came to me next day with a puzzled expression on his face, I thought he'd already got that party money from my mother. But it was basketball he was wondering about. "They tell me you won't play on the Blues team, Boy. I don't get it."

And I didn't know what to say. I didn't know how to make him see that I knew the party money was going to spoil everything with Dan and with the fellows, and that I was already getting away by myself the way I was going to end up anyway. So now I just looked away somewhere and mumbled, "Ah, I don't know anything about basketball, Dan."

"You got the speed and height, Boy. It's time you learned."

"Ah, I don't know." I shuffled my feet.

A couple of fellows passed us and said hello only to Dan, and he shook his head at me. "Boy, you were right on top; Sunday, right in with the fellows. Now you're back where you started. What is it?"

Suddenly he slapped my shoulder. "Come on, Boy—race you to the basketball court!"

We ran over there and Dan got a ball and began dribbling it around the court, shooting baskets from every angle till I itched to get my hands on the ball. He'd grin at me and yell, "Easy, hey, Boy?" till finally I couldn't stand it anymore and I shouted, "Who's supposed to be the coach, anyway? How about letting me try it, Dan?"

"Get it away from me!" Dan arched a shot and I ran in to take it off the backboard and drop one through. We kept that up till we had to flop down on the grass, panting and laughing at each other.

"Dan," I said.

"Yes, Boy?"

"Dan, if my Mother sends you money for a party; you send it back. Will you, Dan? I—I guess I just can't buy being popular the way you said."

"Boy,'" he said, "I'll send it back."

I grinned at him and we just sat on there, taking it easy, and it was swell. Somehow I wasn't thinking of my father so much now, not thinking anyway of his being right there, living the good times over with me as if there wasn't any real today. Right now, it was a good today.

Then I took Dan's knife out of my pocket and gave it to him. "It's a fine knife, Dan," I said, "but I'm going to win a brand new one." And I got up and ran down to the camp store, and made a phone call to my mother.

She wasn't home, she was out with a Mr. Gropher, they told me at our apartment hotel desk. But I left word that she wasn't to send Dan Masters any party money. I just didn't want him bothered with anything like that. It helped a little, leaving that message, helped, I mean, to fight that fear of Mr. Gropher seeing my mother so much.

I didn't know what my mother would do about that phone call. I was surprised when Dan came after me next day about four o'clock. He stuck his head in my tent, where I was staring at a fishing fly I'd been figuring on fixing for about a half hour now. "Your mother's here, Boy," and he started to walk away.

"Dan," I called. "Dan, will you please go with me to see her?"

He didn't want to, I could tell, but I guess it wasn't easy for Dan to refuse a fellow anything. So he went, and I was glad, because I was afraid it was going to be the old story. I was afraid Mr. Gropher'd be along, and I'd get empty inside and not care anymore about being the kind of fellow Dan wanted me to be. It would help if he were there, but

I wondered what would happen when the time came that he could not always be there. I hated to think of that time.

My mother was waiting at one corner of the store, the breeze whipping her dress, and there was life everywhere in her; except in her face; that was set like some of the men my father used to have in for poker, as if she didn't want anyone to know what she was thinking.

While hugging me, she kept watching Dan. Then she stood up very straight in front of him and asked if he had anything to do with my not giving the party.

"The first time, yes," he told her in such a quiet voice. "This time it was his own idea. And this is not Visitors' Day, Mrs. Hadley."

"There are no visitors," my mother said just as evenly. "I am here alone to see my son."

"Alone?" Dan motioned toward the car, parked twenty yards or so away. Mr. Gropher was in it, and I felt as sick as if I could smell his thick cigar all the way over. "Oh." My mother looked at Mr. Gropher, then back at Dan, and color flooded back into her face and she gave a surprised little laugh. "Why, he's—he's nobody."

Dan grinned but my mother was speaking coldly again. "Wouldn't it be wiser, Mr. Masters, to spend a little more time helping Boy have fun, a little less spoiling his party?"

"There are eighty boys in this camp, Mrs. Hadley," Dan said. "If you think I can devote every minute to helping just one, you—" He quit, beginning to laugh, because my mother was beginning to laugh.

And she said, "Why do we go on with this act? I know what you've done for Boy. I could sense something at that swimming meet. I was glad when he phoned not to send the party money because suddenly I was waking up too. It's funny who really gave him the most after all—not presents but the companionship and understanding that really count with a boy." She paused, looking right into Dan's eyes. "But you couldn't have done it all for Boy alone, I think."

"Couldn't I, Anne?" Dan asked. "Was someone else in need of a little honest, inexpensive happiness?"

"I wonder." My mother was wide-eyed, the way she used to play dumb with my father.

And suddenly I knew I must be as happy and normal as any guy, because the devil was in me. "Say—" I looked innocently up at my mother, "—why don't you ask Dan to let you see whose picture he always carries in that shirt pocket, where it gets bumped by his heart?"

I didn't think Dan's color could get any deeper, but it did, and my mother's, too. Very steadily, though, she said, "I don't think I have to see it, Boy." And when she put out her hand it wasn't to take any picture but to clasp Dan's hand, and there was a wonderful warm tingling all through my own body.

For once I was glad to turn away to save them bothering with me. I held up my hands and yelled at some fellows playing catch. "Here you go, Joe!"

I heard my mother give a little cry. "Oh, I see it all now—so plainly!"

Why sure, I thought, I could see it too—see that ball smacking hard and stinging into my hands.

"He isn't shrinking from us," my mother said softly.

Shrinking? Me? "Why," I boasted aloud, "I could throw this ball half way across the lake!"

Dan reached for the ball. "I can throw it *clear* across!"

"Show me!" I jerked away and went running down toward the lake, with Dan after me, laughing and threatening to maul me when he caught me. Just like that memory of my father used to run along with me.

Wherever he was, he must be happy that he could rest now and not have to chase along this way anymore to keep me company. "Dan!" my mother called, but Dan only grinned and yelled back, "Wait around! The boys have to go to sleep sometime!"

But I just laughed to myself, thinking that there was one Boy who wasn't asleep . . .

Oh, I remember all right, then and the wonderful now—so well, and so gladly. THE END

FORGET MY DAUGHTER—
I'LL SHOW YOU ECSTASY!
One man's hot, hard, and hungry body made her forget herself and begin to betray...

Cyrinda is a single mother who grew up in an oppressive, religious home, and her adolescent experiences have affected how she treats her teenage daughter, Tawny. "Too many strict rules had made me rebel," Cyrinda says. "I wouldn't make the same mistake with my own daughter." So she lets Tawny's spiky hairdo and revealing outfits slide, and then gives the thirteen-year-old girl permission to start dating. Barely a year goes by, though, before she's taken up with a 22-year-old man. (25, really, but that doesn't exactly make things better.) Talking with Tawny about it gets Cyrinda nowhere, and somehow she gets it into her head that she can straighten things out if she just can have a conversation alone with Jake.

Cyrinda's boyfriend doesn't think that's such a great idea; he picks up on her attraction to Jake long before she does. Jake figures it out, too, and it's pathetically easy for him to take advantage of her the way he's taken advantage of Tawny . . . and what would be a lurid erotic fantasy if it were told from the man's point of view becomes a devastating melodrama.

My daughter, Tawny, was born smiling as though angels had led her gently into my life. She was a cheerful, easygoing infant, and even a delightful toddler. Since I was a young, single mother, I was inexperienced enough to expect that Tawny would always be the light of my life and never cause me a minute's worry.

Adolescence, of course, changed everything, but before that even as a youngster, Tawny was my green-eyed, perfect doll of a child; she offered me no hint of what was to come until one day just before she turned twelve when she asked: "Mom, what does it feel like to have a baby?"

I cleared my throat. Not wanting to scare her I said "Well, honey, it's painful, but—"

"Not that," she insisted, "I mean, what's it like to have a baby to take care of?"

"Why do you ask?"

Her gaze went heavenward for just a moment, the way it did when she was listening to a new song on the radio. I could only wonder what was going on in that little blond head of hers.

"Babies have to love you, right?" she asked. I nodded, and yet another question popped out of her mouth. "Is it nice to have someone love you so much?" she asked.

"You should know," I replied. "I love you just that much."

She scrunched her beautiful face up playfully and left me alone after that. It's hard to recall those happy days now, after all that's happened, but when I do allow myself to think of Tawny back then, it makes me smile.

Tawny and I mark the time of the change in her personality differently. I say she changed when she began adolescence; she says she changed when Jonah entered my life. I was in my thirties by then, and though I'd dated a bit, I'd never had a serious relationship. Tawny's father was a boy I met in my first year of college. When I got pregnant and dropped out during my very first semester, he transferred to another college and I never saw him again. My family disowned me then, since an out-of wedlock pregnancy hardly suits the daughter of a minister, but hard work helped me get through the most painful parts of my life. Attending nursing school wasn't easy with a toddler to care for but I did it and by the time Tawny was twelve, I was in charge of the newborn nursery in our local hospital, a job I truly loved.

The first time Tawny met Jonah, she giggled and asked, "Are you going to marry my mom?" I swatted playfully at her as Jonah, a man I'd only dated twice before, hedged and stammered.

"Don't let her get away with that, Jonah," I teased. "Tell her she's too young to be running her mother's life."

Tawny danced from the room laughing. Whenever I think of Tawny at twelve, I imagine her dancing, for that's the way she always seemed to me—her little body twirling and floating in and out of rooms.

Tawny's emergence into the teen years began, literally, from the top down. From gorgeous, long, straight blond hair, she one day came home from a friend's house with maroon hair, short and spiked. Inside I groaned, while on the outside, all I did was question why she'd done it.

"Cara likes it," she replied simply, as though that explained everything. I wasn't sure who Cara was, but as far as I knew, all of Tawny's friends were brunettes, blondes—all the regular colors. Tawny had the only maroon head around.

Recalling my own religious upbringing, I forced myself to be quiet. Too many strict rules had made me rebel; I wouldn't make the same mistake with my own daughter. I didn't want her to leave me forever. Still, since by then, I'd been seeing Jonah for almost a year, I asked him what he thought.

"I think you should stop her now before she gets out of hand, Cyrinda," he said.

I considered his comment for about a second before I said, "If I tell her I don't like her hair, she'll do something even more drastic to get my attention. You know, she's not happy that we've been seeing so much of one another."

"Well, it's not like we're getting married or anything," Jonah replied immediately.

I nearly laughed, but held it inside. Jonah, having been married once when he was very young, was quite gun-shy, and that was fine with me. I had a good job and a wonderful daughter; marriage was something I certainly didn't *need*. Besides, Jonah wasn't exactly "Mr. Excitement." I still had some life left in me, and who knew what the future held?

I patted his knee and said, "Don't worry, honey, I'm not proposing." He laughed then, and I was glad. Jonah didn't find much humor in life. I guess being a biologist didn't afford him a lot of laughs. Then a week after my daughter turned maroon, she came home in a very short, flared cotton skirt and a black motorcycle jacket.

"And whose clothes are those?" I asked, noticing that her lipstick matched the color of her hair.

"Cara's," she responded, spinning on her toes for me the way only a thirteen-year-old can. "How do you like 'em?" I shook my head as I sat over my after-work cup of tea. "They'll get you noticed, if that's what you're after." She smiled then, and I got a glimpse of the adorable, blond three-year-old she'd once been. "I hope you're just experimenting, Tawny," I said, immediately wishing that I'd only thought it and not said it out loud.

"You always said I'd go through many phases," she replied, pulling at the spikes in her hair.

"Yes, I did," I answered, wondering how it was that she only remembered the truly innocent, throwaway remarks that I made.

But when she came home that evening for dinner, she was dressed in her regular clothes, and I breathed a sigh of relief.

"Mom," she asked over dessert, "would it be all right if I went out on a date sometime soon?"

I shook my head. "I don't think so, honey. You're only thirteen."

"But I want to," she whined.

I remembered myself at that age, being told that dating before eighteen was a sin.

And so, reluctantly, I made my first, really huge mistake and gave my thirteen-year-old daughter permission to date.

She didn't actually go out until several weeks later, and even then, according to the meager rules I'd set down, her date came inside so I could meet him. I couldn't believe how young he looked; he couldn't have been more than fourteen, but he had a tough edge to him, what with his slicked-back hair, grungy jeans, and layers of well-worn flannel shirts.

"Mom, I'd like you to meet Ryan," my maroon-haired daughter said proudly.

Solemnly, I shook hands with the serious-faced boy, and then watched out the window as they walked together down the street.

They looked adorable.

That evening, I had a date with Jonah myself. Over dinner, I told him about Tawny's date.

"Come on, Cyrinda—are you sure you know what you're doing? She's only thirteen!"

I patted my lips with my napkin and said, "I told you about my own upbringing, Jonah. I decided early on that I'd never be a restrictive parent. I trust my daughter."

"Why?" he asked simply.

"Why do I trust her?" I asked.

He nodded.

"Because I've known her quite a long time." I laughed after I spoke, expecting Jonah to join me. When he didn't, I asked what was wrong.

"She's only thirteen, Cyrinda. She hasn't earned your trust yet."

"Do you really think that's how it is?" I asked, horrified. "Do you think a child has to earn her mother's trust?"

He shifted uncomfortably in his seat.

"Cyrinda—I've never had a child. What do I know? I just think that you should be very careful with Tawny. It's easy for a girl to fall in with a bad crowd these days. Someone could take advantage of her."

I was speechless. Jonah sounded so sensible. Could he be right? Was I giving my daughter credit she didn't deserve?

Those answers would be mine, but not before mistakes were made, serious mistakes.

I left his apartment later than usual that night. Having to go to Jonah's place every time we wanted to be intimate had its drawbacks, but even my liberal attitudes concerning Tawny's upbringing didn't include sleeping with him while she was at home. Jonah heartily agreed.

By the time I got to my house, it was nearly ten. Even though Tawny had convinced me that she no longer needed a baby-sitter, as I parked in front of the house, I was surprised to see that the living room lights were out. Tawny liked a lot of light.

I had to remind myself that I'd called her many times during the evening, and she'd seemed just fine as, hurriedly, I put my key in the lock and opened the door. There on the couch sat Tawny, looking flushed, like she'd just run in the back door.

"What's going on?" I asked.

Her laugh seemed forced, and then she said "That's a funny way to say hello."

Putting my purse down, I walked around to face her. "Tawny, I asked you a question."

She stood, sidestepped me, and said "Nothing's going on Why are you so grouchy, anyway?"

I snapped on the lights. "I'm not grouchy, just curious."

"Sounded like grouchy to me," she muttered, heading up the stairs.

"Where are you going, young lady?" I demanded.

She muttered something and was gone, her bedroom door closing noisily behind her. It was then that I smelled it. Someone had been smoking pot in the living room.

Praying it'd been just another experiment, I didn't question my daughter about it. When I look back now, I wonder how I could've let such behavior go on, but back then, I was so involved in not making the mistakes my parents had made, I ignored the grievous ones that I was making.

As Jonah and I continued to grow closer, Tawny continued to date. All the boys I met were teenagers like her, and some she dated more than once, but I was relieved when she didn't seem to be serious about anyone in particular. I was also relieved when her hair began to grow out and she didn't renew the maroon color. The three extra holes she'd had pierced in her left ear didn't particularly please me, but even Jonah merely laughed when he saw them.

Then, just when I'd begun to relax a little, thinking maybe my instincts were right about Tawny, I met Jake, the man who would change everything.

On that particular evening, I'd been at Jonah's, returning home around nine o'clock. Again, the living room lights were off. But I wasn't upset this time. Tawny had been doing that she'd told me, so she could see the TV better.

But that evening, when I came in and switched the light on, I was shocked to see that although my daughter was on the couch, as usual, she wasn't alone. For, sitting next to her was a boy—at least, that's what I thought at first. But when he stood and extended his hand, I realized I'd been wrong. This was a man. My stomach clenched in an immediate spasm.

"Mom, this is Jake Chesney," Tawny said proudly.

Wondering how on earth my daughter could possibly think that dating this man was all right, I had to force myself to remain calm.

"Hello," I said, shaking his hand, realizing all at once that this relationship had been going on for some time. Out of the corner of my eye, I could see Tawny gazing at him like he'd just been dropped from heaven.

"How old are you, Jake?" I asked bluntly.

"Twenty-two," he answered.

I studied his face, recognizing the lie. He was handsome, with a bright, white smile and trim, athletic body, but he hadn't been twenty-two for several years, that was clear.

"And you're dating my daughter?"

"We've become friends," he answered amiably.

I had a million questions to ask, but Tawny ended that possibility by saying, "Jake has to leave now."

I wish I'd stopped him then, while I was so upset, before he had a chance to get out the door. Then, maybe I could've interrupted the chain of events that was set off. But I was completely flustered. All I could do was fall onto the couch, my head in my hands.

When Tawny closed the door behind her guest, I cried out, "Are you out of your mind?"

She shrugged her thin shoulders. I could see then that her lipstick was worn off, and it didn't take a genius to figure out how that had happened.

Tawny twirled a strand of her short hair with one finger. "I'm almost fifteen, you know. I can date whomever I want."

She turned to leave, but I demanded that she sit on the couch with me. My heart was pounding so hard, I could almost hear its fury coursing through my veins.

"Let me make this very clear," I said to my pouting daughter, "you just *turned* fourteen. That's not even *close* to fifteen, and Jake says he's twenty-two. Do you understand why I have a problem with that?"

Again, she twirled a lock of hair and looked away. The gesture infuriated me. Roughly, I reached out and grabbed her little chin in my hand, forcing her to look at me.

"You may *not* see him again," I said through clenched teeth as she began to cry, trying to pull away. I held tight and said, "And, you may not have company at *all* when I'm not here."

I released my grip and she leapt to her feet, crying. "Well, that's just not *fair!*" she insisted through her tears. "Why should I miss out on *everything?* You're over there having fun with Jonah!"

She knew then that she'd stepped over what few boundaries I'd made for her. Her stance became less defiant, her tears stopped. Seeing the red mark my hand had made on her chin made me feel terrible; I knew I had to calm down.

"Listen to me, young lady," I said in a soft voice. "What I do at Jonah's is none of your business, but what you do here in my living room is of utmost concern to me."

The tears were back. She stood there for a minute trying to figure out what to say before she turned on her heel and fled up the stairs.

I sagged against the couch and put my head in my hands again. Behind my closed eyes, all I could see was that Jake Chesney kissing my Tawny.

The very thought made me ill.

The next morning, Tawny was gone when I got up. I wasn't surprised. She probably had to check with Cara to see how she should react to all this.

Because it was Saturday and I was off for the weekend, I spent a very quiet morning alone in the kitchen, wondering if Jonah hadn't been right all along. Maybe I *was* too lenient.

I was so engrossed in thought, I didn't hear the back door open. When I look back on it now, it seems as though Tawny and Jake were suddenly just there before me, standing hand in hand.

"Tawny," I began, standing, pulling my robe close around me, "I thought I told you—"

"Mom," she replied, cutting me off, "I just want you to know that Jake and I are going to continue seeing one another." Her little chin, still slightly red from my hand, was lifted defiantly while Jake stood there, merely smiling.

"Jake, would you mind stepping outside?" I asked, staring at their entwined hands.

"I don't think so, Mrs. Sykes," he said politely. "I'm here to show my support for Tawny."

"Support for—" I began, and then, taking a step forward, I said, "Jake, let go of my daughter's hand and step outside."

"No!" Tawny cried, backing both of them away from me. I wanted to grab her and shake her and she must've read my mind, for she turned to Jake and said, "She hurt me last night! I don't want her to do it again! Let's go."

Jake, looking slightly amused, allowed himself to be pulled to the door. Just before he stepped outside, though, he turned to me with a grin and shrugged.

I wanted to strangle both of them. Instead, I called Jonah. But I was crying so hard that he couldn't understand me, so I had to wait for him to get to my house before I could spill out the whole, horrible story to him.

"You've got to go to the police, Cyrinda. Tawny's underage, and if this guy is at least twenty-two, he could be in some serious trouble," Jonah said when I'd finally told him everything.

I shook my head. "He says they're just friends. The police can't put him in jail for that. Besides which, Tawny will defend him no matter what."

Jonah ran a hand through his thinning hair. "I'll have a talk with him, then."

Again, I shook my head. "I can't let you do that, Jonah. He hasn't really *done* anything."

"Then what?" he asked, palms raised in front of him.

"I'm not sure," I answered, "but I think I'd better try for some time alone with Jake Chesney."

Jonah didn't agree with me, but I was at a loss for another avenue to take. I couldn't risk losing my daughter, and as long as I forbade her to see Jake, I knew she'd find ways to defy me. Lord knows I hadn't denied Tawny much in her young life. Now, it was going to be really hard to put brakes on my speeding daughter.

Still, when I went to bed that night, I vowed to try and get through to Tawny calmly. Grabbing her the way I had wasn't the way to do it. Just because I'd been beaten as a child didn't mean I had a license to abuse my own daughter. No, I had to find another way. Tawny had come home furious that night, but before she'd gone to bed, I'd made her promise to let me talk to her in the morning. Reluctantly, she'd agreed.

I was up before her the next morning making her favorite breakfast—waffles with strawberries. When she joined me in the kitchen, fully dressed, I put on my best "good mother" smile and wished her a good morning.

"You said all we had to do was talk. Then I'm going out," she announced curtly as I set the meal before her.

"Look, Tawny, I realize you're just trying to assert your independence here, but Jake is much too old for you. I don't even believe that he's only twenty-two."

Tawny took a forkful of waffle into her mouth, smudging her perfectly applied pink lipstick slightly. She chewed, looked at me, and said, "Jake said you'd say that."

Jake's not even here and I'm fighting with him, I thought helplessly.

"Honey, I'd like you to talk to someone besides me to get a fresh perspective," I said reasonably, my jaws aching from smiling.

"Who? Jonah?" she asked, taking another bite.

"No," I answered, "a psychologist. I'm sure they have one at your school. Then you could—"

Her laughter, once so reminiscent of tinkling wind chimes, was now harsh and dry, and it stopped me cold.

"Not a good idea?" I asked benignly, instead of grabbing her chin again, the way I wanted to.

She shook her head, dropped her fork, and said, "I don't need to talk. You don't talk to your mother, or a psychologist, or anyone, do you?"

"I'm grown," I replied.

"So am I," she responded coolly, staring right at me, her perfect pink lips arranged in an unbecoming pout.

"Tawny, I've done the best job I could with you, and up until now, we've had a great relationship. What can I do now to help us get along?" I knew I was pleading, but what else could I do? I'd never before been in such a bind.

Her face softened a bit, much to my relief. "Mom," she said, her voice that of a little girl again, "I'm fine, really. You did a good job raising me, but you're done, and now I have to be with Jake. Please try to understand."

"Honey," I began, but her face had closed up again, her lips in a straight line, pressed against her teeth. I stopped speaking and she walked out the door.

It was then that I knew I had no other choice.

I had to talk to Jake.

But I had no idea where to start looking for him because I knew nothing more about him other than that he was good looking and had lied about his age.

Oh—and he was seeing my daughter.

Nevertheless, armed with those facts, I got in the car and drove. I've always been a believer in fate, so it didn't come as a great shock to me when I found Jake walking along Main Street all alone. Obviously, this confrontation was meant to be.

Quickly, I pulled the car over and beeped the horn lightly. Jake recognized me, flashed that bright smile of his, and came over to the car.

"Get in," I demanded, hating him.

He obliged, easing his trim body into the seat next to me.

"Jake, I need to talk to you," I began, driving out of town toward a new diner that Jonah and I had gone to.

"Sure," he responded genially, sitting back comfortably.

In the diner, I studied his face carefully. I could see how Tawny would be attracted to him. He was very nice looking—tan, with high cheekbones, and dark hair cut fashionably short. Even the little gold hoop he wore in his left ear was attractive.

I looked away from him and asked, "Jake, do you realize my daughter is only fourteen?"

He nodded, sipping the coffee he'd ordered. "I know," he said, "but you've done a good job with her, Mrs. Sykes. Tawny's very mature for her age."

I sighed. It was hard to fight with someone who was clearly not antagonistic. "And what could you possibly see in a child that age? You're not having sex with her, are you?"

He shook his head before I'd even finished the question. "No," he said, his cheeks coloring slightly. "I couldn't do that. Tawny—she's just a kid."

"Well, you've kissed her," I insisted.

He nodded shyly. "We kiss, yeah. Sure. It's hard to be around her without kissing her. She's so pretty. She looks just like you." He studied me boldly, the way I'd studied him. I felt my cheeks burn.

"Why are you seeing her, then?" I asked. "You're a good-looking guy. You could have anyone you wanted."

"Even you?" he asked coyly, a little grin playing at the corners of his lips. I stared at him until he laughed and said, "I'm seeing Tawny because I like her, that's all."

Still, I said nothing.

Jake lost his grin then. Lowering his voice, he said, "My little sister, Gwen—she died when she was about Tawny's age. I—I guess I just never really got over it."

"I'm sorry," I muttered, watching as he brushed briefly at his eyes, as though he was crying. Suddenly, I felt terrible. "Did she took like Tawny? Is that it?"

He nodded, sipped his coffee again, and since he didn't seem able to continue talking about his sister. I let it drop. "What do you do for a living, Jake?" I asked.

"I work in a sporting goods store." he said, brightening again. "It's called Titans."

"I know the place," I said, nodding. "Is that where you met Tawny?"

"Yeah. She came in with a few of her friends looking at Rollerblades." He laughed a bit and said, "They were so cute, the group of them, pretending to be so much older than they were. I just couldn't resist talking to them."

It was getting harder and harder for me to dislike Jake. Except for that playful crack about me, I found him really engaging. And if he wasn't lying about the reason he was seeing Tawny, then honestly—what could it hurt? Hurriedly, I banished that thought from my mind.

"Of course, working in a store isn't what I plan to do for a living," he told me. "I'm going to college in the fall to become a gym teacher."

"How long have you been out of high school?" I asked, a sneaky way of finding out his age.

"I know what you're doing," he said in a singsong voice, grinning. "All right," he said then without further prodding, spreading his palms out in front of him on the table, "I'm not twenty-two. I lied. I'm really twenty-five."

I took a deep breath, let it out, wondering what else he'd lied about.

"But the rest is true," he insisted, as though reading my mind. "I—I guess I had to recover from my sister's death, so I put off going to college. Gwen was sick so long..."

The nurse in me perked up. "What was wrong with her?" I asked.

"Leukemia," he answered, looking away for a moment. "It was hard to see her just waste away like that . . . it took a lot out of me."

He looked so sad; I reached across the table and squeezed his hand for a moment. "Where are your parents? Do they live in town?"

He shook his head. "They moved away after my sister died. I have my own apartment."

I sipped my coffee, wondering where I would go from here. He was making it hard for me to attack him.

"Look, Mrs. Sykes, if you really don't want me seeing Tawny, I won't. That's all there is to it. I'll just stay away from her."

That's what I wanted, all right. The trouble was, all of a sudden, I wasn't so sure I wanted this man completely out of my life.

I covered my eyes with my palm for a moment, and then said. "That's a good idea, Jake. I really would rather you didn't date her." Then, captivated for a moment by his clear, bright eyes, I blurted out, "However, if, in a few years, you're. still not attached and still interested, then maybe—"

Shocked at what I'd been about to say, I stood, threw a few bills down onto the table, and began to walk away.

Jake grabbed my hand from behind as he caught up with me. My fingers closed around his.

"Hey, you drove me out here remember? How about a ride back to town?"

I blushed and walked with him to the car.

On the way to town I talked nonstop about my job at the hospital, needing very much to occupy the conversation. I just didn't want to hear Jake's voice again. When I left him at the store, he got out of the car, flashed that great grin at me, and said, "Hey, I'll call you someday if I need medical advice, okay?"

I nodded, willing to say anything to make him leave. To say that I was conflicted about my feelings for him would have been an understatement.

I called Jonah the minute I got home.

"I saw Jake," I told him right away. "He promised he'd stop seeing Tawny."

"Do you believe him?"

"I want to," I replied truthfully, "but, honestly Jonah, I need to forget about all of it today. Let's do something fun this afternoon."

Miniature golf is what Jonah came up with for fun, and that was fine with me. It wasn't especially exciting, but, after all, I'd only asked for fun. After we'd played four holes, Jonah leaned on his club and looked at me.

"Why do you look like that?" he asked.

"Like what?" I responded, confused.

"Like you were faraway for a minute there. Are you still thinking about Jake? I mean, you said he was off-limits, and yet you haven't stopped talking about him. You're thinking about him right now, aren't you?" Stung, I hit my golf ball and said, "I'm not thinking about anything."

"Oh, really? Listen, Cyrinda, are you sure you're not attracted to this guy yourself?"

I laughed, feeling my cheeks burn. "Are you kidding? He's got to be five or six years younger than I am."

"Five or six years?" he asked, stopping again, drawing annoyed stares from the people behind us who were waiting to play.

"Yes," I answered, avoiding Jonah's stare.

"So, you figure him to be about thirty?" I nodded uncertainly. Even though Jake had admitted to being twenty-five, I thought there was a very good chance that he was actually older.

Or maybe it was just wishful thinking.

"And you really believe him when he says he's not having sex with your fourteen-year-old daughter, and that he's going to college this fall?"

"Why are you grilling me, Jonah?" I cried.

And then, too furious to wait for an answer, I tossed my club to the ground and stomped off. I heard Jonah calling after me and I could feel the stares of the people around us, but I didn't care. Tears stung my eyes.

I didn't speak to Jonah during the entire drive home. He didn't seem to mind. I

began to think then that maybe we weren't really right for one another. After all, I deserved some fun out of life, and what kind of a fun date was miniature golf, anyway? Maybe Jonah was just too boring for me.

We parted without words.

Once, home, I went into my bedroom and studied my reflection in the mirror. It was easy for me to imagine that Jake and I looked closer in age than Jonah and I did. Jonah, at forty, was gray and growing a paunch. I, on the other hand, was still trim. I worked really hard at looking good. Just as I came to that conclusion, the phone rang.

"Mrs. Sykes, I'm really sorry to bother you, but remember when I asked if I could call you if I ever had a medical problem?"

He didn't identify himself, but that wasn't necessary. I knew who it was.

"What's wrong, Jake?" I asked.

"Well, after you dropped me off this morning, I went running in the park and I did something to my knee. I sure hate to ask this, but do you think—"

"What?" I pressed during the moment of silence as my heart pounded.

"I shouldn't have called," he said. "I'm sorry."

"It's okay," I insisted. "What do you need Jake?"

"Well, would you mind terribly coming over here? I mean, I'd come to your house, but the pain—"

"Where do you live?" I asked, feeling my professional self spring to life.

Jake gave me his address, which turned out to be an apartment above the sporting goods store, an easy place to find. Since Tawny was out with friends, I didn't have to worry about her, so after throwing a few things I thought I'd need in my purse, I headed out the door.

When I knocked on Jake's door and heard him call to me to come in, I began to feel suddenly shy. Cautiously, I opened the door and followed his shouted directions to the bedroom. There was Jake, his trim athlete's body dressed in running shorts only, sprawled out on the rumpled bed. Putting my purse down, I walked toward him, feeling overdressed and very warm in jeans and a T-shirt. Sweat began to trickle down between my breasts.

"Which knee?" I asked.

Grimacing in pain, Jake pointed to the left. Skillfully, I palpated the knee, my fingers touching his kneecap and the surrounding areas. When I reached the muscle on the right side of his knee, Jake jumped and stifled a shout of pain.

"Looks like a tendon tear," I said, glancing up at his flushed face. "You'd better stay off it for a couple of days. I brought what I thought you'd need."

"You?" he asked playfully as I went to my purse.

I held up an Ace bandage, smiling. "This. I'll put it on. I brought some muscle relaxants, too. I'll leave them for you. If you're not better in a day or two, you should see a doctor."

I said all this while I was bandaging his knee to distract myself from the feel of his muscular leg beneath my fingertips. I had to keep reminding myself that I was a nurse; Jake, my patient. When I was done, I stood and faced him.

He lay back against his pillow and said, "I feel better already. Thanks so much, Mrs. Sykes."

"Cyrinda," I corrected automatically, pulling at the neck of my T-shirt a bit in the heat. "No air-conditioning?" I asked needlessly.

He shook his head. "I've just been lying here, sweating," he said, drawing a fingertip slowly down his bare chest, brushing through hair and sweat.

I looked away, picked up my purse. "Will you be all right?" I asked, my mouth suddenly dry.

"I guess."

"What is it, then?"

"Nothing," he said, grinning slyly. "I guess I can call for a pizza."

"Would you like me to get you something from the deli across the street?"

"I can't ask you to do that," he answered, still smiling.

"Nonsense," I responded happily.

Why was it I couldn't do enough for this man? On impulse, I bought lunch for the both of us and brought it back up to his place.

"Hope you don't mind if I join you," I said as I walked back into his bedroom with the lunches.

"Not at all," he answered eagerly, pulling himself up so that he was sitting against the headboard.

I tried to ignore the way the sweat made his chest hairs shine. Instead, I dug into my sandwich.

In the middle of lunch, Jake yawned and said, "You were right about those muscle relaxants. They sure do relax you." He grinned a silly grin and I laughed, recognizing the effect the pills were having on him.

"Just finish your lunch and take a nap," I advised. "Maybe you'll be cured when you wake up."

He took the last bite of his sandwich, then let his hand fall loosely across his bare chest. "If I'm not better, can I call you again?" he asked in a tired-sounding voice, his eyes half closed.

"Yes," I answered quietly as his eyes closed and he eased himself down in bed. In seconds, he was breathing deeply in sleep. Somewhat reluctantly, I let myself out.

Tawny was home when I got there. I was shocked at how she looked, for there, before me, was my little girl, all traces of makeup gone, her now light amber hair hanging loose around her face. Even her four-times-pierced left ear held only one small stud, which matched the one in her right ear. Impulsively, I kissed her cheek, and then poured us both a soda.

"You look beautiful," I said, sitting across from her.

"Thanks," she replied shyly. "You said I'd be going through a lot of phases."

I nodded and swallowed the cold orange soda, forcing the picture of Jake, his finger trailing sweat down his bare chest from my mind.

"Well, I think I just passed through the pot-smoking punk phase," she said as she screwed her face up in a cute grimace.

"I'm so glad you're through it," I said quietly after I went to her and gave her a big hug.

"I'm through with Jake, too," she announced. "I won't be seeing him anymore."

I studied her face. "What did I ever do to deserve such a brilliant young lady for a daughter?" Tears stung my eyes, so before she could answer, I pulled her to me again and gave her another hug.

"I'm going to the movies tonight, okay?" she asked then.

"Fine. Are you going with Cara?"

She nodded. "Thanks for trusting me, Mom. I know you don't

know Cara, but she's shy. Someday you'll meet her."

I blew her a kiss and she was on her way.

Jonah didn't call that night, and though I was surprised, I made no effort to call him. Instead, I rented a couple of videos. Trouble was, no matter what I watched, all I could see was Jake Chesney lying there in his running shorts.

You've got to stop this, Cyrinda, I told myself. *This isn't good for you.*

Tawny came home from the movies at around eleven, and although I would like to have talked to her a bit, she merely gave me a kiss and went on to bed. She seemed a little down from her earlier mood, but I chalked that up to adolescent hormones. Right after she went to bed I turned off the television and headed to my bedroom. Sleep came for me easily as I pictured my beautiful daughter in my mind, minus makeup, with a new attitude.

The next morning my phone rang at six o'clock right as my alarm went off. I figured it to be Jonah, so I let it ring a couple of times before I picked it up. When I did, I was surprised to hear Jake's voice on the other end.

"I'm sorry to call so early," he said right away. "I hope I didn't wake you."

"No," I answered, feeling heat climb up my throat, warming my face. "How are you feeling?"

"Well, that's why I'm calling, actually," he said in a little-boy voice. "Do you think you could come by here? I'm not any better and I just don't know what to do."

I sighed. I almost never called in sick; I was too dedicated for that.

"Look, Cyrinda—I'm sorry I asked. Never mind about me," he said in that same boyish voice.

"I'll be there in half an hour," I said. He needed to be assured that that was really all right with me, and I gave him that easily.

After he hung up, I called the hospital and told them that I was taking a sick day.

Tawny was still asleep, as she was most of these summer mornings when I left for work, so after I got dressed, I loaded my purse with more medical supplies and left.

As I was driving to Jake's I was aware of what I was doing; I just didn't know why I was doing it. I'd successfully chased Jake away from my daughter, and now here I was, driving to his apartment instead of work at six-thirty in the morning. I realized then that I should've taken more time to think this thing through, but I'd already gone too far. I just didn't realize how far that would end up being.

"You're crazy, Cyrinda," I muttered to myself as I got to his door. I knocked first, then let myself in and walked to the bedroom, calling Jake's name. He looked just as he had when I'd left him the day before, only now, he had a stubble of dark beard shading his jaw.

"Cyrinda, thanks so much for coming," he said, looking troubled and in pain as he lay in shorts again, sheets carelessly strewn about the bed.

"Still hurts?" I asked, while looking at, but not touching, his knee.

"Yeah," he said, frowning.

Empty Chinese takeout containers decorated the dresser and windowsill. It was easy to see he couldn't have eaten all that food by himself. Someone had to have been with him. Fleetingly, I wondered who it was.

Taking a deep breath, I began to unwrap the Ace bandage.

"I was better, but last night around midnight, it really began to hurt a lot," he said, frowning.

The knee still wasn't swollen or red, but when I pressed the tendon that had seemed sore the day before, he winced.

"It's not any worse, Jake," I said, standing again, glad that early morning made it cool in the room. I began to think that I shouldn't have given myself the day off. There was nothing really *wrong* with Jake. But, then, I wasn't really sure why I was here. I'd known from the start that his knee wasn't badly injured.

"Cyrinda," he said then, drawing my gaze to his face, "could you just pull this sheet out from under my shoulders? It's twisted."

I saw something dancing in his eyes, something dangerous. Like a curious kitten, I moved closer. When I reached behind his shoulder, his arms quickly encircled my waist.

"Jake," I said, sending a warning in my voice.

Still staring at me, now grinning, Jake moved his hands up until they were pressing my breasts. His eyes were burning my face.

"We can't," I whispered as he began to pull me down on top of him.

Ignoring my words, he pressed his lips to mine. He tasted of toothpaste and orange juice. I pulled away from him and looked into his face, his heavy-lidded eyes. A warning shouted out in my brain. I ignored it and let my body fall onto his. In moments, we were naked.

By the time the noonday sun heated the room, we'd made love twice and lay sweating on damp sheets.

"You were great," Jake whispered in my ear after we woke from a nap. I lay with my back to him, his bare body pressed against me. Staring out the window, I began to wonder about what I'd just done.

When Jake's phone rang, I took that moment to go into the bathroom to wash up. Looking in the mirror, I hardly recognized the woman who looked back at me. A feeling of dread filled me. I could hear Jake's hardy laugh as he talked on the phone, and briefly, I wondered who he was talking to.

Quickly, I dressed, and when he hung up, I was trying to pull my damp hair into something that resembled a ponytail.

I'd lost track of Jake in my haste, but as I looked around the room for my purse, I caught sight of him standing at the window, smoking a joint, his back to me, still wearing just those shorts. The Ace bandage had come off his knee the first time we'd made love. It lay tangled in the mass of sheets on the unmade bed.

"Listen, babe, when you get home, tell that hot little number of yours, Tawny, that I can't make it today. Knee hurts too much."

He'd turned slowly as he spoke until he was facing me, that smile I once found so attractive decorating his face, mocking me. I stared at him in horror, wanting to rush out the door, and at the same time, wishing I had a weapon so I could kill him.

"Cat got your tongue?" he asked playfully as he rubbed his bare stomach with an open palm.

Suddenly, in my mind, I saw it all crumbling to pieces. "You lied about everything?" I asked, feeling the terrible taste of bile in my mouth. "Your little sister—everything?" My knees felt week.

"Yep," he nodded, laughing a bit. "Oh, I once had a gerbil named Gwen, but it got flushed down the toilet or something. I forget."

My heart was pounding so hard, it actually hurt my chest. "Why?" I asked as tears of fury began to fill my eyes.

He shrugged. "I like women. I like women of all ages, all sizes. And I *love* the hunt." He paused, put out his joint. "Once the challenge is over, though, I like my women gone. Except, of course, for virgins. Them I keep around for a while. They're usually so grateful. Tawny sure has been." Bending down, he retrieved my purse from the floor and threw it to me. "Bye-bye, Nursey," he said, heading to the bathroom. "Lock up on your way out."

Three fast steps started me across the room, my arms outstretched. I knew I could kill him with my bare hands. He met me halfway, roughly grabbed my wrists, and threw me away from him as easily as he'd thrown my purse.

"Get out," he ordered as I struggled to my feet.

"I'll have the police here tonight!" I said, nearly breathless from emotion. "You won't get away with this. You raped a minor!"

"I didn't *rape* anyone, but that doesn't matter. I'll be gone by tonight. But good luck, anyway," he said as he entered the bathroom.

Every emotion I'd ever felt filled me. I didn't know whether to try to break down the door, or scream rape, or wait for him to come out so I could kill him with a kitchen knife.

In the end, I did none of those things. In the end, I merely picked up my purse and left.

I cried all the way home, realizing what a fool I'd been, what a stupid fool. I'd believed in him, and all the while, he'd been abusing my daughter.

How could I have slept with him?

Jake Chesney was the devil himself.

I knew I was a mess when I parked in front of my house, but I didn't try to straighten myself out, figuring that Tawny could be out at this time of day. I pulled myself out of the car and stumbled into the house, still crying.

"Mom?" I heard the minute I got in.

Quickly, I wiped my nose, blotted by eyes.

"I've been looking all over for you, Mom. Where were you? Why weren't you at work?" Tawny cried, running down the stairs to meet me. When she didn't mention the sight I had to have been, I knew there was still more trouble facing me. And I knew that somehow, it involved Jake Chesney.

"Mom, we have to talk," Tawny said, taking my hand, leading me into the living room.

Yes, Tawny, I thought, *we do have to talk. You've been listening to a monster instead of me.*

I did my best to pull myself together, despite the terrible headache I felt pounding inside my skull.

"Mom," she said after we both sat down on the couch.

I waited. In seconds, her face went from one filled with resolve to that of the three-year-old she'd once been.

"What is it, honey?" I asked.

She shook her head, her hair falling in her face. I made her sit back so I could face her.

"Tawny, I know it's something bad. Tell me."

She stared at me, tears running down her face. "I'm pregnant," she said in a harsh whisper.

I sat there staring at her for one beat, two. Then I sagged against the back of the couch feeling weak.

Not pregnant, I thought, *He couldn't have done that to her.*

Tawny got hysterical then, and I left her on the couch, went into the kitchen and poured myself a small glass of scotch from the bottle I kept over the stove. I felt I'd be needing it.

Tawny had calmed a bit by the time I came back into the living room. "Who's the father?" I asked in a tone so normal, one could have thought I'd planned the pregnancy.

Please let it be someone else—anyone else. Please, I prayed.

Tawny looked away at first, then back at me. "Jake," she said in a harsh whisper.

Shattered, I stared at my daughter. *Of course*, I thought. Even though he's used a condom with me, he didn't need one with Tawny. Tawny was a virgin. What could he catch from my innocent daughter?

"Oh, God!" I cried, my head in my hands.

This was a nightmare. The scotch I'd drunk had no effect on me at all, and I considered getting more, when right in front of me stood Jonah. I hadn't even heard the door open.

"Cyrinda, can I help?" he asked.

"Tawny told you?"

He nodded and said, "Tawny said she couldn't find you, and I didn't think she should be alone."

I stood and hugged him. "Thank you, Jonah. Thank you."

"We can work this out, Cyrinda. I know we can," he insisted quietly.

I stared at him—at his thinning gray hair, at his slightly thick waistline, knowing in my heart that I didn't deserve him.

Like most problems in life, ours had a solution. Since Jake was the father of Tawny's child, I took the decision about the pregnancy right out of her fourteen-year-old hands. Tawny had an abortion. It wasn't an easy decision to make, but Tawny accepted it. I'd given my teenager way too much rope; she'd almost hung herself with it.

Tawny and I talk a lot more about things that are really important to her now. She confessed to me that the fictional character Cara was really Jake, but I don't blamer her for any of that. Tawny was a child when she met him; Jake Chesney took callous, cruel advantage of her.

When I start worrying about whether or not I made the right decision, I remind myself that Tawny's still just a teenage, after all. Then I'm glad I decided to let her continue adolescence without the burden of early motherhood. I think she'll survive the mistakes I've made raising her.

I've tried to be more open with her, too, explaining about the very religious upbringing I'd had, which caused me to raise her without limits whatsoever. The only thing I've never told her is that her mother slept with the father of her aborted child. Tawny doesn't need to hear that; no one does, for that matter. It's something that will haunt me for the rest of my life.

Jake left town just as he said he would. Apparently he's just a drifter—a mean spirited user of women, mind you—but no more than a drifter nonetheless. I pity the next woman he steals from, for he did steal from me. He took my money, my time, my attention, and closest to my heart, my beautiful daughter, Tawny Evangeline.

Jonah and I were married a short time ago, and Tawny was my maid of honor. She brought a date to the wedding—a boy as young as she is. They looked adorable dancing together. THE END

THE STEPMOTHER CURSE: "I'M WICKED NO MATTER WHAT I DO!"

Now that we've seen a few stories about single moms trying to find their second husbands, here's a young woman who's fallen in love with a man who already has a child of his own. Serena met Trace standing in line at a fast-food place, and they were married just two months later. Trace only has custody of his eight-year-old daughter on the weekends, but that's still plenty of time for Olivia to act resentful toward her stepmother.

"This wasn't the way it was supposed to be," Serena admits. "I had married the man of my dreams, and part of the dream had been to be the perfect mother to his child." But while that dream may not be off to a great start, the fact that she's the one telling us this story is strong evidence that she's not going to quit trying anytime soon—especially since she remembers all too keenly what it was like to be the confused little girl adjusting to a new adult in her life.

"**I** hate you! I hate you! You're a mean old stepmother—even worse than Cinderella's!" I stood there, watching Olivia sob into her pink-checked pillowcase, and my blood ran cold. Her small body shook with grief, knotting itself into a tighter ball with each tremor.

Wicked stepmother? That couldn't be true. Not about me. I had married my Prince Charming, and that made *me* Cinderella. Didn't it? Anyway, I certainly understood the pain of a cold and uncaring step-mother; I'd vowed when I married Trace Snyder that I would treat his eight-year-old daughter as if she was my very own little girl.

I sat down on the bed and pulled Olivia toward me. Her body stiffened and my heart twisted with remorse. Not five minutes earlier,

I'd lost patience with Olivia and screamed at her like a New York City taxi driver. And it wasn't the first time.

"I'm sorry I yelled," I said, my own voice shaking, "but you had told me that your bed was made, and when I checked, the comforter was thrown on the floor." I reached to pat Olivia's hand, but she pulled away from me. "Everyone in the family has chores," I tried again, determined to stay calm. "One of your chores is to make your bed every morning."

"You're not my mother! I don't have to do what you say!" Olivia pulled herself up against the headboard. Rebellion twisted her face into a pout.

Resentment spiraled through me. I had worked hard all week and I didn't need a hateful little girl to deal with every weekend. But I sighed and tried again. "I know I'm not your mother, but this is my house and I make the rules. Everyone makes their own bed here."

"My mommy doesn't make me do work at home. She says you're mean to make me work all the time!" Olivia hiccupped between sobs. The same words she'd said a few minutes earlier in the living room. "My mommy says I don't have to do what you say, and I'm not going to!"

My temper flared. Without any conscious thought, I raised my arm and swatted Olivia on her bottom. Hard. I saw the red imprint of my hand below the edge of her T-shirt.

I stared in horror, remembering the times when my own stepmother had taken my father's belt and whipped me with it until red welts lined my legs. I'd sworn years ago that I would never raise my hand against a child.

"Daddy! Daddy!" Olivia screamed at the top of her lungs. "Serena hit me! She hit me!" Her screams echoed through the house and could probably be heard by the neighbors.

The sound of Trace's footsteps pounded down the hallway, the door swung open, and my husband's handsome head peered inside.

"Hey, what's going on in here?"

"Serena hit me!" Olivia screamed.

"Oh, come on, Olivia. Serena wouldn't do that." Trace looked questioningly at me. "She doesn't believe in hitting children."

Heat rose in my cheeks and I dropped my gaze.

"She hit me!" Olivia propelled herself off the bed and into the arms of her father. "She's mean and she hates me and she makes me do all of the work just like Cinderella's wicked stepmother!"

"Olivia," I gasped. "That's not true. I only wanted you to make your bed. And I never meant to hit you." I paused, struggling for an explanation that didn't seem to come. "That was an accident, sweetheart."

"Was not!" Olivia wrapped her arms and legs around Trace's body. "She hit me really hard because she hates me and she's mean!"

I wanted to peel the child from her father and shake her until she was limp. Then I went weak with horror at even having such a thought. Shaking could kill a child! How could such a small person unleash such anger inside of me? But was I really mad at Olivia? Wasn't I actually angry with her mother, Nicole?

"I think that Nicole has poisoned Olivia's mind against me," I blurted out, then wished I hadn't. It was wrong to speak against a mother in front of her child, but I seemed powerless to control myself. "All I asked her to do was make her bed before watching TV. She lied about it, then said that I wasn't her mother and she didn't have to do what I said." Too late, I bit my lip. I had descended back into childhood, screaming accusations back and forth with a child, almost as if I was vying for Trace's approval. What was I doing? Trying to compete with an eight-year-old?

"Is that true, sugar?" Trace asked his daughter patiently. "Did you lie and then say those hurtful things to Serena?" I saw his forehead crease and I cringed knowing that I had put him in the position of having to take sides between his wife and child.

Olivia hesitated, then burst into fury. "Yes—but she's not my real mother, and I don't have to mind her, do I, Daddy?" Olivia kissed Trace's cheek and patted his hair, a method calculated to wrap Trace around her little finger. My earlier remorse evaporated into annoyance.

Trace shot me a desperate look, but instead of helping, I put my hands on my hips and narrowed my eyes. A silent reminder of our many discussions about the need to discipline Olivia.

I saw his face cloud with frustration, then darken with the anger that inevitably followed. Trace seldom lost his temper, but when he did, it wasn't a pretty sight. I began to wish I'd held my tongue as he separated himself from Olivia and set her on the floor.

"Young lady, you do indeed have to mind your stepmother."

I cringed, wishing he'd picked another word—like Serena, or my wife.

"I won't, I won't!" Olivia screamed in red-faced rage.

Trace seemed to snap. I could almost see the anger coursing through him. My wonderful husband, whom I jokingly called Prince Charming, stood over his cowering daughter and screamed at her, his face red with fury. And it was all my fault.

"You won't mind your stepmother? You lied about making your bed?" he yelled. "You won't watch TV again this weekend! You've got to show some respect for your stepmother's wishes!"

"Trace," I whispered, not quite sure what to do. I didn't want to undermine the discipline, but I was horrified at his overkill tactics. Besides, if she didn't watch TV, what would she do all weekend? Make my life miserable? "Don't you think that's a little drastic for not making a bed?"

"Too drastic?" Trace ran his fingers through his black, curly hair. "First you complain that I never discipline Olivia, and now you complain that I'm too tough? There's just no way that I can please you. You're getting to be just as much of a whiner as Nicole!"

Anger filled me. It was on the tip of my tongue to yell that maybe Nicole had reason to whine, but I didn't like badmouthing a mother in front of her child, not even when the mother and child were Nicole and Olivia.

"I think this is an inappropriate conversation to have in front of a child," I said, with a meaningful glance at Olivia.

"You're talking to me like I'm some little kid!" Trace said. "You think I'm wrong no matter what I do! You want to handle this, you handle it!" He stormed out of the bedroom.

"All right, I will!" I shouted through the slamming door, determined to have the last word. Then I saw the smirk on Olivia's face, and I knew I'd played right into her hands. I ground my teeth together to keep from scolding her.

You're a daycare professional, I reminded myself, *Why don't you use the skills you've worked so hard to develop at work? Everyone at the Sunshine Center thinks you hung the moon. Surely you can handle one kid!*

I took a deep breath, then smiled at Olivia just to prove that I was in charge. "Olivia, why don't I show you how to make up your bed? We can make a game of it," I said brightly.

"I don't want to make my bed! I don't have to make my bed at home and I don't have to here! I don't have to mind you. You're not my real mother!" Olivia hid her face in her hands, but her sobs were dry sobs. I determined to keep my cool.

"That may be true, but this is my house, and while you live here on the weekends, you're going to obey my rules." I forced myself to smile.

"Am not! Am not! I hate you! You're worse than Cinderella's wicked old stepmother! You make me do all of the work, and now you won't let me watch *Sesame Street!*"

"Young lady, don't you dare speak to me like that! You can just stay right here in your room alone until you can keep a civil tongue in your head!" As soon as I'd spoken the words, they echoed in my ears. My hands went clammy. It was the exact speech my own stepmother had screamed at me twenty years ago when I was eight years old. The painful memory of that speech was the motivation behind my need to be a good stepmother to Olivia.

I vividly remembered the anger I'd felt toward my father's second wife. Hateful memories, years old, flooded my mind while I stared at Olivia's obstinate little back as she rolled off the bed and marched herself to the corner to sit down and pout miserably. Suddenly, she looked very small and alone. I wanted to call her back, to put my arms around the stubborn little shoulders, so like her father's when he was angry.

This wasn't the way it was supposed to be. I had married the man of my dreams, and part of the dream had been to be the perfect mother to his child. It was almost impossible to believe, when I thought of how well everything had begun, that it could all be falling apart so horribly.

It had been one of those perfect autumn days about a year ago when I first met Trace. The air was crisp and clean and the sun warm—Indian summer is what you'd call it. The day had a positively magical feel to it. I'd awakened glad to be alive, almost certain that something wonderful was going to happen to me that day.

And it did. His name was Trace Snyder. He was tall and slender, with broad shoulders, curly black hair, and beautiful brown eyes that twinkled with the warmth of golden sunshine.

I had never believed in love at first sight—in fact, at the time, I wasn't sure that I believed in love at all, since I'd seen so little of it in my twenty-eight years. But when I saw Trace behind me in the line at that fast-food restaurant, laughing because I couldn't make up my mind about whether I wanted a Mega Cheese Supreme or a Deep Sea Filet, my legs almost melted beneath me.

We shared a booth and laughter, and split the Mega Cheese Supreme and the Deep Sea Filet. By the time lunch was over, Trace knew the story of my life and I knew his.

He'd had a bittersweet childhood, not unlike my own. His parents had divorced when he was ten and he'd lived with his mother, while I'd gone with My father. Trace told me he'd met his ex-wife when he was in the service, and married her after she'd gotten pregnant. The marriage had been a failure from the start, but he'd never regretted the birth of his daughter, Olivia.

When Nicole had decided she was unhappy in the marriage and wanted her freedom, Trace confessed that he'd felt conflicting emotions—relief at receiving his freedom, and guilt at not providing a solid, stable home for his daughter. Talking to him, I just knew I could make all of his dreams come true, and he mine.

I told him about my own life—how my parents had also gotten divorced when I was just a child; how my mother had been more interested in her boyfriends than in raising me; and how miserable and lonely I'd been throughout my growing-up years.

Trace was delighted to learn that I worked at the Sunshine Center. I told him about how all of the children called me Miss Serena, and that someday, I wanted to have a whole house full of kids myself. Later that night, when I remembered all of the things that I'd told him, I blushed with embarrassment, figuring he probably wouldn't ever want to see me again.

But he did. Trace called the very next day to take me to dinner, and we were married two months later. We were perfect for each other because we both wanted the same things, and one of them was to provide a good home for Olivia, even if it was only on the weekends.

But it hadn't worked out the way we'd planned. The one child in the world I couldn't get along with had turned out to be my own stepdaughter.

"Well, if I can't watch TV, what can I do?" Olivia had turned away from her corner and was glaring at me. "I'm bored."

"After you make your bed, we could go to the park," I suggested, looking out the window and seeing that it was a perfect autumn day, very like the one a year ago when Trace and I had fallen in love.

Olivia rolled her eyes, stalked over to where her comforter was lying on the floor, and picked it up. She spread it haphazardly on the bed.

"There," she said.

I opened my mouth to object, then closed it. I just wasn't up to another fight.

"Fine," I said.

After the usual amount of whining from Olivia, we arrived at the park. I could tell by the way that Trace was playing up to Olivia that he was sorry he'd come down so hard on her about the bed and wished he hadn't taken away her TV privileges.

"Want a ride, princess?" He lifted her up onto his shoulders and they trotted down the sidewalk ahead, leaving me to trail along behind, feeling like a stranger. I wanted to be a part of the family, not some third party of little value.

"Don't you think she's a little old for that?" I remarked. I knew it wasn't a nice thing to say, but right then, I just didn't feel like being nice.

"She'll never be too old for her daddy to lift," Trace said, laughing and zigzagging along the sidewalk. "Last one to the swings is a wet blanket!" he said, lowering Olivia to the ground.

They both sprinted away, leaving me walking slowly behind. When I reached them, Olivia was sailing high into the air on a swing. She cast a triumphant look at me and suddenly I realized that she looked on this as a game, and that she was clearly the winner.

A cold shiver slid down my spine.

Later on that night after Olivia had gone to bed, I tried to discuss the matter with Trace, but he had the football game on and I could tell he didn't want to talk. I tried anyway.

"Things are going badly with Olivia," I said, trying to stand between him and the 36-inch TV screen. "It seems like the harder I try to be a good mother to her, the worse things get."

"Can't this wait until later, hon?" Trace asked, leaning sideways in an attempt to see around me.

"It's not something we can discuss in front of Olivia, Trace," I said. "There never seems to be a good time for us to talk lately."

"After the game would be a good time," Trace said.

But after the game, Trace had other ideas. He pulled me close and nuzzled my neck.

"Mmmmm ... you smell *good*," he said.

"I thought we were supposed to *talk*," I answered, remembering how hurt I'd been at the park and pushing him away.

"Actions speak louder than words," Trace said with a laugh, sweeping me off of my feet and carrying me toward the bedroom.

I giggled in spite of myself. It was exciting to be swept off of your feet, and I didn't want him to think of me as a whiney wife. He threw me onto the bed and began to smother me with kisses, and soon I didn't care that I had been mad; all I wanted was for him to keep kissing me.

After we'd made love, Trace rolled over onto his side with his back to me. I could hear his soft snoring almost immediately.

I felt empty and frustrated and blinked back tears, but comforted myself with the thought that there was just one more day left of "our" weekend with Olivia. Then I would have Trace all to myself for another week—until the next in an endless line of weekends from hell arrived. It struck me how selfish this thought was and I took a painful little breath, then determined to try even harder tomorrow to be a better stepmother.

I was packing a picnic lunch for a trip to the zoo when the doorbell rang. Nicole stood in the doorway holding a pillowcase full of Olivia's clothes and wearing a phony smile. It always made me feel funny talking to her. I knew it wasn't my fault that she and Trace had broken up; I hadn't even met him until they'd been divorced for over a year. But she was the mother of his child, and I never knew quite what to say to her.

"Is Trace here?" Nicole glanced back toward a red sports car with a man behind the wheel parked in front of our house.

"Mommy?" a small, scared voice asked from beside me. "Did you come to get me, Mommy?" Olivia sounded wistful, but the expression in her eyes told me that she had no hope.

I caught my breath. This was exactly the same scene that had played out twenty years ago between my mother and me. I remembered how scared I'd been when I saw my stepmother's angry face and my father's worried one.

"Come in, Nicole." I stepped toward Olivia and pulled her against me to open the door for her mother. Olivia stiffened, but for once, I didn't take it personally.

Nicole declined, then took exactly two minutes to hand me Olivia's clothes in the pillowcase and tell me she'd be gone for a while with her new boyfriend. He was moving to Tampa, and she wasn't exactly sure when they'd be back.

Hearing her mother's words, Olivia threw herself against Nicole, clinging desperately to her long, slender legs. "Mommy, Mommy! Please don't go!" she wailed, the sound of her voice and the look on her face breaking my heart like it had broken all those years ago.

"Now, now, Olivia. Tears will make your face ugly." Nicole pulled away. "Be a good girl and Mommy will bring you a pretty new dress when she comes back." She glanced toward the man in the car, then bent over to peck a kiss at Olivia's head. "Bye-bye," she said, and ran for the waiting sports car.

"What's going on?" Trace asked, coming to the door from the kitchen. "Olivia, baby, what's the matter?"

Olivia wheeled on her heels and fled upstairs to her room, screaming all of the way.

"What happened?" Trace asked, glancing first at the car speeding away, and then at the pillowcase full of clothes that I was still holding.

"Olivia will be staying with us now," I said quietly.

I handed him the clothes and went up to Olivia's room, pausing for a brief moment at the closed door, and then knocking.

"Olivia," I said softly, to give her the feeling of the sanctity of her own room, "it's Serena. Can I come in, honey?"

"No! No! I don't want you! I hate you! You're mean! I want my mommy! She's nice to me!"

I opened the door and walked over to the curled-up ball of misery lying on the bed. My heart ached. I sat down and rubbed my hand gently against her back. Olivia stiffened instantly.

I drew back, rebuffed, and listened to the strangled sobs of an eight-year-old. I sat there remembering. And then I decided to tell her the truth.

"Olivia, sweetheart, it's true that I'm not your real mommy, and that sometimes, I do the wrong things." I heard Olivia's breathing soften ever so faintly. "I don't really know how to be anyone's mommy. But I'm trying to learn, honey."

"You think I'm a bad little girl." Olivia's voice wavered. "You don't like me very much."

"Sometimes I say things that I don't mean," I said softly. "Especially when you hurt my feelings."

Dead silence.

"I hurt your feelings?" Olivia sat up in bed, tear streaks staining her cheeks.

I nodded. "And when you called me your wicked stepmother, it hurt my feelings really badly, and that's why I got so angry with you, Olivia." I slipped my hand over her fingers. "But I'm sorry now. I really am."

"Why?" Olivia asked, tears streaming freely down her cheeks now.

"Because even though I get mad at you sometimes, I really love you, Olivia."

"You can't love me—I'm not your very own little girl," Olivia said quietly, looking down and pulling her hand away from me to rub at her tears.

"Yes, that may be true, but you're my very own little stepdaughter; and I love both you and your daddy very, very much." I pulled Olivia onto my lap and she leaned her face against me. The softness of her delicate little body went straight to my heart.

"You do?" Olivia asked. "Are you sure?"

"I'm sure." I rocked back and forth with her. "And it doesn't matter if we get mad at each other. That's okay, too. We're a family now, and sometimes family members get angry with each other, but things always get better in the end."

"They do?" Olivia's tearful eyes were round with wonder.

"You bet. And no matter who gets angry, this is your room, Olivia, and you can live here forever."

"I can?" A half-smile spread over Olivia's face. "Are you sure?"

"I'm absolutely sure," I said.

Olivia's gaze lifted and her grin widened. "Hi, Daddy," she said.

I turned and saw Trace watching us from the doorway, his eyes filled with tears of love.

"Hi, sugar." Trace came over to the bed, smiling at us. He sat down and pulled both of us into his arms.

I had never felt so safe. THE END

SLAVE MOM: MY FAMILY WOULDN'T LEND A HAND
It Took The Military To Free This Woman

Diana works a full-time job, which doesn't leave her a lot of time to clean up after her husband Ralph and their two sons. And because her mother-in-law believes it's a woman's duty to clean up after her man, Ralph isn't likely to be much help dealing with the dirty dishes and the laundry. "When I suggested he help with the cleaning," Diana remembers, "he informed me that since he made most of the money in our family, he deserved to relax when he came home." You can guess how well that went over.

Housework was one of the first concessions True Love *and* True Romance *made to the feminist movement, in terms of adjusting their vision of what makes a perfect marriage—and yet, even after decades of stories where husbands and sons realize they can make women happy by offering to split the household stores, the idea that "there is no such thing as men's work or women's work" was still treated as an almost radical concept… at least for the characters. You get the sense, from Diana's narration, that the women reading her story would be shaking their heads in sympathy the whole time.*

The edge in my husband's voice could've cut through steel. "Are all the dishes dirty? I can't find one single clean glass. Do you want me to have to drink out of the faucet? Why didn't you run the dishwasher this morning?"

Unfinished housework was the story of my life. "I didn't have time to finish loading it. If you look in that cabinet, you'll find some paper cups. Use one of them."

Ralph didn't bother to look where I was pointing. "I don't want to use a paper cup. I want to drink out of a real glass. I thought you were going to try harder to keep up with everybody around here."

Eric, our younger son, walked into the kitchen. "Mom, you know my basketball jersey? I want to wear it, but I can't find it."

"It's probably with the dirty clothes. Wear something else."

"But, Mom, I want to wear that shirt. Can't you just wash it now?" His ten-year-old face looked as serious as if wearing that shirt were the most important thing in the world.

"Not right now, Eric."

"Oh, Mom!"

"Well, wash some glasses then," my husband insisted. "I want a drink of water."

About that time, Marty, our twelve-year-old, came in from soccer. "What's for dinner, Mom? I'm starved."

"Chicken, but first I'll have to run to the grocery store and get a few things." I picked up my purse. "I'll be right back."

"Wait," Ralph said. "What about my glass?"

"Use a paper cup, and I'd really appreciate it if you could finish loading the dishwasher."

He mumbled something about it not being his job to clean up our pigsty of a house, and that I should try harder, but I didn't stick around to listen. I'd heard it all before. So I hurried out the door.

Ralph was right. The house was a pigsty. Every dish we owned was always dirty, and our clothes were all piled in the laundry room. The bathrooms needed scrubbing. The trash should have been taken out, and every room needed to be cleaned and straightened. The problem was that I just couldn't keep up with it.

I worked full time as a receptionist for a family practitioner, but my husband was brought up to think that housework is the sole burden of women. I've tried to train our sons to clean up after themselves, but they take their cues from their father.

Ralph's mother, Ann, had always let him think that a man was too good to worry about mundane chores like cooking, cleaning, and doing laundry. She said that since men work for their families, fight for their countries, and lead more stressful lives than women, it is the duty of the women of the world to take care of them. While that attitude might have been common a hundred years ago, Ann didn't seem to grasp the fact that these days women were doing everything men have always done. So my mother-in-law criticized my housekeeping, and my husband echoed her sentiments.

My own mother had passed away not long after I married Ralph, and my father, a colonel in the Air Force, was always stationed in some exotic part of the world. He wasn't around much when I was growing up.

I had suggested to my husband that we hire a woman to come in and clean a couple of times each week, but he had pointed out that his mom had raised four boys without help. When I countered that Ann hadn't worked a job, Ralph argued that since we had only half as many boys, I should only have half as much housework as his mother had.

One time, Ralph offered to take the boys to the park to give me a chance to clean up; but when I suggested he help with the cleaning instead, he informed me that since he made most of the money in our family, he deserved to relax when he came home. We had a bad fight after that. From then on, whenever he criticized my housekeeping, I just determined to try harder.

I was sick of the whole situation, but I couldn't stop thinking about it I guess that's why, as I drove home from the grocery store, I didn't see the truck that ran a red light and crashed into the side of my car.

I woke up in the hospital with a broken leg, and broken ribs. Between the pain and the painkillers, I wasn't aware of much of what was going on.

I remember Dr. Mercer, my boss, coming to see me and telling me not to worry, that I was in good hands and everything would be all right. When I asked my husband how he and the boys were getting along, he patted my hand and said he had everything under control. I was too sick to wonder what he meant.

My father called my room while I was still in the hospital. "How, are you doing, pumpkin?"

"I'm all right, Dad."

"Your doctor says you're lucky to be alive. Now listen, I can't get away for a few days, but I've spoken to Ralph, and I should be there before the end of next week. Don't you worry about a thing."

"You don't have to come, Dad. I know you're busy. I have a few broken bones, but I'll be all right."

"I want to see you for myself, pumpkin, and I'll be there just as soon as I can."

When Ralph took me home from the hospital, I was surprised to discover that the house was clean, the laundry was done, and dinner was on the table.

"How did you do this?" I asked him.

"We managed," was all he said.

Marty told me that the neighbors came in and cleaned the house, and they had been taking turns bringing supper for my family while I was in the hospital. They had been very nice to Ralph and the boys, and I was grateful for their help, but once I was back home, their job was done. I was on my own.

So much for being on my own, I thought. My head hurt. My broken ribs kept me from taking a deep breath. All I could do with my crutches was hobble from my bed to a chair in the living room. Ralph couldn't stay with me. He had to go back to work. Marty and Eric went to school, and I was left alone in the house. Not that I minded being alone. I closed my eyes and let the peace and quiet soak into my broken body.

But too quickly, Ralph and the boys came back, all with the same question on their lips.

"What's for dinner?"

"I don't know," I told Ralph. "You'll have to tell me what's in the kitchen, and maybe I can explain how to cook it."

"Don't worry about dinner, honey," my husband said. "We'll order a pizza. Marty, call and get a jumbo with everything on it. Have them deliver some sodas, too."

We ate pizza the first night, submarine sandwiches the next, and Chinese food on the third night. After that, I tried to get my husband to take over the cooking.

"Ralph, we can't order food for the rest of my recovery. We'll go broke. You'll have to try to cook something. I know there's spaghetti in the kitchen. It's easy to make. You won't have any trouble. I'll tell you everything that needs to be done." But my husband couldn't boil water without burning it. He forgot to stir the spaghetti to keep it from sticking together, and he couldn't find the sauce. So we ended up eating something that tasted like ketchup poured over a mass of starchy goop.

The clothes piled up, the dishes piled up, and everything else went downhill. That was when Ann came by for a visit.

"Somebody ought to clean this place up," she told me.

"Well, now that you're here, Mom, maybe you can help," Ralph said.

"I'm sorry, but I'm on my way to a bridge luncheon. I just popped in to see if Diana needed anything," his mother told him.

"She could use some help," her son pointed out.

"I think you should call a maid service," Ann suggested. "There are several good ones listed in the phone book. My friend Betty uses one."

"Good for Betty," I muttered after she was gone. "Ralph, did your dad ever do any housework?"

He glared at me. "He didn't have to. He had Mom to take care of him. She never wrecked the car."

"I didn't wreck the car either," I snapped. "In case the police didn't tell you, somebody else ran into me."

"I know," he said. "I'm sorry. It's just that I feel so helpless. I don't know what to do. I wish we could afford to call a maid service."

I wish we could, too, I thought.

Dad arrived on Saturday morning. "Hey, pumpkin, I'm home," he called.

"Come on in, Dad. I'm in the living room."

He was barely in the door when Eric and Marty surrounded him. "Grandpa, we didn't know you were coming!"

"So, how are my favorite grandsons?"

"We're your only grandsons," Marty pointed out.

"You're still my favorites. Now, take me to your mother."

"It's good to see you, Dad," I said as he bent over and kissed my forehead.

"I wish it was under better circumstances. But your old dad is here now. Don't you worry about a thing. I'll have this place shipshape in no time."

"But, Dad, don't you want to sit and visit first?"

He smiled. "Now, you know I've never been much for sitting. We'll have plenty of time to visit." He turned to Eric and Marty. "Boys, I'm going to need your help."

"Sure, Grandpa,"

Marty answered.

"What can we do?"

"We'll start on the kitchen first. Eric, I want you to bring all the dirty dishes over to the sink. Marty, you rinse them, and I'll load the dishwasher."

"You mean you want us to wash dishes?" Eric asked.

"For a start. Then we'll wipe the counters, mop the floor, fix lunch, and move on to the next room."

"But Grandpa," Eric said, "that's women's work."

"Women's work? Who told you that?"

"Well, Grandma always says—"

"Janet never said anything like that." Janet was my mother. Dad suddenly realized that the boys weren't talking about her. "Oh, you mean Ann. She said that, huh? Well, I don't agree with her. You see, Eric, that attitude has limited man's potential for hundreds of years. The truth is, there is no such thing as men's work or women's work. There is only work and it all needs to be done. Do you think General Fredral Chennault took his mother along to clean up after him?"

"Who was General Fredral Chennault?" the boys wanted to know.

"Let's get started on the dishes, and I'll tell you all about General Chennault and the Flying Tigers."

Ralph came in while Dad was fixing lunch. "Something smells really good. Oh, Colonel, I didn't know you were here."

"Haven't I told you to call me Fred? You're just in time. Lunch is ready. If you'll set the table, I'll go help Diana into the kitchen."

"How long will you be in town?" Ralph asked Dad over lunch.

"I'll stay as long as my little girl needs me. I have some leave due, and it looks like you can use my help."

"Fred, we don't want to ruin your visit by asking you to--"

"Nonsense," Dad interrupted. "You're not ruining my visit. That's what family is for. Now, Ralph, tell me about the insurance business. I've been wanting to talk to you about whether I should get more term life."

Dad hadn't been there an hour, and he had my family eating out of his hand. My husband was happily explaining insurance options, and my two sons hung on every word as though they knew exactly what their father and grandfather were talking about.

After we had finished eating, Dad and the boys cleaned the kitchen, made a grocery list, and left for the supermarket. "I'm going to teach you how to make a stir fry," Dad told them as they went out the door.

"I'm amazed," Ralph told me. "I didn't know your dad was so efficient."

"I didn't either," I admitted. "I hate to say this, but I don't know my dad very well. The few times he was home, he was always so imposing. I was kind of afraid of him."

"Well, I'm glad he's here. I hope he's serious about staying for a while."

Ralph must have meant that, because when Dad explained that he had taken a room at a motel, my husband insisted he stay with us and sleep on the fold-out sofa in the family room. The boys echoed the invitation, and I was relieved when Dad agreed.

"Are you really a pilot?" Eric asked as he helped his brother carry Dad's bags into the family room.

By the time a week had passed, my father had everything straight and running smoothly. He had taught the boys and even Ralph how to clean, cook simple meals, and do the laundry. Instead of complaining, they seemed to enjoy the work.

Ann appeared on Friday afternoon. Dad answered the door wearing one of my aprons.

"Come on in, Ann. You look as though you just came from the beauty parlor."

"Hello, Colonel. As a matter of fact, I did. Thanks for noticing. But if you don't mind me asking, what in the world are you wearing?"

"An apron, ma'am. It keeps the cleanser off my clothes. I was just cleaning the bathroom sink. When Ralph gets home, we're going to tackle the windows."

"Ralph? Wash windows?"

Dad gave her a cold look. "Yes, Ann. You raised a good man, but he needed a little guidance."

"Guidance?"

"He suffered from the misconception that women are the only ones who clean up in the world."

Ann's face turned pink. "I don't understand."

"I know you don't," Dad said. "More's the pity. Now if you'll excuse me, I'll get back to the bathroom sink. Diana's over there on the sofa. As you can see, she's fine."

"Your father's an amazing man," Ann told me. "I never would have thought—I mean, he's such a *man's man*. To see him wearing an apron and doing housework, well, who would have thought?" She shook her head. "I'm glad he's here taking care of you. I've got to hurry to meet Betty. Tell Ralph I'll call him later."

A few days later, Marty surprised me by saying, "I want to be just like Grandpa. He can do everything, and I want to be able to do everything, too. Don't worry, Mom. From now on, you'll never have to tell Eric and me to clean up our rooms, and we'll help with everything else, too. Grandpa says if we keep helping like he showed us, he's going to take us to an air show. He's going to fly us there himself!"

After another week, I could get around on my crutches well enough to take over most of the household chores myself, and I began planning to go back to work.

"Dad, I'll never be able to thank you for what you've done," I told him gratefully.

He smiled. "You don't owe me any thanks, Diana. It was my

pleasure. I didn't get to do much for you when you were little. I'm glad I could do this for you now."

"We'll miss you after you've gone."

Eric came into the room just then. "Are you leaving, Grandpa?"

"Sure, Eric. I'll have to get back to the Air Force. They can't keep on operating without me."

"But, Grandpa, you can't go," Marty said. "Who knows when we'll see you again? You promised to take us to the air show."

"And so I will. As a matter of fact, from now on you'll see me all the time. I've been transferred to the base just across town. I'll be moving into a house near the base, and I'll need all of you to help me turn it into a home."

The boys jumped up and down, Ralph shook his hand, and tears sprang to my eyes. "Oh, Dad, I'm so glad."

He took my hand. "The only thing in life I've ever regretted is that I let the Air Force separate me from you and your mother. From now on, I won't let anything take me away from you, Ralph, or the boys. I can't make up for the past, but I promise the future will be different."

After he left, I headed toward the kitchen.

"Hey, where are you going?" Ralph asked. "I'm cooking dinner tonight. It's a special dish your dad showed me." He grinned. "Mom told me your dad said I needed guidance. He was right. Can you ever forgive me?"

"What do you mean?"

Ralph put his arms around me. "I love you so much, Diana, and I've been such a jerk. Can you ever forgive me?"

My words were lost in his kiss. But not for long.

Marty's voice called from the kitchen and interrupted us. "Hey, Dad. Eric and I soaked these ribs in this sauce like you said. Want me to light the grill?" THE END

I SAW MOMMY KISSING THE DELIVERY BOY!

After eighteen years of marriage, 37-year-old Marlee's fallen hard for the new delivery boy at her local grocery store, "a young Marlon Brando" who can set off "a wild kind of thrill" just by putting his hand on hers. Pretty soon, she's got a standing appointment for afternoon delight—until the afternoon when her eight-year-old daughter and her classmates spot Marlee and her paramour making out on his doorstep.

From there, it's only a matter of time before her husband finds out, but that's not the only revelation Marlee will need to deal with. Fortunately, Baxter's one of those sympathetic spouses who responds to his wife's adultery by saying, "I'm sorry I didn't give you what you needed." Then again, his forgiveness just makes Marlee's shame that much more acute.

Whenever I went to Hunter's apartment, it was always during the day, when my husband, Baxter, was at work, and my daughter, Cammie was at school.

Hunter reminded me of a young Marlon Brando. He wore tight jeans, a leather jacket, and black biker boots. The first day I'd met him, when he'd looked me over in the grocery store, I'd felt like lightning had struck me.

I was deciding between two different boxes of cereal when the darkly handsome young man came walking up the aisle. I moved my shopping cart, in order to get it out of his way, and accidentally bumped into a pyramid of soup cans, knocking the entire display to the floor.

The young man just laughed, then he picked up every can and stacked them back into a perfect tower. It was then that I noticed the white apron he had tied around his waist. I realized he must work at the store.

"Thank you," I said, embarrassed by my clumsiness, and relieved that the store manager hadn't had to come over.

"My pleasure," he answered softly, his gaze holding mine.

My heart pounded; I could hardly breathe. He stood so close to me that I could smell the light, spicy scent of his aftershave.

"I'm Hunter Shaw." He smiled and put out his hand.

"Marlee. Marlee Cooper." I guess I was nervous. He made me nervous. I shook his hand.

"Well, then, Marlee, I don't suppose you're available right now. I'm about to go on my break. But a beautiful woman like yourself couldn't possibly be—"

"Yes, I am," I stammered.

He very slowly slipped his hand out of mine. The action was so erotic, I felt shivers go up and down my spine.

"Would you consider having a cup of coffee with me at the café next door? I'm a lonely guy in a strange town who needs a friend," he said, his voice smooth and low.

I hesitated. I was a married woman. Yet, I immediately knew that I would go with him. I wanted to. I'd never felt so much excitement in a man's look. Not even my husband's.

I felt tingly all over by the time I'd paid for my groceries and put them in the trunk of my car.

The café next to the market was a small take-out restaurant with a few booths. It was deserted this time of day. Hunter led me to a booth in the back. While I slid into the seat, Hunter went up to the counter and ordered two cups of coffee. In a few moments, he brought the steaming mugs to the table and sat down.

We sipped our coffee. I could tell it had just been freshly brewed, and it warmed me inside, taking away a sudden chill I had. Perhaps the unnerving feeling came from being in this handsome stranger's presence.

Hunter told me all about himself. How he'd driven up from Louisiana looking for construction work. A friend of his had told him there was plenty of work in the area, but he'd taken the grocery store job to make ends meet in the meantime. He enjoyed going from state to state. He'd learned a lot about the country that way. He wasn't married. Had never been married. He said he'd never found the right woman.

"Now, what about you, Marlee?" Hunter smiled, his gaze intent on my face. My hand shook as I put my mug down.

"Well, I've lived here all my life. I'm married, and we have a seven-year-old daughter. Her name is Cammie."

"The way you say her name, I can tell she's the apple of your eye."

"She is. She's my whole life."

"Are you happy, Marlee?" Hunter asked, his voice soft, like a caress.

The question startled me. It was so personal. Had I given him any reason to think I wasn't happy? Did agreeing to come here with him send that message? Of course I was happy. But when I didn't answer him right away, I suddenly felt the warmth of his hand over mine.

"I think I get the picture," he said.

I caught my breath at this inference and quickly blurted out, "Of course I'm happy!"

From the corner of my eye, I saw the lady behind the counter staring at me. Guilt and feelings of disloyalty flooded through me. Hadn't my husband provided for me and our child? Hadn't he been a caring husband, lover, and father?

So why was I sitting in this café with a stranger, letting him hold my hand? Wishing he would take me in his arms and hold me, kiss me? My face burned with shame, yet I didn't get up and leave.

Hunter kept his hand over mine and shook his head. "I don't think so, Marlee. I think you're about as lonely as a beautiful woman can get."

Pure heat, a wild kind of thrill, swept through every inch of my body. In the back of my mind, I heard the warning bells, but my body had already accepted this stranger's unspoken invitation. I suddenly felt bound to him.

As the waitress came to offer more coffee, I pulled my hand away from Hunter's tender grasp. I had to get home before the frozen dinners and ice cream in the trunk of my car melted.

"I have to go, Hunter."

"Sure. I'll walk you to your car."

We quickly finished our coffee and headed for the door.

Outside, it was windy, but the sun was warm, so I didn't bother to button my coat. Hunter walked on my right, his deep brown eyes riveted on my body as the wind flipped open my coat. I had worn brown slacks and an old sweater that was tight from too much washing. His gaze roamed freely, and I welcomed it.

When Hunter took my hand, I didn't pull away. I knew what I was doing was crazy, especially in a public parking lot where everybody in town came to shop. Any second, I could run into someone I knew, or someone Baxter knew. I also knew that I was older than Hunter, but that piece of knowledge didn't stop the hammering of my heart.

Hunter took the keys out of my hand and unlocked my car door. "It's been quite a while since I've driven a car," he said slyly. "Those are my wheels." He nodded over toward a huge, gleaming motorcycle parked a few feet away.

"You came all the way from Louisiana on that?" I asked, astonished.

"Yes, ma'am. Now, don't tell me you've never rode on one?"

"Well, no, I haven't. It looks dangerous." My body shivered from the imagined risks and exposure he'd met riding that thing for hundreds of miles.

"Sometimes, Marlee, a little danger can be a lot of fun."

Hunter smiled, his warm breath brushing my ear as he leaned in close to me. Again, I made no effort to pull away or to tell him to stop. Instead, I welcomed the closeness of his hard, youthful body, his masculine scent, the muscles under his tight T-shirt.

Warning bells pounded through my head, but I dismissed them. This stranger made me feel young again, desirable—and, for the first time in my eighteen years of marriage, I wanted to be free.

Baxter and I had been college sweethearts. When we'd gotten

married, I'd dropped out to be a wife, and hopefully a mother. Baxter had graduated and started his own computer software business.

Motherhood didn't come until ten long years later. Cammie was born on a cold December morning after a hard, two-day labor. Exhausted and weak, I couldn't enjoy my baby for several days after she was born, but Baxter bonded with her immediately. At the time, feelings of jealousy gnawed away at me. I'd somehow felt cheated. After all, I had been the one to go through all the agony of her birth, not my husband.

After my recovery, though, when I was finally able to hold Cammie in my arms, all the hurt feelings instantly disappeared. I was a mother. I couldn't have been happier.

We settled into being a family. I devoted all my time to my baby. I knew there were times when Baxter felt left out, but I couldn't help it. Having a baby was something I'd always longed for, and I wanted to savor every moment of this most precious of experiences.

Then, Cammie started school, and I suddenly had an enormous amount of time on my hands—which, I admit, I didn't put to good use. I lived for the moment each day when Cammie got out of school and I could pick her up.

But then she started making friends, and I realized she was growing away from me. My husband had his business, which allowed him to retreat even further from the daily life I'd created for myself—and unconsciously excluded him from. Suddenly, when I looked in the mirror every morning, there were new lines on my face. At thirty-seven, I began to think of myself as old.

"If you can get away sometime, I'll take you for a ride," I heard Hunter saying just then. I jerked back to reality. The smell of spice.

"When the wind blows through your hair and you're traveling on an open road at the speed of light, there's nothing closer to heaven."

"I'd like that," I heard myself saying, like some naïve schoolgirl.

Was I insane? Didn't I realize where this could lead? I had a husband and a child. Where were my morals? Didn't I care about the people I loved?

I managed to leave Hunter in the parking lot that day.

If only it had been the last time I ever saw him. . . .

That night, I couldn't get Hunter out of my mind. I made dinner, then gave Cammie her bath and put her to bed. Baxter ate his dinner in silence. I knew he was tired. He'd put in a fourteen-hour workday. When you owned your own business, long hours came with the territory.

I hadn't realized until that moment how unsettling it was to have us apart for so long. Baxter had asked me several times over the years to join the business. He'd been encouraging in letting me know I'd be an asset to him. But I had no interest whatsoever in computers.

No, a little voice inside me said, *your interest lies in having an affair with a younger man, and destroying the lives of your husband and your child.*

That night, I hoped Baxter didn't want to make love. I was relieved when he went to bed early with just a kiss on my cheek and a warm embrace.

"Dinner was great, hon," he said as he walked wearily up the stairs to our bedroom.

I lay awake all night, my mind totally focused on the handsome stranger who'd come into my life. The tight jeans, the crooked grin, the brown eyes that bore into mine—the warmth of his breath, his hard body. And he'd found me attractive. Desirable. He could appreciate an older woman.

I could hardly wait to see him again. He'd given me his telephone number, tucking the piece of paper he'd written it on into my coat pocket.

I felt powerless to resist Hunter; I knew it was only a matter of time.

I opened my eyes and stretched, looking out the window. The park across the street was turning green, and spring flowers were beginning to bud in their circular beds. Groups of children played on swings and chased each other around picnic tables. A few people walked along paths, while some seniors sat at tables, talking and playing chess.

I felt Hunter's hand slip across my waist. His nose nuzzled my neck, and I giggled. I lay my head back on the pillow, my lips eager for his kiss. He kissed me, long and hard.

My desire for Hunter's body grew, but I knew I had to get home. I'd already stayed longer than I should.

Much longer. I'd been coming to see Hunter almost every afternoon for the past three months.

Hunter watched me as I dressed hurriedly. I had to force the zipper up on my slacks. I must've gained a little weight and not realized it.

"When will I see you again?" Hunter asked, rolling over and sitting up on the edge of the bed. "This bed's gonna be cold until you get back in it."

"I'll call you," I said, bending to kiss him.

He rose off the bed and took me in his strong arms. I didn't want to leave him. What I wanted was to get back into bed and have Hunter make love to me all day long.

But I finished dressing, and Hunter followed me outside.

The sun felt warm, almost hot on my face. I could smell the first, fresh hint of summer in the springtime air.

Hunter kissed me good-bye—a long, lingering kiss. Then I headed down the steps to my car.

"Mommy! Mommy!"

The child's voice sounded familiar. Had I not been in my usual, lust-filled daze, I would have recognized it immediately.

"Mommy, wait!" the child's voice called.

I stopped suddenly, putting my hand over my eyes to shield them from the blinding sun.

Across the street, in the midst of a group of children and a lone adult, I saw my daughter frantically waving at me. Cammie's smile was perplexed, and her teacher, Mrs. Dobbins, did not smile or say hello to me as I approached.

I glanced back at Hunter's apartment building. He'd gone inside and closed the door.

Thank God!

"Hi, honey," I said to my daughter. Then I smiled at Mrs. Dobbins.

She arched an eyebrow, her face a block of ice. She stared at me accusingly. Of course, she'd met Baxter at the last open house and had seen him at the other school activities that Cammie had been involved in.

"Who was that man, Mommy?" Cammie asked me innocently.

"Oh, just a friend, honey." I tried to dismiss her question, but Cammie was having none of it.

"You were kissing him, Mommy. Who is he?" she demanded, eager curiosity in her high-pitched voice.

My daughter had never seen me kiss any man but her father.

"I'll—I'll explain later," I stammered.

The other children were all staring at me, watching wide-eyed. I could feel my face burning. Obviously, they all had seen me kissing my lover.

"It's time to get back on the bus, children!" Mrs. Dobbins announced, still looking at me coldly.

I kissed my daughter's cheek. "I'll see you at home, baby."

There were tears in Cammie's eyes. And, as young as she was, I could read shame there, too. Shame for her mother, who'd been seen kissing a stranger the way she was supposed to kiss her husband.

I began to tremble. The enormity of what I'd been doing suddenly overwhelmed me, to the point that I nearly thought I would faint.

Would my daughter mention this to her father? How could she not? Would her classmates tell their parents? Would everyone find out that I was an adulteress?

I drove home, my heart pounding, my nerves shattered. For the first time since I'd started meeting Hunter at his apartment, I was seeing myself as I supposed I really appeared to others. Suddenly, it became very clear—what I'd done. I'd jeopardized my life, my marriage, my child's stability.

And what I felt for Hunter was uncontrollable lust—certainly not love. I'd known this in my heart, and yet still, I'd still pursued him. There had never even been any thought of divorcing Baxter and marrying Hunter. I'd just wanted sex from Hunter. I'd relished the idea that a younger man wanted my body. It had been exciting to walk into his small studio apartment, strip off my clothes, and fall into bed with him. I was living out a fantasy.

But now, my fantasy had turned into stark reality—the worst nightmare of my life.

What was I going to do? What could I say to Cammie—how could I expect her to keep silent? What about what Mrs. Dobbins and all those children had seen?

I wondered what Cammie was saying on the bus. Was she crying? Were the other kids saying mean things to her about her mother? I couldn't bear the thought of my daughter being hurt—I couldn't stand the thought of losing her trust.

I pulled my car into the driveway, got out, and ran into the house, slamming the door behind me. I felt as if everyone on our block had seen me kissing Hunter and knew about every sordid detail of our affair.

I looked around at my lovely home—the happiness and security my husband and daughter had given me, I'd sold cheap. I knew Baxter's love for me was real. Lasting. Honest. Because he loved me with all his heart and soul.

I fell onto a kitchen chair and cried. I sat there crying my eyes and heart out for a long time; it wasn't until I heard the squeaking breaks on Cammie's school bus that I realized two hours had passed.

Quickly, I splashed some water on my face in the kitchen sink and dabbed myself dry with 'a paper towel. Then the front door opened and closed.

I waited for Cammie's usual, "I'm home, Mommy!"

It never came.

"That you, honey?" I called, trying to sound normal.

She didn't answer. I went into the den. Cammie was running up the carpeted stairs, her schoolbag dragging in one hand, pictures she'd drawn in the other. Her little body looked old, somehow.

"Cammie, we have to talk."

She stopped, turned and came back down the stairs. The hurt in her big, blue eyes filled me with remorse. I took her hand and drew her into the den where we sat side by side on the sofa.

God, help me, I prayed. *Help me to straighten all this out. I can't lose my child or my husband. Forgive me, God, please.*

I was so choked up, it took me a long time before I could speak. I could only hope God heard my prayer. I was determined to do anything necessary to hold my family together. I took a deep breath.

"Sometimes, mommies make mistakes, Cammie. The man you saw me kissing isn't someone I love, or someone important to you, Daddy, or me. As a matter of fact, I won't ever be seeing him again."

"Is he going away forever?" Cammie asked, her eyes pleading.

I didn't want to lie, but I didn't want her to think that Hunter would still be in that apartment across the street from the park. Often, the children went there on school trips. Baxter and I took Cammie there on Saturday afternoons. We had picnics there in summer.

"Yes, he's going away," I answered.

Something stirred in my mind, then instantly crystallized. Hunter had been telling me for a long time, only I didn't want to hear it. I was having too much fun.

"There's a good job in New York," he'd told me. "Pays good money. It's about time I got started doing what I want to be doing."

I'd muttered something and started kissing his chest to arouse him for another hot round of sex.

Suddenly, I realized that Hunter had been giving me an opportunity to end our relationship gracefully. As he'd surely done with countless other women in the past. He was moving on again.

"Then you were giving him a good-bye kiss?" Cammie asked hopefully, her face still clouded with worry.

"Yes, honey. I was giving him a goodbye kiss."

"Sarah Jean said he was your boyfriend. That you only kiss on the lips if you love somebody. Is he your boyfriend, Mommy? Don't you love Daddy anymore?"

What had I done? I swept her into my arms and held her to my breasts. I could feel her little heart thumping fast.

"Of course I love Daddy. Your daddy is the only man in the whole, wide world that I could ever love."

"But who is he?"

"Just—just a friend, for a short time, Cammie." I panicked. My daughter obviously didn't understand. What could I tell her that could make it all go away?

"Honey, my friend was the delivery boy from the grocery store. He'd been very helpful to me, but he got a new job, so I was just . . . saying good-bye to my friend."

Did I say it right? Did she understand? Would she let it go and forget all about it?

A slow smile replaced the frown. "See my drawings, Mommy?" She lifted up a drawing of a big green frog, and another of a house with three people standing next to it: a man, a woman, and a little girl. The little girl held a dog on a leash and a cat in her arm. I hadn't thought that Cammie wanted a pet until now. I made a mental note to talk to Baxter about getting her one.

"They're wonderful, honey. I'll hang them on the refrigerator. Wait till Daddy sees them."

"You really love Daddy, Mommy? Cross your heart?"

Still so troubled? Would it ever go away? My heart ached to make all the bad thoughts disappear from her mind.

"Oh, Cammie, I love you and your daddy more than anybody in the world. I always will. No one can ever change that."

"Well, that's good to hear."

"Daddy!"

I hadn't heard Baxter drive up and come in. Cammie ran to her father. He picked her up and planted a noisy kiss on her waiting, puckered lips.

"How's my girl?"

"Fine. Friends kiss on the lips sometimes, Daddy."

I froze, my heart in my throat.

"They do, huh?"

"Wanna see my pictures?"

"You bet."

When Baxter put her down, Cammie ran to the sofa and picked up her pictures, showing them to her father.

"You are quite an artist, honey," Baxter said, hugging her to him.

Cammie beamed.

"Now, how about going upstairs and changing? Mom and I will hang these masterpieces on the fridge."

Cammie grabbed her schoolbag and hurried up the stairs.

"Hi, I'm home early. I hope that's okay with the lady of the house." Baxter grinned at me.

For one agonizing moment, I wanted to hold him against me and tell him what I'd done. I desperately needed the honesty between us, after all the lying I'd been guilty of. Yet, I knew how much the truth would devastate him.

Dear God, I prayed, *work some kind of miracle for me!*

I looked at this man, with whom I'd shared so much in the past eighteen years. Baxter had lines around his eyes that crinkled when he laughed. He was tall and strong, kind and gentle, solid in every way. He had a wonderful sense of humor, and when he made love to me, he always thought of my pleasure first.

Having all this, I'd still wanted to go to Hunter. I'd accepted—welcomed—that fascination with the unknown. The danger, as Hunter had put it. I'd wanted to prove to myself I was intriguing, desirable, sexy, wanted.

I'd felt driven to Hunter. Even now, as I thought of confessing everything to my husband, just the thought of Hunter's hands roaming over my body filled me with uncontrollable desire. There had to be something wrong with me. I loved my husband. And I hated the feelings I still had for Hunter. I could only pray that, in time, they'd go away.

I stepped into my husband's open arms. I knew I loved him with my whole heart. Baxter's love was honest, strong, nurturing. My body began to respond to his gentle, soothing hands, and I reached up and kissed his lips.

"Hmm, where did *that* come from?"

Baxter asked teasingly.

"From here," I answered, placing his hand over my heart.

I thought of how my life had been for so many years. I'd spent most of my time waiting for Cammie to come home—cleaning the house, arranging and rearranging my daughter's room, reading, browsing through catalogs, watching television. Baxter would complain that I never saw my friends anymore, that we hardly ever went out together without Cammie, and no one ever came over. More and more, he'd buried himself in his work.

Then, when Hunter came into my life, I forgot about all of that. I'm ashamed to say that when Baxter and I had made love during the past three months, I'd fantasized that he was Hunter.

Leaning against Baxter, I prayed again that somehow, God would make what I'd done come out right.

Baxter left me with a kiss to go and take a shower. Cammie sat at the kitchen table where I could help her with her homework as I prepared dinner. I'd hung her pictures on the refrigerator where three others still hung.

During dinner, I smiled and joined in the conversation between my husband and daughter. But when Cammie began to talk about her trip to the park with her class, I froze. She chatted on about swinging, and the flowers and the monarch butterfly they'd seen.

Then she blurted out, "And I saw Mommy, too. She kissed her friend goodbye."

"I see," said Baxter. "It sounds as if you had a wonderful day."

"Can I be excused now?" she asked.

"All right. Why don't you play in your room for a while? I'll be up in a little while and give you your bath," I told her.

She bounded from the table and ran up the stairs to her room.

"Was it Hope?" Baxter asked.

"What?"

"Were you saying good-bye to Hope? You two were always as close as sisters."

Baxter was right about that. Hope and I had known each other since high school. But I'd cut her off when Hunter came into my life. I didn't feel I could confide in Hope about my affair. She liked and respected Baxter too much. She'd think I was crazy to even think of such a thing, let alone go through with it. I also knew she'd be the one person to talk me out of it. And I didn't want that.

"Oh, yes—I was with Hope," I managed to say.

"What were you two doing at the park?"

"We had a little time to spare, so we took some coffee there and enjoyed the beautiful day. It was almost like summertime." The lie came easily, like all the others.

"Yeah, it was. I want to try and get some yard work done this weekend," Baxter remarked.

"Good! I'll help you. I'm thinking about planting a small flower bed around the mail box."

Baxter's face lit up. "We could drive down to the nursery on Saturday. See what they suggest. I noticed, driving by there the other day, they have boxes of pansies in all colors out front. They hold up well in cold weather."

"Sounds like fun," I said, meaning it, even though my voice didn't hold any enthusiasm. I'd suddenly felt the food in my stomach turn over.

"What's the matter?" Baxter asked.

I swallowed forcefully to try and keep it down.

It didn't work.

I ran into the downstairs bathroom and slammed the door. I threw up in the toilet. When it was over, I sat down on the cold tile floor, exhausted, a washcloth over my face.

There was a soft knock on the door. "Marlee, are you all right?"

Still feeling dizzy, I managed to pull myself up and open the door.

"Honey, why didn't you tell me you were sick? I would've cooked dinner. Go lie down. I'll take care of everything down here."

With his strong arm around my waist, Baxter led me to the stairs.

"I can make it now," I told him.

I climbed up the stairs to our bedroom and fell across the cream-colored cotton bedspread. I felt like I could sleep forever.

Sunlight filled the room, dancing off the crystal lamp on the dresser. I felt completely disoriented as I looked around. What time was it? Where was Baxter? Cammie?

I bolted up and ran to Cammie's room. She wasn't there. Neither was her schoolbag. I hurried down the stairs to the kitchen.

A lined piece of paper from Cammie's binder lay on the table.

Baxter had written me a note:

I got Cammie off to school. Hope you feel better. See you tonight.

I looked around. The kitchen was spotless. Baxter had cleaned everything. In the den, I found a blanket, and pillow on the sofa, where he'd spent the night. He hadn't wanted to disturb me.

Back in the kitchen, I made a pot of coffee, drank a cup, then went back upstairs and took a long, hot shower. Again, my stomach felt queasy. I'd no sooner dried myself off than I needed to throw up again.

When it was over, I took my temperature. Normal. I brushed my teeth and washed my face. Again, tiredness overwhelmed me. I wrapped myself in my terry cloth robe and went back to bed.

With my arm resting over my eyes to keep out the light, I tried to think about what I should do. I didn't know if I could live with Baxter without telling him what I'd done. But then, of course, my husband would be hurt beyond all reason. Should I protect him from my betrayal? What about Cammie? What if she tells Baxter someday that she saw me kissing the delivery boy?

My thoughts became jumbled, and I fell into a deep sleep.

When I awoke, the small clock on my nightstand read two o'clock. It was amazing how much better I felt now.

Apparently, rest was what I'd needed. I decided I must've had a short bout with the flu bug.

I quickly dressed and went downstairs to see what I could make for dinner. I defrosted hamburger to make meat sauce for spaghetti, took down a package of pasta, and decided to make a big salad and garlic bread, with ice cream for dessert. I was suddenly famished.

As I busied myself with cooking, I thought how lucky I'd been that Hunter had never come to see me at home. He'd never even asked for my phone number, and I never offered it. I realized now that this was all part of his no-strings-attached plan. I guess I'd known all along that we were just using each other. It wasn't freedom that I had wanted or needed. That had been an excuse to help calm my guilt. In reality, I'd wanted this affair. I wanted to experience a wild relationship filled with sex.

Cammie came home, acting like her usual self. She did her homework at the kitchen table, had a glass of milk and a coconut cookie, then sat in the den to watch a video.

By the time Baxter got home, dinner was ready. I'd put candles on the table and put on a nice dress. I wanted things to be nice for my husband. I wanted to create a warm, romantic atmosphere. It wasn't the shallow lust I'd experienced with Hunter that I felt, but something deeply honest and good that I wanted to share with my husband.

Instantly, I knew something was wrong. Did Baxter have a bad day at work?

"Hi," I said kissing him on the cheek.

He didn't pull away, but he didn't kiss me back, either. Nor did he ask me how I was feeling.

Dinner passed quietly. Cammie chattered on about school and said her friend Sarah Jean had gotten a new charm bracelet and a tube of lipstick.

I'd never asked Cammie if she had mentioned the man I'd kissed to her father. I kept hoping she'd forgotten about it. Thankfully, she seemed involved in other matters now.

"Can I have a lipstick, Mommy?"

"When you're older, honey."

"But Sarah Jean isn't older, Mommy."

"I know, honey, but you're just a little girl. Maybe later, you can play with one of mine, okay?"

"Okay!" She grinned, satisfied.

I kept glancing at Baxter. He seemed so lost in thought. And when he finished his dinner, he got up quietly and went into the den without a word.

I cleared the table, washed the dishes, and had Cammie help me dry. She continued to remind me about the lipstick, until I finally took her upstairs to let her play with mine in the bathroom. I gave her a box of tissues, a light pink lipstick, and an old compact of blush, and left her alone. She was joyous.

I found Baxter at his desk in the den. He just sat there, rubbing his forehead with his hand. I knew something was wrong and could only pray it had nothing to do with Hunter and me. Then Baxter turned his chair around and looked at me.

"Cammie told me," he said quietly.

My heart hammered so loud, I thought I'd pass out.

"What are you talking about?"

"Who was this 'delivery boy' our daughter saw you kissing, Marlee?"

I took a step into the room and closed the door. I didn't want Cammie to hear a word of this. I stood in front of my husband's desk and looked into his hurt and bewildered eyes.

Tell him the truth, a little voice said. I took a deep breath.

"His name is Hunter Shaw. He helped me pick up some soup cans I'd knocked over in the store. He invited me for coffee at the café next door. Then I came home."

For a long moment, I couldn't go on. My husband waited patiently. That was something Baxter had a lot of—patience.

"We got together a few days later at his apartment. And I I. . . I kept going back."

I'd never seen so much sorrow on a man's face as I watched my husband take in what I'd just told him. For fear my trembling legs would give out, I sat down in the leather chair opposite his desk.

"I'm so sorry, Baxter. But it was nothing."

"You slept with another man. It was everything, Marlee," Baxter said, so softly I barely heard him.

I twisted my hands in my lap. What was I to do now that I had destroyed all of our lives? How could I make amends? How could I save my marriage? Was it even possible?

A sudden wave of dizziness and nausea overwhelmed me. I ran from the den to the bathroom just in time.

I lost my entire dinner. I leaned my back and head against the cool tile wall and closed my eyes. Then I heard the bathroom door open and watched through tear-filled eyes as my husband came in, wet a washcloth, and pressed it to my forehead. And I knew in the depth of my soul that Baxter loved me, in spite of what I'd done.

But could he ever forgive me?

"How far along are you?" Baxter asked quietly.

"What?" I didn't understand what he meant.

"You're pregnant. How far along are you?"

"I'm not. . . ." I didn't finish. The truth hit me, cruelly. It hadn't been the flu that had made me ill. It was the hormonal changes in my body as it prepared to accommodate a new life.

If I could have died, I would have, right then and there. I was carrying Hunter's child. I couldn't look at Baxter.

My periods had always been irregular. And for the past two years, I had gone two, even three months without one. I'd thought it was the beginning of menopause. My best friend, Hope, had experienced these same changes when she was only thirty-eight. So had her mother. I'd assumed my body was making those same changes.

When I'd been pregnant with my daughter, I'd felt wonderful for the first few months, then I had morning sickness until my seventh month, when it all went away. Nothing guaranteed you'd have the same pregnancy experience the second time.

"How did you know?" I asked Baxter.

"You're restless; your breasts are tender; your wedding ring is too tight."

He was right. I looked at my wedding ring; the flesh around it was puffy and swollen. I hadn't been able to sleep. My breasts hurt when Hunter made love to me. They'd hurt with Baxter, as well.

With Baxter. . . . Was there a chance this baby could be Baxter's? Did I dare hope?

I'd wronged my husband in the worst possible way. I couldn't blame him if he hated me. For three months, I'd snuck around with Hunter, going to his apartment and engaging in wild sex, totally unashamed. The thought now sickened me. I'd never been careful going in and out of the building where Hunter lived. The whole town could have seen me. People could be talking about me now. My husband and child would be publicly humiliated by what I'd done.

Too late, I understood how saying yes to one moment of temptation could ruin lives forever. I'd given in to my bodily urges, to the desire to feel young again, wild, free. And with that single, willful decision,

I'd shattered everything I ever believed in. "You better go and see Dr. Sears," Baxter said, leaving the room.

Tears streamed down my face. I felt more sickness in my soul than I ever could in my body.

I don't know how I managed to get Cammie bathed and into bed. Baxter slept in the den. I slept in our bed alone.

The next morning, after Baxter left for work and Cammie got on her bus, I called Dr. Sears' office. Luckily, there had been a cancellation, and I made an appointment for that afternoon.

"You're fine, Marlee. Due date should be around October. That sound right to you?"

I was three months along.

"Yes, that sounds right," I replied.

"Want to know what it is? I can schedule you for an ultrasound early next week."

"I'm not sure," I answered.

"Well, talk it over with Baxter. And take these vitamins." Dr. Sears wrote out a prescription and handed it to me. "I want to see you in a month."

I made an appointment, then went out to my car. For a long time, I just sat there, thinking. I wanted my life back the way it was. I wanted my husband, a happy child, my friends. But not yet. There was some thing I had to do first.

I had to call Hunter. One last time.

I drove home and rushed inside to the phone. I dialed Hunter's number, hoping he hadn't left town for his new job. On the fourth ring, he answered.

"Hunter, it's Marlee. I'm glad I caught you before you left town."

"I am, too. Come on over," he said, his voice low and husky.

But his invitation had no effect on me. "I have something to tell you, Hunter. I'm pregnant."

"Hey, no kidding. Well, congratulations!"

"You want me to have your baby?" I gasped.

"Whoa! Hold on there. This baby isn't mine. Never could be."

"Why not?" I asked him, amazed.

"Marlee, I'm sterile. I had a bad case of the mumps when I was young. I can't ever have kids."

"Hunter, you never told me. . . ." I started to cry.

"Marlee, is there a problem?" Hunter asked, sounding concerned.

"None at all. Good-bye, Hunter. And good luck."

"You, too, baby."

I hung up the phone, my hand shaking, relief pouring through me like a gentle, cleansing waterfall. This baby was Baxter's. Gratitude filled me.

What I'd done had been stupid and dangerous. I'd met Hunter one day, and went to bed with him two days later. For all I knew, he could have been a killer or a rapist, or he could have been HIV-positive. Would Baxter believe me if I told him what Hunter had said? Or would doubt hang over our marriage like a heavy shroud, forever?

That night, when Cammie was tucked into bed, I went to talk to Baxter.

He probably can't stand the sight of me, I thought, opening the door to the den where he'd been shut up all day.

He looked up at me from a stack of papers he'd been working on. The computer monitor showed a list of client names, and a fax was coming in. I waited until he read the fax and placed it on his desk.

"I'm sorry for what I did. I need your forgiveness, Baxter. I can't go on without—"

"I forgive you, Marlee," he said, sounding more tired and lost than I'd ever dreamt possible. "I just don't know what to do about this broken trust between us. I keep asking myself if I can ever trust you again."

"I could never do this to you again. I love you, Baxter." I let the tears flow, my heart aching for what I put him through. Oh, how I wanted to hold him against me and take away all the pain I'd caused him.

I put my arms around him. Instantly, his hands went to my waist, then up to the small of my back.

"Marlee," he whispered. He kissed me. Our passion grew with each moment, then he drew away.

"It's going to take time," I said. "Maybe lots of time. I don't want to lose you. Please, help me through this, and let me help you."

He touched my cheek with his fingertips.

"Do you still love me?" I asked, not recognizing the tortured voice of the woman who spoke.

"I will always love you. That won't ever change. But why did you do it, Marlee? Did you stop loving me at some point?"

"Baxter, no!" I swallowed hard, knowing I had to make him understand so we could put this behind us. "Hunter—he's younger than me. I felt, I don't know, desirable, young. . . ." I couldn't finish. I had no words.

"And you don't feel that way—desirable—with me?"

"Of course I do. I feel a passion with you I could never feel with another man. I have my priorities straight now, Baxter. What I felt . . . did with Hunter, it wasn't love. It was fantasy, lust. I made a terrible mistake giving into temptation, but it won't ever happen again. I've learned the difference between lasting love and a loveless affair."

"I'm sorry I didn't give you what you needed," Baxter said, his voice heavy with sadness.

"You did. I was the one who didn't appreciate your love. Baxter, this baby is yours."

He looked at me with the same hope I'd felt in my own heart.

"You don't know that," he said.

"Oh, yes, I do."

Six months later, William Baxter Cooper was born. I'd explained everything to Dr. Sears. He took care of the paternity test and showed the results to Baxter and me, together. I could see the weight lifting off my husband's shoulders.

Cammie is enchanted with her new baby brother. Baxter's and my life is back to normal. I've gotten back in touch with my friends. They think I had a difficult time with my pregnancy, and that's why I fell out of touch with them. We leave it at that.

Mrs. Dobbins, Cammie's teacher, is pleasant again when we meet. And no one else in town seems to have found out about my affair with Hunter Shaw. At least, neither Baxter nor I have heard any rumors.

At night, after Cammie and Billy are in bed, I help Baxter with the business in the den. I've learned a lot about computers, and working together has brought us closer together. And our mutual trust is growing.

I don't crave danger and recklessness anymore. I have the best husband in the world who loves my unconditionally, and whom I love in the same way. I can only hope that Hunter will learn what real love means someday, and I hope that, when he does, he can hold on to it.

Once, I prayed that, somehow, God would make what I'd done turn out all right. I've learned from my terrible mistakes, and I'm so thankful for the forgiveness I've received. The love I've felt from my family has even been enough to help me forgive myself. THE END

FOUND—BY THE BLACK DAUGHTER I HID FOR YEARS

This story unfolds with all the drama of a TV-movie. At first, you're not sure what drives Ingrid's obsessive interest in having a baby girl, while her husband can't wait for their two teenaged sons to leave home and give them an empty nest to play in. Colin is beginning to get tired of the subject, and Ingrid's own mother thinks she's being unreasonable. Then she gets a letter from the institution where she'd placed the daughter she'd had years ago, before her first marriage, up for adoption. That girl found a good home; she's just turned eighteen, though, and she wants to meet her biological mother...

Ingrid has never told Colin about that little girl (and the father, a graduate student from Nigeria, is long since out of the picture). So she tries to keep the reunion, and the relationship that develops after it, a secret—and Colin leaps to some fairly natural, but completely wrong, conclusions about what's going on that give the story an added emotional tension.

(The race issue, by the way, is basically melodramatic. Although Ingrid is prompted to give her daughter up to spare her mother embarrassment, it's essentially presented as being about having a child out of wedlock; her concerns about Ingrid's interracial romance are raised very subtly, and prompted by an excessive fear of gossip rather than any overt prejudice.)

In the fishbowl where I live, the waters are always clearer to everyone else. Especially my mother. Her advice is freely given, but rarely taken. I should know. I listened one time too many.

I'm part of a large family in a small town, and whenever someone hangs out their dirty laundry, everyone else seems to know about it.

I learned this the hard way, but it happened so long ago, it's become old news. No one talks about it anymore; they've moved on to juicier subjects. But that doesn't mean they've forgotten. Not by any means. I know how hard I've tried, but I can't forget. And neither can my mother.

But Colin didn't know. He didn't share the same driving need, or feel the pain I hid so deeply inside.

Put the past behind you, everyone said. Get on with your life. After all, they all had. But then, they weren't directly involved—not like I was. And I *was* trying to get on with my life. With all my heart, I was trying, but Colin was the first one to admit that even he didn't understand my desperation. That's why, even though I'd promised myself that I wouldn't, that morning, I simply couldn't stop myself from bringing it up again.

Colin was finishing his coffee. I cleared away his toast crumbs and egg-smeared plate before slipping my arms around his neck from behind.

"I want so much to have a child with you," I whispered, before the rumble of footsteps brought Evan and Andrew into the kitchen. "Wouldn't you like a child of your own? A little girl?"

"Uh-oh, not the little-sister routine again," Evan groaned.

"No way, Mom. I do *not* want to share my room," Andrew piped in emphatically. "My room's just the way I like it. When I used to have to share a room with Evan, I couldn't leave anything on the floor. If I did, I never knew where to find it again—or if I *would* find it again."

"If you'd put your stuff away, you wouldn't have to look for it; it would always be there," Evan retorted.

"Without you in my room, my stuff is always right where I leave it. Handy," Andrew snapped back.

Evan pulled a face and gave Andrew a shove, making the toast in his hand fall on the floor, buttered side down.

"Now look what you made me do! You have to clean it up, Evan!" Andrew shouted crossly.

The arguments of the two young men in my life will always be the same. Evan and Andrew are incompatible, the courses of their lives set. But I'd always believed that when they were little, things might've been different. They could have had time to appreciate a sister. They might have welcomed her presence then, or even sought her female advice. But I'd never given them that chance. And now, their lives were filled with sports, friends, and school.

"Honey, you know I don't want any more kids." Colin added his standard argument, pushing his chair away from the table as he rose. "Your boys are my kids. And I think we have enough to handle with these two ballerinas."

"Hey!" Andrew and Evan growled in unison, turning their antagonism away from each other to meet Colin's humor.

"When you guys are finished with World War III, come on outside. We're going to clean the garage this morning," Colin told them.

More grumbles and groans.

"Because this afternoon, we have tickets to the game," Colin added with a grin.

"Yeah!" Evan cheered.

"Awesome!" Andrew added, and the two of them shared a high five.

Evan picked up the lost piece of toast, tossed it on the counter, and hurried to eat something before beginning his usual rush through the day.

While my two teenaged sons wolfed down food, Colin came over to the sink beside me and smoothed the curve of my neck and shoulder with his broad hand. He kissed my temple and turned me around, into his arms. From the first moment I'd met him, he could always make me melt with hunger for him.

"You know I love you, Ingrid, but I just don't understand this need of yours to have another child." He tickled the inside of my ear with the tip of his tongue, knowing it would send flames of desire curling all the way down to my toes. I leaned into his solid strength.

"Look, in a few short years, we'll have this whole house all to ourselves," he whispered hotly. "Then we can spend all day showing each other exactly how much we love each other. And in how many, varied ways..."

I tried to make his dreams for our future enough. I loved Colin with all my heart. He was my soul mate, the man I'd searched for, the man I'd thought I'd never find.

Dishes clattered behind us. The boys were oblivious to our embrace. They, too, felt secure in our little family circle of love.

So how could I possibly want more? How could I even think about jeopardizing my life with Colin?

I knew he loved me more than I'd ever dared hope for. And the most special part about him was that he loved my sons as if they were his own flesh and blood.

Maybe that genuine love was precisely what had given me the courage to dream of more.

To dream of the daughter I couldn't forget.

But how could I explain something that even I didn't understand? Still, I only knew that I couldn't let it go.

Watching my three men together, I told myself firmly that this family was everything I'd always worked toward. Colin was the kind of man I'd searched for, but never thought I'd find. And yet . . . I needed my little girl. No matter how hard I tried, I couldn't stop thinking about her.

I tried again. "Wouldn't a little girl with curls, and lace, and giggles add some lightness to this houseful of rough-and-tumble boys?"

"We have *you*," Colin said roundly, stepping back with a teasing smile. "You keep things feminine and happy around here."

"Yeah," Andrew chimed in with his mouth full. "And girls don't giggle. They shriek."

"Not you, of course, Mom," Evan said with an impish smile that reminded me of his biological father.

Derek had been my high school crush; I'd pursued him relentlessly. Of course, he hadn't been too difficult to catch. We were two young people high on life and love, or so I'd thought. At graduation, I wanted to get married, but Derek had already decided to move in with his brother in Philadelphia and get a job there. He would be too busy to come home, he said, and it was best if I found someone else.

Heartbroken, I couldn't even think about finding someone else, but I did find work as a cashier in a grocery store. Then my father was killed in a car accident, just before Christmas. My mother had her own grief to deal with, and Derek was gone. I felt positively abandoned.

It was during that time of total loss that I met Femi. Femi understood just how I felt. He was from another country, far from home, swimming alone in an unfamiliar sea of people. I found great comfort with him.

A year later, I heard that Derek had moved back to town, but I didn't seek him out. I was so confused by all the curves life was throwing in my direction that I just wanted to be left alone. But Derek didn't see it that way. He was sorry he hadn't been there for me when Dad died, and maybe even a little jealous of Femi. Suddenly, it was Derek's turn to pursue me relentlessly, and finally, I gave in. More than anything else at that time, I needed to be loved, and Derek offered me that.

Derek and I were married in a simple ceremony just before my twentieth birthday. I think, now, that the marriage was basically destined for failure right from the start. My mother had always said that I loved too easily, and that I should try to be easier to love. To this day, she thinks I drove Derek away with my constant talk of little girls, and maybe she's right. We had two little boys, one right after the other, and the responsibilities were instantly more than we could handle. After all, Derek and I were barely more than kids ourselves back then.

When Andrew was seven months old, a month before Evan's second birthday, I bought a set of beautifully illustrated children's encyclopedias. I wanted our kids to have more than we had, but Derek blew up.

All his friends were having wild, single fun, and he couldn't even afford to invite them over for potato chips—while I could spend a bunch of money on something we couldn't even use. I promised to return the books, but Derek said forget it, and walked out. At first, I was frantic, but after a couple of weeks, I knew he wasn't coming back.

Derek and I are friends now, but it wasn't that way at first. It took a lot of years for us to sort through the anger and disappointments. Eventually, though, we came to realize that what had happened between us in the past simply didn't matter anymore, if it ever really had. It was the boys who mattered most to both of us.

Derek had been married to Holly for twelve years now, and they had two girls and a boy of their own. They seemed happy, and though they didn't see much of Evan and Andrew, the boys both knew they could contact their father whenever they wanted.

I was so lucky to have found Colin. Because of him, Evan and Andrew had grown up with a wonderful father figure in their lives. When life was so complicated and out of control, Colin made everything good again.

So, why did I want to rock the boat?

"Besides, another child wouldn't necessarily be a girl," Colin rationalized as he headed for the door.

"And he—or she—would ruin our foursome," Evan added, clearing his plate. He shrugged matter-of-factly. "We're perfect for four sides of the table."

"And twelve donuts, and eight pieces of pizza, and—"

"As if I ever get my share of those!" I pointed out with a grin.

With two strapping teen boys and a six-foot man in the house, I was often left with little more than table scraps! But, doggone it, girls tend to think with their hearts, not reason with their minds like my guys were trying to do! They could analyze the situation all they wanted, but what I *needed* was a deeper connection, someone to share that feminine bond with me.

I shoved the chairs under the table and brushed away the crumbs. "I know I'll always be outnumbered, but sometimes, I'd just like to tip the balance a little more in my favor." I zinged the soggy dishcloth, water droplets and toast crumbs flying, between my two sons. It dropped squarely into the sink.

"Ooo, way to go, Mom!" Andrew hooted.

I ignored his levity, refusing to let it lighten my mood. "Since the three of you are going to clean the garage anyway, I'll get the car out of your way. I'm going for a drive. These dishes can wait—since I have to do them alone whenever I do them, anyway."

Colin caught me gently by the arm before I could flounce from the room, "You keep saying you want a child with me," he confided with an uneasiness that bordered on anger, "but I'm beginning to think that this need of yours is becoming an obsession. You know, no child can dissolve the shadow that's darkening between us, Ingrid. Maybe all you really want is a daughter. And not me."

That's not true! I shouted in my mind. But I couldn't force myself to say the words. This was a new argument—one I wasn't prepared to deal with.

Andrew was carrying out the trash and Evan was sweeping when I backed out of the driveway.

Colin waved and called, "You'll be back in time for the game, won't you?"

I nodded and headed for my mother's house. It had been a while since I'd last seen her, and the longer I waited between visits, the more irritable she tended to become. I composed myself and my thoughts during the ten-minute drive over to her place.

Mother had always made it very clear where she stood on my need for a daughter. Whenever there was a disagreement between Colin and me, she'd say I was being petty or unreasonable. She'd sided with Derek all the time when I was married to him, too.

When I stopped to think about that, I often wondered why I did want a little girl so badly. The bond between my mother and me was so frazzled and tenuous. But it hadn't always been that way. I could remember a time when I could share any confidence with my mother, and it had seemed like she could solve the problems of the world. Somewhere along the way, though, I'd grown up and learned that there were some things she couldn't, or wouldn't, fix.

But how I missed that closeness, that thread of female kinship that I'd known growing up. I wanted so much to share that with my own little girl.

"You and Colin had a fight, didn't you?" Mother asked when she met me at the door. "Your eyes are glassy and your nose is pink."

So much for composure. Or hiding anything from her. She knew me far too well.

"Hello, Mother, it's good to see you, too."

"Sorry, dear, but you look so *unhappy*. I hope it wasn't that same ridiculous fight about you having another child, was it, Ingrid?"

As she set about making coffee, I hung my jacket on the back of a kitchen chair and took a seat.

"It wasn't a fight," I clarified wearily. "It was a discussion. And it isn't ridiculous."

The ritual of words and actions was the same as always. I could have mapped out her movements about the sink and stove, and predicted exactly how long it would take her to execute each of them. But suddenly, when she sat down across from me at the table, she did something totally unexpected. She stared at me with long and unnerving intensity.

"Ingrid—" she began firmly, but then her whole face seemed to cave in on itself with doubt. Her gaze fell away, and she stirred cream into her coffee.

Her hand trembled, and I noticed for the first time how tired she looked. But I didn't push. I knew if I did, she might not share what she was having so much trouble getting out. Somewhere in the shadows of my mind, a light went on, Not only did my mother know me—sometimes too well—but I also knew her, her methods and frailties. So I waited in silence.

"Ingrid," she said finally, "I—I almost didn't tell you this, but—" She removed the spoon from her mug and reached for a napkin.

I sipped the steaming liquid in my cup and tried to calm the flutter of fear that suddenly rose in my chest.

Was she ill?

"I got this letter in the mail—about a week ago." She slowly pulled an envelope from the pocket of her slacks. The anxious frown on her face was as deep as the creases in the envelope she handed me. "I wanted to—but I couldn't quite bring myself—to throw it in the trash."

I looked up at her, fingering the envelope in my hands. "Mother, but—it's addressed to me. At least—it *was* addressed to me, before I got married. My maiden name is written here. But—how could you even think about throwing it away?"

"Because—because I already know how shaky your marriage is, Ingrid. I—I was afraid this would upset you. That you might even..."

"Might even what? Embarrass you again?"

How could I ever have thought she knew me? She didn't. Didn't at all. Wasn't that what had started all this business between us in the first place? Yes, Colin and I had our differences, but I knew without a doubt that he was the best thing that had ever happened to me.

So why did my heart leap into my throat when I saw the return address on the envelope?

St. Mary's Home.

I could hardly breathe as I opened the letter and read it carefully. Finally, I looked up at my mother, tears shimmering in my eyes.

"Oh, Mother, I'd always hoped... but I never dreamed she might... oh, Mother—my baby, Eva... she wants to meet me!"

Mother clasped her hands over mine, but her voice was hard again. "You'd better think on this, Ingrid. Think long and hard," she said.

My eyes burned. My throat burned. My heart burned most of all.

As much as I wanted this, needed this, I couldn't pursue it. If Colin ever found out, after all this time, what would he think? Would he still love me? Or believe in me anymore?

"If only I'd told him in the beginning," I whispered fervently. "Even if it had meant he wouldn't have married me."

"How can you say such a thing?" Mother's hands fluttered with as much intensity as her words. "How would you ever have raised those boys alone? You know I didn't have the financial means to help you after your father died. All I had to give was my advice, but I've always stood by it, Ingrid, and you know it. You did the right thing."

I stared at her, wiping listlessly at the hot tears that streamed down my cheeks. "For who, Mother? For Eva? Or for you? Because it certainly wasn't the right thing for me!"

I could tell the accusation stung, but I didn't care. Mother wasn't worried about Eva or me. She was worried about what the gossips in our little fishbowl would say if I stirred up the muddy waters all over again.

I drove to the city and roamed the streets from here to forever, searching faces, looking for my baby. Our town was white, for the most part, but every time I saw a girl about her age at the mall, I would wonder, Could this be her? The day she turned five, I cried all day long, thinking about her starting school, without me there by her side, watching her, helping her, guiding her, loving her. I hadn't even gotten to witness her first baby steps, and on that day, she'd begun her walk out into the world.

After that, every September was unbearable. September meant another new year of school. Another birthday gone by. For eighteen years, I studied every black-haired toddler, every dark-eyed little girl, every dark-skinned teenager that I saw, and wondered, could this be her? If only I could see her smile, touch her, and know for myself that she was happy.

In time, my search became second nature, almost a constant internal radar, fueled by a hopeless ache.

The more streets my car traveled, the more hopeless that ache became. But now, it seemed, my non-stop radar had brought her close, so close that I could have touched her. I could have held her in my arms and hugged her in reality, instead of just in my mind and heart. Did she need to fill the emptiness as much as I did? She must, or that letter would never have been sent.

I was on my way home from Mother's house by then. I fingered the paper that held so much potential in my pocket. It was real. I pulled over to the curb, read the words again, and knew what I had to do.

Three weeks passed like an eternity while I struggled to hold back the tidal wave of excitement that was rising inside of me. I couldn't tell Colin, nor could I let my mother guess. But I had to do this. I had to see for myself that my child was all right. I so longed to touch her, to see her smile, to finally *know* her.

At last, the day finally arrived, a gloomy Thursday that threatened rain. It didn't matter. We had agreed through a social worker to meet on neutral ground and chosen a restaurant, a seafood restaurant, for lunch. While I love shrimp and scallops, Colin hates them, so I knew it would be safe.

I was early. I waited in the lobby, watching the ceaseless flow of people pass by. Then, when a pretty, cocoa-complected girl entered with two women, something inside of me—maybe that long-alert radar—instinctively sensed that this was the group I'd been waiting for.

I approached them, and asked softly, "Is one of you Mrs. Ivers?"

The shorter, rounder woman turned to me with a smile. "I'm Marie Ivers," she said.

My heart raced. "Mrs. Ivers," I said, "I'm Ingrid Hagen."

We shook hands, and she introduced me to Della James, a tall, thin woman with closely cropped black hair. While it registered on some level that this was the woman who'd raised my little girl, my real focus was with my child, my daughter, and had been with her ever since the moment when she'd first walked in through the door. No, even longer than that. Since the day I'd had to let her go.

Tears streaked silently down my face, I couldn't help it, and then she was in my arms, hugging me as tightly as I held her.

"Eva! Oh, Eva! My little Eva!" I wept joyously.

"Her name is Regina now," Della gently corrected. "Regina James."

I took a step back and held her at arm's length, beaming proudly with fresh tears shimmering in my eyes. "I'm so happy to meet you at last, Regina," I told her earnestly.

She smiled, wiping away her own tears. "I'm happy, too. What—what should I call you?" she asked, somewhat hesitantly.

I glanced from Mrs. James to Mrs. Ivers. The moment seemed awkward. I realized that "Mom" or "Mother" was too much to ask, though I ached for it.

"How about Ingrid?" I suggested finally, gently squeezing her hands for reassurance.

"Ingrid it is, then." She nodded and smiled, then hugged me again.

"Your tables are ready," *the* waitress announced. The arrangement was for the two women to eat on one side of the restaurant garden, while Regina and I sat at our own table on the other side, so that we could have a chance to get acquainted.

The first real thing Regina said to me was, "I'm glad you chose this place. I love seafood!"

"So do I!"

I stopped putting the napkin in my lap and looked straight into her sparkling midnight eyes, thrilled at even so little as that tiny scrap of common ground. My heart swelled to bursting with pride and a sense of kinship. The emotion was followed instantly by a flash of guilt for having deceived Colin, but I quickly pushed that thought from my mind.

We ate, my daughter and I—what a glorious combination of words! My daughter and I. The phrase is so common, but there is absolutely nothing common about a daughter. The food must have been good that day, but I didn't notice. I listened to Regina as she told me about her life—about school, and her friends, her family, and her hopes for the future.

"You're so beautiful," I told her, getting all choked up with tears of prideful happiness, "both inside and out. And your thirst for knowledge reminds me so much of your father. You look a lot like him, you know."

Regina grinned. "Do you think I look like you?" she asked, somewhat bashfully.

She had this beautiful, exquisite way of looking up at me through her thick, dark lashes. I could tell she was a little shy. I studied her for a moment.

"Your smile, I think, and the shape of your nose." The truth is, our physical resemblance was subtle, if not slight. Regina was truly striking—not anything like me, with my blond hair, fair skin, and blue eyes. She was also considerably taller than me, and athletically built, as her father had been.

"My parents have always told me how much they love me, and they showed it with unlimited hugs and support," Regina began gently. "But the one thing they refused to let me do was search for you. And I begged to—ever since I can remember. I just couldn't stop wondering about where I really came from. But my parents were worried about what would happen to me if you refused to see me, or if the meeting didn't go well, so they made me wait until I turned eighteen." She shook her head incredulously, grinning from ear to ear.

"And now—well, I just can't believe it! Here you are!"

My heart flooded with emotion. "Here *we are,*" I said, feeling fresh tears well in my eyes as I reached across the table to stroke her face.

"Why didn't you keep me?" she asked suddenly, her face serious, her voice barely above a whisper.

I sat back in my chair and closed my eyes for a long moment. I prayed for the means to explain to her in a way she could understand. I assured her that it wasn't because I didn't love her. I always had, and always would. But sometimes, the things we want in life, and the things that are best for us, are not the same.

Regina sipped her water thoughtfully. "That's what my mom always says—like when I was younger, and I wanted my own room. She told me I needed to learn to share with Shereese. She's my sister."

I smiled. "It's taken me a long time to realize that I need people around me. I really don't do well all alone. Most of my life, there have been people all around me. A brother, a sister, and cousins as I was growing up, and then Derek."

Regina asked about him, and I told her all about how he'd gotten a scholarship, and how I'd felt left behind. Soon after, when my father was killed in a car accident, I felt very lost and all alone. I went to a bar.

I'm not proud of the amount of drinking I did, but that's where I met Femi, Regina's father. He was a doctoral student from Nigeria. He, too, knew what loneliness was, and we spent a lot of time talking, walking, and simply sharing. Femi made me feel like a whole person again. Like a woman. He made the hurt go away.

For six months, I thought my life was full again. But then Femi received his degree. He'd promised to return to his country, and he was a man of his word. There was no changing his mind. My family pointed out that if I went with him, I'd be a stranger in a strange land, and Femi was quick to agree—perhaps too quick. Without his support,

I knew I couldn't survive the isolation of an unfamiliar culture.

It wasn't until after he was gone that I learned I was pregnant. My mother demanded to know what I was thinking, or if I'd been thinking at all. She finally agreed to help me have my baby, as long as I promised to give it up for adoption.

"So, you see, Regina, at the time, as a frightened, lonely young woman, I really felt like I had no other choice available to me," I explained to her gently.

Regina nodded solemnly. "Is your mother still alive?" she asked.

"Yes."

"A grandmother," Regina said longingly. "I wish I could know her. My father's parents are both dead, and my mother was raised by an aunt and uncle. I've always wanted grandparents. . ." She colored slightly then, and asked, carefully, "Does your mother—does she still hate me?"

I gasped in utter surprise. "Oh, Regina!" I took her hands in both of mine, squeezing them reassuringly. "Oh, darling—she never hated you! It was because of me . . . and because of the circumstances . . and the lack of money—but never because of you, Regina! Never because of you!"

She smiled tremulously. "Do you think she would come—next time?"

Next time?

The thought, both heartwarming and terrifying, stole my breath away.

"I—I don't know if she'll come," I admitted honestly.

"Please ask her to," Regina insisted.

Well, I couldn't promise something I wasn't prepared to deliver, so I tried to explain to her, in a roundabout way. "Unlike me, I can tell that you've been a real blessing to your parents, Regina," I said warmly, proudly.

She hugged me again then, and an hour or so later when we left, we made plans to get together again real soon.

When we did, and Regina asked about my mother again, I admitted I hadn't been able to tell her about our reunion yet. Regina didn't bring up the subject again, and neither did I. After that, things were fantastic for a while, until Colin began asking questions.

Where was I spending more and more of my time? And why was I being so secretive about it? After a couple of months of flimsy excuses, he held me one night and said I seemed different. Something about me had changed. While he was pleased that I seemed happier, he was also worried. "Are you seeing another man?" he asked.

The words were like an arrow in my heart. "No! Oh, Colin—no! Never! I'm not seeing another man! I would never do that to you, Colin! I love you too much!"

I showed him how much he meant to me when we made love that night, and afterward, when he held me in his arms as we were drifting off to sleep, I said softly, "I know you don't want me to have our own little girl, but maybe if we—"

Colin groaned loudly. "No adoption, Ingrid. We've been through this before. A hundred times at *least*."

"Maybe a foster child?"

Colin turned over and put his pillow over his head. "Good night, Ingrid."

A week later, I was on my way out the door to see Regina when Colin stopped me.

"Where are you going?"

"To my mother's," I lied. I knew I was compounding the problem, but I didn't know what else to do. I had to see Regina. I had to get to know her better, make up for all the lost time.

Colin nodded slowly. I wasn't sure he was convinced, but I didn't want Regina to think I wasn't coming, so I hurried out without another word.

"You're late," Regina teased when I got to the restaurant and found her waiting for me at our usual table. After several failed attempts to engage me in meaningful conversation, she finally asked, "What's wrong?"

I looked at her sideways and knew this was the moment I'd been dreading from the moment I saw her walk into the restaurant that very first time. "I didn't want to give you up the first time, my little Eva.

And now, Regina, I'm afraid I'm going to have to give you up again," I said quietly, brokenly, tears welling in my eyes so that she seemed to blur in front of me.

Regina looked stricken. "Why?" she asked in a very small voice. "Is it—is it because of your mother?"

"The first time, it was because of my mother. This time, it's my husband. Regina, Colin doesn't even know you exist," I admitted frankly, tears streaming down my face as I took her hands in mine.

"So you had to choose—choose between him and me. Well, I know it wasn't easy for you to decide," she said bravely, "because I think you like our visits as much as I do." She hesitated, then plunged on with, "You know, when I had to choose between finding a job to stay close to my friends, Lisa and Kerry, or going away to college, my mother really helped me. First, she said I had to make up my mind about what *I* wanted. Sometimes, that's the hardest part. But after that, it was easier to see that I needed to go away to college, and still stay in touch with my friends. I guess for you, it must be best if Colin doesn't know about me."

My heart shattered into a thousand, tiny pieces. Regina hardly knew me, yet she believed in me, and trusted in my decision. What *did* I want? What was best for others around me? Those were some hard, difficult questions that I had never really confronted before. Not ever. Now, suddenly, I realized that maybe if I'd at least addressed what I wanted back when Regina was still my little Eva, even if I hadn't acted on it by keeping her, maybe facing the results of what was best for those around me would have been easier, and more constructive. Maybe then, I could have dealt better with giving up my daughter.

Well, those were all questions that should have been answered a long time ago. Now, the turn of events in my life was coming full circle, and demanding that I face those very same questions, or lose everyone who'd come to mean the world to me.

"I don't know what I'm going to do, Regina," I told her honestly. "I only know that I love you, that I've always loved you. And I always will."

Before I left, I held that child of mine tight in my arms. What a wise, remarkable young woman she had become.

"You weren't at your mother's," Colin said, meeting me at the door when I got home. "Where were you?"

"I, um—I went to—uh, I had an appointment."

"An appointment? With who?"

"Well. . . ."

He grabbed me by the shoulders and made me look into his face. "Are you seeing someone else, Ingrid?" he demanded. But in his eyes, there was no accusation. I saw only distress. "He's willing to give you the daughter you want, isn't he?" he said then, his voice breaking.

Tears filled my eyes. I couldn't hold back the sobs. "Oh, Colin, what am I going to do?" I leaned into him, weeping, and he slid his arms around me.

"Trusting me with the truth would be a good place to start," he murmured into my hair.

He was right. Too many things in my life had been secreted away. It was time to brush the dust off those choices I'd made so long ago, and bring them into the light.

Regina had asked me if I knew what I wanted. I think even then, I knew—maybe I've always known—but I hadn't realized it until that moment. Or maybe it was just that I'd never found the courage to face what I wanted until I surrendered myself as a mass of boneless jelly into Colin's loving arms. It was there that I found the strength to risk it all.

Yes, I wanted Colin in my life. And yes, I wanted to play an active part in Regina's life. But most of all, I needed to be able to live with myself, and that meant being open and honest. No more secrets, no more lies, no more half-truths.

"I am seeing someone else, Colin," I said quietly then.

He took me by the shoulders again, and this time, he set me firmly away from him.

A tremble ran from where his broad hands had left my shoulders, all the way down to my shaking knees. The look of hurt in his eyes made me hurry on.

"It isn't what you think. It's not another man; it's—she's my little girl. Only now, well—she's a beautiful, grown woman." I took a deep breath and steeled myself. "Colin, I have a daughter."

There. I'd said it. I took another deep, calming breath and braced myself for his reaction.

"A daughter? But—how, Ingrid? When—? Why?"

"It was long before I met you. I was only eighteen. . . ."

Though we weren't touching, I could feel the tension melt from Colin's body. The initial shock that had drawn his dark brows tightly together was replaced by concern, not the anger or censure I'd always feared. There was only an aching, obvious disappointment.

"But, why, Ingrid?" he asked sadly. "Why didn't you ever tell me?"

"I think—because I was afraid. Afraid I'd lose you. Colin—I'm *still* afraid," I said anxiously then, reaching out to grip his arm.

He closed his eyes and shook his head, and continued to shake his head as he dropped into his favorite chair, and pulled me down with him into his lap.

"That isn't going to happen any time soon, my love. Come now, Ingrid," he murmured gently. "I think it's time you told me everything."

I thought I'd cried all my tears when I was reunited with my daughter, but tears came again, this time overflowing with relief. Colin held me close and listened quietly until I was finished.

"So that's the ache I've felt in your heart all these years, the pain you would never share," he said sadly after a long, silent moment.

"You've always said you don't want a daughter, but, you know what?" I sniffed to keep from bursting into tears all over again. "I—I don't know if I can ever give her up again, now that we've found each other after all these long, painful years."

"Could I meet her?" Colin asked, his deep voice barely above a whisper.

I turned in his arms, wondering if I'd really heard the words, or if they were only a repeat of my endless dreams. "Did—did you say what I think you said?" I asked him, almost breathlessly.

He nodded solemnly.

"Are—are you sure, Colin?"

"Yes."

I threw my arms around his neck and kissed him with more love than I'd ever known could possibly exist.

The following week, Colin and I stopped at my mother's house on our way to meet Regina.

"I can't imagine where you're taking me," she said, as Colin closed the car door for her. "Such a big secret! All hush-hush!"

She was enjoying the mystery, but I wasn't. Why hadn't Colin warned me that he'd invited my mother along? Was this an act of revenge for keeping him in the dark for so long?

"Have you arranged to pick up Evan and Andrew somewhere, too?" I demanded when he got in behind the wheel.

"We can if you like, but wouldn't that overwhelm our hostess? I thought you'd want to save that for another time."

Another time? There would be another time? How could I suspect revenge from Colin when there wasn't a malicious bone in his body?

I will always remember the look of surprise, and then joy, on Regina's face when we pulled up in front of her house that day. I held my head up high when I introduced her to her grandmother, and to Colin.

"This is my daughter, Regina Yvette James. Isn't she beautiful? Her parents did a marvelous job of raising her. She is so happy, and so very insightful. I know now that I absolutely did the right thing when I gave her to them."

When my mother's eyes met mine, I knew, in that moment, that we finally shared a deeper understanding of each other. At last, we were on that same, mother-daughter wavelength we'd shared when I was growing up.

I've known and lost two men in my life for very different reasons, and I'm at peace with that. I feared I'd lose Colin, too, but finding Regina was exactly what I needed. I have great love in my life—from my mother, from Colin and the boys—but my daughter Regina completes me. She is the part of me that was missing all these long years—the broken part of me that needed to be fixed before I could ever feel whole again. I hope I can be the same for her, if she'll continue to let me. I don't feel the driving need for a little girl anymore. And, strangely, in finding my daughter, I found my mother all over again.

Now, we all know Regina. And she knows us. Colin knows all of my secrets, and I know that nothing can threaten our love for each other.

We've rid our family fishbowl of its murky secrets, and the waters are crystal clear again. With my mother behind me, my daughter and sons before me, and my husband at my side, the future looks both warm, and dazzlingly bright. THE END

CELEBRITIES ADOPT— I STEAL BABIES!

But before you call the F.B.I. and turn me in, read on to find out how it all happened. You see, my most unlikely and unusual journey toward forgiveness—and redemption—all started with one of those unsettling, middle-of-the-night phone calls...

Vera isn't a very sympathetic narrator. She's quick to judge Giselle, the former receptionist in her husband's office, for leaving her daughter in a daycare center: "I don't approve of that," Vera sneers, "but I wasn't going to tell her how to care for her own child." When Giselle calls Vera's husband, Shane, late one night after taking an overdose of pills, Vera assumes they're having an affair and decides to track them down. She eventually reaches the hospital where Giselle is dying—and the woman's body is barely cold before Vera decides to take little Elissa home.

If Ingrid's excessive desire for a baby girl in the last story is about healing a wound from her past, Vera's obsession is pure selfishness: "I have to have somebody to take care of!" she screams at Shane, but she basically thinks of Elissa (and Min Hee, the daughter she's already adopted) as dolls she can dress and play with. She's dumbfounded when Shane doesn't buy into her plan, which drives her to a foolish plan of action—and though she's saved from her own recklessness, this is one of those cases where the upbeat spin at the end of the story rings just a bit false. At least, it does to me... but see what you think.

The first person I saw that Saturday night in the ER was Giselle Malloy. She was lying on her back, not moving or breathing.

Next, I saw Shane, my husband. He was staring at the white

uniforms of the circle of busy nurses and interns who were working on Giselle. He looked pasty-faced with fear. In his arms lay Giselle's baby daughter, Elissa.

One intern towered above the others. Kneeling on the bed, he was astride Giselle's chest, giving her CPR. Perspiration covered his face as he pressed down and rocked forward.

"Have you got a heartbeat?" an older doctor asked, rushing into the room from the hall.

"I can't feel or hear anything. When we got the electrodes on, there was a tracing, but I couldn't find any pulse."

The older doctor placed one end of his stethoscope on Giselle. He listened over the heart, moving his hand across her firm breasts. Flecks of blood were on Giselle's pale lips. The doctor shook his head and muttered, "Looks terminal."

Thirty minutes later, Giselle Malloy was pronounced dead.

To be honest, I never liked Giselle Malloy. I didn't trust the way she was so quick to volunteer to work overtime during the busy season in Shane's contracting company, where she was a secretary.

When Shane first told me about her job interview, he said, "Poor kid! She's had a rotten deal. A coast-to-coast truck driver married her and three months after their baby came, deserted her. Everybody in our office liked her right away, though. I guess I'll give her a job, even though she's slow on the computer."

I didn't say anything, but I had my own thoughts. *Sure, slow on the computer—but fast in bed. Thirty-year-old divorcée with tears in her baby blues . . . she probably knows how to vamp all the men in the office, including my Shane.*

Of course, whenever Giselle Malloy and I chatted, we both pretended to be friendly. We compared our children. While she went to work, Giselle took Elissa to a daycare center. I don't approve of that, but I wasn't going to tell her how to care for her own child. However, I will admit that my fingers itched to fix Elissa's hair and to dress her in some cute dresses.

When I reached out to take the baby girl from Shane's arms, I don't think he was aware I did it. His eyes were glassy with pain.

I hugged Elissa. She stirred without opening her eyes and said, "Mommy?"

I whispered, "Your mommy is not here right now, darling, but it's okay for you to have a cookie." I dug into my jacket pocket where I usually keep a supply of snacks for the kids.

Elissa's yawns stopped instantly. Her eyes opened. "Chocolate?"

We settled for a broken graham cracker. We were on our way to becoming good friends as I rocked her back to sleep. *How can anyone turn away from this innocent child, who has no family, no home?* I felt a surge of warmth. I knew my inner feelings were right— *I must protect this child as if she were my own.*

What a strange world, I mused. Earlier that evening, I'd started out from my home with hate in my heart for Giselle Malloy. Now, I was holding her beautiful child and wanting to take care of her.

My thoughts went back to the phone call that started this strange night. . .

I woke up slowly when Shane groped in the dark for the ringing phone in our bedroom. The receiver did not fully cover his ear and I could hear a female voice calling, "Shane! Are you there? Shane?"

"What's the matter?" His words blurred together. He was groggy with sleep.

"This is Giselle. I called to say . . . good-bye."

Shane was still half-asleep and seemed amused by her sense of humor. "Okay. Where are you going?"

"Took sleeping pills . . . all of 'em . . . everything's a mess . . . so tired . . . can't pretend anymore. Goodbye, Shane. . . ." There was a crashing noise from the phone.

Shane was instantly wide awake, talking steadily into the mouth-piece. "Don't do it! Giselle, listen! Hold on, hang on!"

Then the loud hum of the dial tone took over.

Shane swung his long legs out of bed. He was out of his pajamas before reaching the closet. He threw on his clothes.

"What was that?" I stirred as if just waking up.

"Go back to sleep." He was zipping up his jeans.

I snapped on the bed light. "What are you doing?"

"Don't worry about it. It's nothing."

"Nothing? Three in the morning, someone calls up and you say, 'Don't worry'?"

"There you go, overreacting again."

"Who called?" I demanded. I wanted to see if he would lie to me about Giselle.

"Only a friend who needs help. She took some sleeping pills."

"Who?" I pretended I hadn't already overheard.

"It was Giselle Malloy. Remember? She used to work for me."

"Giselle?" He dropped the name of his former secretary so fast I could hardly believe my ears. "Why did she call you?"

The look he threw back at me was pure anger. "She has a big crush on me, okay? Does that make you feel better?" He went out the door in a trot. I heard his station wagon grind its gears and speed away from the house.

I snapped the light off, determined to go back to sleep. But it was no use. Bad memories, mostly about my failing marriage, floated through me.

There was a time when everything was right between us. Shane was doing well as a carpenter and I was taking home a weekly paycheck for being a receptionist in Dr. Cotrell's office. We saved our pennies and made the first payment on a house before our first baby arrived.

Dylan was a spunky kid and he made Shane very happy. At that time, Shane seemed more in love with me then than ever before. When Dylan was almost three, we tried urgently to have another child. Nothing happened. We started bickering about anything and everything. After many months, we decided to adopt.

Through Dr. Cotrell, I found a darling, Korean infant girl, Min Hee. For weeks, Shane worked hard to straighten out the legal problems. Min Hee was the best thing that happened to me that entire year. I got out all of Dylan's baby clothes and re-fitted them to her tiny frame. I was delighted to have a "doll" to play with and to talk to once again. The year flew past.

Shane started his own contracting business. He put most of our savings into the firm. For a while, he did very well. He was busy and happy building homes for other people while I was thrilled to make a nice home and family for the four of us.

Then, the unexpected happened. The bottom dropped out of the housing market. Shane's business slid under. He cut his office staff from eight workers to one; Giselle Malloy worked without pay until the end. I always felt she was a jinx.

Because Shane was so depressed about his failing business, I went to the office each day for a few hours to use my office skills from earlier years. I was rusty, but Shane kept saying how wonderful I was at it. Poor Shane—he always wanted to be successful in business, but it wasn't happening. I ran my own home and his office better than he and Giselle did together. I wondered at the time if I was doing too much for him.

Losing the company was hard on Shane. He not only lost the company, but he also lost his self-confidence. He was always so proud of being the boss-man, the head of everything. He thought of himself as stronger than any man working for him. When he was unemployed and moping around the house all. day, I could not resist making a few sarcastic remarks.

"I thought you were so strong! What happened to my big hero?"

Through all those hard times, whenever we made love, I ignored using any contraceptives. I didn't tell Shane, but each month I was hoping to get pregnant. It had always been better between us when there was a little one for me to take care of and to love. When nothing happened—that is, when my periods came right on schedule—my suspicions turned into a nagging, constant worry. I called Dr. Cotrell about having a complete checkup. Just as I expected, he found a growth on my uterus. He insisted on a total hysterectomy; I would never be able to have another baby. I felt trapped—and my tears didn't solve a thing.

As soon as I got home from the operation, the quarrels with my husband worsened. I was angry and depressed; I wanted to adopt a baby, but Shane was dead set against it.

"I'm telling you—we cannot *afford* it. My business is at a *standstill*. I can't even find a carpenter's job for myself!"

"Doesn't my happiness count?" I pouted and cried.

"That's not the point."

"It'll be better for us if we have a new baby in the house. It was that way before! Don't a home and family mean more to you than your stupid business?"

"We can't have one without the other, Vera."

"I have to have *somebody* to take care of!" I cried, louder than necessary.

"You have two growing kids, a cat, four tropical fish, seventeen potted plants, a house with a garden—isn't that enough?"

"No. I want a *baby!*" I shouted, pounding on the kitchen table. I was in hysterics.

Shane, unable to handle my anger, disappeared until the next day. I never did find out where he spent that night, but it didn't matter. All I could think about was having one more chance to take care of one more baby. I fell asleep with the pillow against my breasts, pretending to nurse.

Not long after that fight, Shane left me. He said he was going to look for work; there was not enough construction happening in our part of the state. He came home only on weekends; I could see by his hangdog look that no jobs turned up.

And that is why, while I was listening to Shane's station wagon roar away into the darkness, several questions jumped into my mind: *Where has Shane been these past weeks? Is he living with Giselle?*

The abrupt, middle-of-the-night phone call made me certain he was seeing her. The more I chewed on these worries, the more anxious I was to get dressed and to follow Shane. I know Giselle's home address from the files at the office. Her home is across town, on 183 Belvedere Road.

"Wake up, Dylan!"

His twelve-year-old face looked like a wrinkled newspaper on which someone had been sitting. He yawned. "Time for school, Mom? It's still dark outside."

"No, we have to go help a sick friend."

"Who? Who's sick?" He was obedient and put on his jeans.

"Never mind. I'm going to wake Min Hee. You warm up the car. Try to be quiet with the garage doors."

Dylan scooted down the stairs, delighted to he handed the ignition keys to my cranky, old sedan.

I wrapped Min Hee in a blanket and placed her in the backseat. She hardly moved or mumbled.

I had only driven through Giselle's neighborhood a few times. I wasn't sure whether she lived in an apartment building or a house. *Maybe I'll see Shane's station wagon parked outside. If so, though—what next? Crash Giselle's front door to catch them in the act? What will happen if I do find them together? Does that mean it's the end of my marriage?*

My brain seemed to whirl as I looked for dimly lit street signs and house numbers. I soon found Belvedere Road. But which direction? I turned right with a prayer. There! House number 183, a brick bungalow with porch lights blazing, stood as big as life.

Shane's station wagon was nowhere in sight. I stopped the car, got out, and then eased the car door shut. I signaled to Dylan to stay with Min Hee. Feeling as if someone were watching me, I moved carefully up the front walk to the house and crossed the porch on tiptoes. The silence seemed to intensify the thumps of my pounding heart.

Suddenly, I heard footsteps behind me. I whirled about.

"Evening, ma'am. You here to help Mrs. Malloy, too?"

I saw a white-haired man come from the shadows. He said, "It must've come over her very suddenly. My wife and I saw the ambulance lights flashing and we came right over. We often babysit for her kid and we—"

"Ambulance?" I was openmouthed in front of this elderly gentleman.

"Yup. County Hospital, it was from. They just left. And that nice, young guy who used to bring Mrs. Malloy home from the office when she worked late followed along."

"In a white station wagon? He took the baby with him?"

"Yup. Scary thing, isn't it, the way it comes on you so suddenly?"

Without answering, I ran to the car. I turned it around in a speedy exit, and headed toward County Hospital.

Then, there I was, walking down the polished hospital corridors just like any other visitor, holding a sleeping child in my arms. *Who's better able than I am to save this child?* I asked myself. Already I was planning how to divide Min Hee's room to fit in another bed. *If I simply move the toy chests into the alcove and stack the dressers, it could all work out. . .*

Dylan quickly settled into the backseat with Min Hee. I managed to snuggle all three kids under one blanket. They looked like little cherubs deep in happy dreams. I headed home, driving carefully with my precious cargo.

With a chuckle, I thought Shane would certainly be surprised when he discovered Elissa had been "added" to our family. I was not aware of any other relatives of the child, except for the long-distance truck driver, who had not been around since the divorce. All the legal problems about adopting Elissa could be settled later, in the same way Shane took care of everything with Min Hee. All I wanted to think about was the thrill of taking care of one more baby—at last!

At home, I gently laid the sleeping children in various beds. I put Elissa alongside me in the big bed as I took a quick nap before breakfast.

When the phone rang at eight that morning, my head was jumbled with too little sleep. I knew it must be Shane calling.

"I'm still at County Hospital. Giselle Malloy . . . she's dead."

"Shane, are you okay?" I could tell he was weeping.

"God, Vera, it was awful. They kept pumping on her and shoving needles into her, but they couldn't bring her around! I never saw anybody die before!"

"Shane, please come home now."

"I can't. I brought Elissa here with me, but now I can't find her. Some nurse must have held her for me. I don't remember. She's probably sleeping somewhere in one of their beds. They're looking all over—"

"Shane, listen. I have a surprise for you. Come home."

"No. I can't leave here until I find that kid."

"Shane, listen! I have Elissa."

"You . . . what?"

"That was me, not a nurse! I brought her home with me, and she is *just so cute!* Simply *adorable.*"

"What did you do that for?"

"Because ... I was trying to help. I only wanted—"

The sharp click and dial tone warned me of the wrath Shane was about to bring home to me. I decided to get up and prepare a big breakfast. It would help us get through what was sure to be a bumpy morning. I busied myself with Shane's favorites: fresh-squeezed orange juice, flapjacks, bacon, hot syrup, and a pot of steaming coffee.

Shane started in on me before he was even fully through the front door. "What kind of a dumb stunt is this? Don't you know kidnapping is a serious *crime?*"

"Why are you yelling?"

"I had the whole hospital turned upside down looking for that kid! Why the hell did you bring her here?"

"Where else? A park bench? That child needs a *home.* I can take good care of her."

Shane was fuming, red-faced. "That's not *our* responsibility. There is a social worker in the hospital for these situations. We're going to take her back!"

I saw his intent glare. I side-stepped his anger by saying, "Not now. She needs her sleep. We can talk about it later."

Breakfast was mostly in silence. Shane's mind was replaying the grotesque hospital scenes he'd witnessed earlier. "If only I'd reached her sooner," he muttered. "Calling the ambulance from the highway phone wasn't soon enough. I should've called them before I left here."

"You did all you could. You can't think of *everything.*"

Obviously, Giselle wasn't a threat to me anymore, but I was still curious about their possible romance, wondering, *Was he planning to ask me for a divorce?*

He went on, "I should have listened to her. Everyone needs somebody to talk to sometimes. But I was always too busy with my own problems—closing the firm, you, the kids. . ." His face was full of regrets and tears.

"I am a 'problem'?" I bristled.

"Oh, Vera, let's admit it. Things haven't exactly been so peachy around here lately."

"I don't have to listen to this," I snapped. "I do my part. This house is always nice and clean. Our kids are well behaved. It's not *our* fault *you're* a failure!" I hit him hard where it hurt—I saw him flinch.

"Why bring that up now?"

I didn't intend to stop. "You run off for days at a time. How do I even know where you're living? Or with whom?" I banged the pots and pans in the sink—it's my safety valve during our fights.

"I run off because I am *hurt*. When someone gets hurt, they run. Or cry. Or both." He sounded barely alive.

I stared at his twisted face—the pain-filled mask of a small boy who disappoints his mother and begins to weep.

He was trembling. "I tried. First, the business fell apart. Then our marriage. And now, Giselle is dead—"

Before I could reach out and stop him, Shane picked up his coat and was moving toward the door.

"Where are you going?" I tried to grab at his arm. He dodged away.

"To tell the hospital social worker to contact the Teamsters' Union. They'll find him."

"Who?"

"Don't act so dumb." He slammed the door and ran down the porch steps.

Of course, I knew he intended to return Elissa to her real father. I noticed that Shane's plan of action didn't include any consideration for me. Or for Elissa. He was only concerned about his own problem; he knew it would be too difficult for him to have little Elissa around the house, reminding him of Giselle. He wanted to forget both of them.

I pulled open the door and ran out onto the porch. "Don't you have any *feelings?*" I shouted. "How *dare* you throw an innocent child away? I won't let you do it!"

He didn't answer as he got into his station wagon and sped off.

There was no point in shouting at his retreating exhaust pipe. But there was a good reason to go indoors, go upstairs, and pack two suitcases. Which I did. I decided if I had my way, he'd never see Elissa again. Or the rest of us, for that matter. Still, it was hard to decide what to pack. Where are we even going? For how long? Are we ever coming back?

After a breakfast with their "new baby sister," I told my kids they would not be going to school that day, since we had to go on a "secret mission." I chased them outdoors to play on the swings while I over-watered the plants, overfed my fish, and captured the cat inside her travel case. Then I sat down to write a note to Shane:

Dear Shane,

People often say, "Behind every great man is an even greater woman." Well, soon the woman who worked so hard pulling her man along the path of life is older, less pretty, and no longer needed—just like I am, apparently. I've helped you enough. Now, the job is over and done. From now on, I'm going to get what I want, which is mostly to be left alone with these kids. I am very calm and reasonable now, but if I have to do it, I will give you more trouble than you can handle. So just leave me alone with these kids. They are all mine.

Good-bye.

I put the note on his bureau, where I knew he'd find it. I locked all the windows and whistled up my three traveling companions to be packed into the car, alongside two overstuffed suitcases, an assortment of toys, and a disgruntled cat. I remembered to also take along all my sugar-bowl money. We were a tangled group, but happy to be going on an adventure together.

"Did you pack my swimsuit?" Dylan believed we might be on our way to Winoreddy Lake, our usual summer vacation spot.

"When will we get there?" whined Min Hee. She's usually the strong, silent type.

I couldn't answer her. Tension iced up my neck muscles.

The next complaint came from little Elissa, in a more direct way.

"Mom, she wet herself," reported Dylan.

"We'll stop at a gas station in a minute." We were on the expressway, headed west, although I wasn't sure why. It could've been any compass point, for all I knew.

At the next gas station I plopped Elissa down on the front seat to change her diaper.

She whimpered, "Mommy?" In her thoughts, a trip in the car no doubt meant a search for her missing mother. *Poor little Elissa, I thought. She will never see her mother again. Can I supply this child with enough love to take Giselle's place?*

I continued driving toward a destination I didn't know, and then stopped the car to study the road map. The long, curving lines seemed to reach out endlessly, and I wondered what was ahead for us. *Another town? A chance to find our own apartment? Can I land a part-time job while the kids are in school? Can I find a nursery school for Elissa?*

I used to say about Giselle Malloy, "How can she raise a child in only a few hours a day? She never has time to play or talk with her own baby. She must be a stranger in her own house!"

Suddenly, though, there I was, facing the same kind of problems.

There was no one to count on, no one to share my daily troubles of raising kids. I didn't like this new, strange feeling of being completely *alone*. I began to clutch inside.

"Where are we going, Mom?" Dylan noticed we passed the same street corner three times. "I'm trying to remember what I forgot," I lied. Through my tears I saw blurry road signs, familiar street corners, and finally—the houses on our own block.

Shane's station wagon turned the corner just as we stopped moving. His face dropped when he saw suitcases and toys piled high in my backseat.

"What's going on?" A boyish look of confusion clouded his face.

"I came back to share the good news with you, and you're taking off?"

"What good news?" It was my turn to look confused as I climbed out of the driver's seat.

"The hospital reached Elissa's father through the Teamsters, just like I said. He's making a run to the West Coast, but will be back here next week."

"He's taking her away *next* week?" A bolt of lightning shot through my stomach.

"No. He wants to talk to us about adoption. He believes it would be best for the child to grow up with a normal family, since his job doesn't let him settle down in one place for any real length of time. He wants to visit with us for a while, and then talk about the legal part of it."

"Oh, Shane, I love you!" I blurted out as I hugged him tight. "We can make it work!"

He was holding back from my eager kisses. "What's with the suitcases?"

"Oh," I responded casually, "the kids and I decided we needed a vacation up at Winoreddy Lake for a couple of days. Want to come with us?"

The children beamed with delight, thinking they knew all along what my secret mission entailed.

"Can we afford it?" Shane asked.

"The sugar bowl will cover it," I said, smiling.

Dylan was hanging out of the car window. "Come on, Dad. We can have a swimming race out to the raft, just like last year!"

"I'll get my swimsuit," said Shane, smiling directly at me for the first time in weeks.

"No!" I shrieked. "*I'll* get it for you." Before he could move, I ran into the house, up to the bedroom and to his bureau, where my angry letter was waiting.

As I tore the note into shreds, I thought of Shane. He'd been badly hurt by his own personal failures and suddenly, I realized he was *still* trying to find himself. Perhaps he *did* have an affair with Giselle Malloy—maybe I'll never know. But I *do* know he still tries to please our kids and me. His decision to come back home to us and not drop out forever, as many men do, means to me that he is a good man. Clearly, he knew for many years what I am just learning—that love doesn't depend upon never making mistakes. In fact, real love gets stronger *through* forgiveness. Shane silently gave me years of understanding and support; now it's my turn to do the same for him.

As I went outside, hugging Shane's swimsuit to my chest, I saw all three children cuddled in Shane's lap. And I just *knew* then that there's more than enough love in my heart for all of my family—kids, cat, fish, plants, and needless to *say—especially* for my loving husband. THE END

I STOLE A CHILD

Once I had a child—and gave it up—but the hunger
for my baby never lessened. Day by day my craving
grew, till desperate forces drove me to a deed of cruelty

Carol's husband dies in a highway accident right after she gets the results
of her pregnancy test, and once her doctor convinces her that "a baby needs
a home, a father and a mother," she agrees to give the child up for adoption
when it's born. She's unable to let go emotionally, though, and soon she's
buying baby clothes and toys, keeping them in her apartment for a phantom
child. Then she meets a young mother in the park, who makes the mistake
of voicing her frustrations with raising a baby in front of Carol. "She didn't
deserve to have him!" Carol thinks. "I loved him more than she did, more
than she ever could!"

There's never any doubt that Carol is unhinged, although she makes
a point of emphasizing that she's learned her lesson and is ready to finally
start living in "the real world—the only world where I can find true love
and happiness." Carol's story makes for an interesting contrast with Vera's.
Carol has to face very real consequences for what she does, and it forces
her to rethink her state of mind during all these events. Vera, though, is let
off the hook by a lucky break, and never considers whether or not taking
another woman's baby was really the right thing to do.

Never, as long as I live, can I blot that terrible Saturday night from
my mind. It wasn't only the tragedy of what happened, but the endless
hours of waiting—of staring into the storm-swept street—searching
for Frank's car. He was due home from a long run between New
York and Chicago. Frank drove a trailer truck for United Autoways,
and sometimes he'd be gone on his route for as long as a week. The
separation was hard, but at least it always meant we'd have a few days

together afterwards. Only sometimes, like that Saturday night, I wondered if the waiting and anxiety were worth it.

And yet those long days together were always like a second honeymoon. We used to load our old car and take off on trips, sometimes up to Boston or out on the Cape, and once we drove way up to Maine to swim at Old Orchard Beach.

I thought of our happiness now, as I turned restlessly from the window. You're *being foolish, Carol*. Why didn't he come? It was so late and the weather was so miserable. I shook my head. It was more than just being over anxious. Frank had been late before, but that night was different. That night I was going to tell him about the baby. I hadn't told him yet, because I had gone to the doctor after he'd left on this long haul.

The results of the test had come through today. I knew now there wasn't any doubt, and I couldn't wait to tell Frank. We were going to have a baby —after five years of marriage. Both of us wanted children so much. To me especially, life seemed so empty without a baby. Every part of me yearned to hold a child in my arms, to feel the touch of a baby's cheek pressed close to mine, to comfort and love and protect—to be a mother—and now it had finally happened. If only Frank would hurry home so I could tell him!

Though I tried not to, I watched the clock. Four o'clock, five and six—he was two hours past his usual time. I started to dial the trucking office, and then I realized they were closed at this time on Saturday. Frank would put the trailer in the garage and drive home.

I finally did call the garage, but there was no answer. I went back to the window then, trying to peer out into the street, hardly able to see the lampposts now through the dark rain. What was wrong?

"Frank, Frank—" I whispered. "Why don't you call?" Where was he? I put out the fire on the stove and I sat and waited another endless hour. And then, just as I was going to try the garage again, the phone rang.

I ran to it and caught it up eagerly. "Hello?"

At the other end a strange voice answered. "This is the State Police, Ma'am. We're calling about Frank Sperry. Are you his wife?"

Startled and frightened I gasped, "Yes! Why? What's happened?"

There was an awkward pause, and then the voice went on. "We want to know if we can pick you up to come down and identify him. It's routine—"

"Identify him!" The receiver slipped out of my fingers, and I was trembling as I bent to pick it up. "Hello? What are you talking about? Who is this? I don't understand—what's wrong with Frank?" The words tumbled out of me as I stood there, terrified. There was a roaring in my ears and the whole room seemed unsteady, unreal.

The man at the other end of the wire was speaking choppy, meaningless words. "Sorry—I didn't realize you hadn't been told. The trailer skidded on a wet curve and your husband was—killed instantly—terrible that you had to find it out like this. Look, we'll send a man right over—"

I hung up and sank back into a chair, staring at the phone with horror.

No, I wouldn't believe it—I wouldn't! They had made some mistake. Of course, that was it—some other trailer, some other driver. I rushed to the closet and pulled on my coat frantically. I was halfway out the door when a police radio car pulled up at the curb. Two State Troopers came up the path.

"Mrs. Sperry?" His voice sounded miles away, unreal, and it kept echoing through my head, Mrs. Sperry, Mrs. Sperry, Mrs. Sperry. I tried to speak, but my throat was tight and my lips numb. I started towards them, and then suddenly I was screaming, a long, agonizing scream. They rushed forward, I remember that, and it was as if they were frozen in mid-stride while the whole thing became a flat, meaningless picture. Only my own voice rang in my ears, and then I can't remember anything but blackness.

When I opened my eyes I saw a white ceiling, and looked around at a hospital screen and a nurse writing on a chart while a doctor bent over me. I struggled to sit up, and he pushed me back gently. "Now you rest for a while. You've been pretty upset."

"Frank!" I whispered. "What happened?"

He looked at the nurse and she stepped forward, her face twisted with pity. "You must be calm, Mrs. Sperry. Your husband was in a—an accident."

"I know—was he—" I couldn't finish the question, and there was no need to. I saw the answer in her face. I closed my eyes and sank back, and the sobs caught at me, tearing their way out from the core of my being. Frank was dead. Frank, my husband, my lover—my whole life! How could I face it? How could I on living without him? Where would I find the strength? Oh Frank, *my darling, my* darling!

I heard the doctor whisper, "Give me the hypodermic, nurse," and then there was the cool touch of alcohol on my arm and the quick prick of the needle.

I turned my face toward the pillow.

How could a man die? How could someone who was so much a part of me cease to exist? I could remember every tone of Frank's dear voice, the way his hair used to curl back on his forehead, the way he'd stretch out in his chair in the living room—the thrilling touch of his lips.

Frank, gone now, finished—how could I believe it? How could I face it? Frank was my whole life. Why, I was going to tell him about the baby—and now he'd never know, never.

The baby, our baby. The baby Frank would never see. I was crying, but softly, without the cold despair I had felt before. The sedative was working. Mercifully, I didn't think of all the other implications of Frank's death right then—that I'd be alone with a child to raise, that there was no way I could support myself and my baby. I couldn't think of anything then except the desolate emptiness of losing Frank.

The trucking company took care of the funeral arrangements, and I was grateful for their kindness. There was no one else I could turn to. I had no relatives, and Frank had an only brother somewhere in California. But I didn't even have his address. We'd both been alone, but neither of us had ever felt the need for anyone else.

"As long as I've got you, baby, I've got the whole world," Frank had said that night we had driven over to Fall River for a dance. I remember the way he held me while we danced, his face so proud. "You're the prettiest girl on the floor, Red."

I had looked up at him, smiling happily. "Why, thank you, Sir.

You're pretty smooth yourself."

He had drawn me close then, his lips whispered against my hair. "Let's duck this joint Mrs. Sperry, and take a little ride. I want to park somewhere and show you the stars. It'll be such fun—" Memories! Do they ever stop, ever lessen? Would they always burn my heart like this?

I think the most terrible moment of all was at the cemetery. I couldn't bear to watch the coffin slowly disappear down into the grave. I turned away blindly while one of the men led me back to the car.

I sold the house the week after the funeral, and one of the accountants from the trucking firm was good enough to help me with my finances. "The sale won't bring you much," he explained. "You were carrying a pretty big mortgage, and you've only had the house a few years. You'll get the down payment back and what you've put into it—but of course, there's your husband's insurance policy," he said, as I looked bewildered.

I shook my head. "I don't know. I don't think Frank had any insurance. We talked about it, but—" I bit my lip. "We hated to make any plans like that. We thought—after the baby—"

I began to cry then and he sat there awkwardly. "I'm sorry, Mrs. Sperry."

"No, I'm acting silly. It's just—if I could get used to it. If I could only accept it!"

But I should have known then you never accept it. You walk along the street and someone passes and out of the corner of your eye you see a slight resemblance—and you turn around almost wildly.

It's hope, I guess. You can't give up hope I easily. I left New York after that and took a room in Boston, where Frank and I had been so often, but it wasn't any better. I knew I'd have to find work, though I'd had no experience. I was only sixteen—the year after Dad died—when Frank was discharged from the Navy and we were married.

Finally, I found a job as a salesgirl in a book shop. The pay wasn't much, and I had to keep dipping into the money I had left from the sale of the house and the car. I stopped working in my seventh month, and then, week by week, I saw my pitifully small bank account dwindle, while I felt a growing sense of panic. I counted the days to my confinement uneasily.

There was barely enough money for the hospital now. In another few months there wouldn't be enough. I had only paid the doctor part of his fee. Where would I get the rest?

In desperation I finally told Dr. Lawrence my story. He was the only person I knew in Boston. "But what about your family?" he asked slowly.

"I have no family." I looked down at my hands. "Frank only had a brother, and I don't even have his address."

He shook his head. "And you have no friends?"

"None. None that I could go to at a time like this. They're all young and they have their own problems. None of them are rich and I doubt if I could even borrow money from them."

He took his glasses off and looked at them. "You don't have to worry about my fee. That can always wait, and there are free hospital wards where you can have the baby. But—" He hesitated. "What about afterwards? How will you get along? If you work, who'll take care of the baby?"

I clenched my fists hopelessly. "I don't know. Everything has happened so quickly, Frank's death, and now—he never knew about the baby—not even that." I stopped, fighting to keep my voice level. "What can I do?" I asked finally.

He didn't answer for a long time, and then finally he sighed. "There are charitable organizations where you can go for the last month of your pregnancy. They'll take care of the expenses of the birth, and they'll give you a start afterwards."

I didn't see what he meant. "You mean, they'll help me take care of my baby?"

He looked uncomfortable. "If you have no family—well look, Mrs. Sperry, a baby needs a home, a father and a mother. They could find a home for your child, a good home."

I just looked at him. "You mean, give my baby up for adoption?"

He frowned. "The way you say that—look at it from your baby's point of view. What can you offer the child? How can you possibly keep it?"

I leaned forward, covering my face with my hands, but I didn't cry. I just sat there, letting his words sink in. *What could I offer my baby? How could I possibly keep it?*

"Don't decide anything now," he said gently. "Just think about it."

I left his office, my brain in a whirl. I knew what he meant. Without the baby, I could find work, earn a living—build some sort of a life. With the baby, what could I do? How could I earn enough money to support the child and myself?

But to give up my baby—how could I do that? How could I ever dream of it? I had waited so long for this child.

And yet, wasn't the doctor right when he said a baby needs a home, a mother and a father? I knew how carefully adoption agencies screened parents. Surely they'd find a home for my baby among good people, and the baby would never know.

I think that was what hurt the most, that the baby would never know. And yet in the end, that was what decided me.

I fought and struggled with my own heart, but how could I do anything that would hurt my child? How could I expose it to insecurity and hunger, to the humiliating dependence on charity that I would be driven to?

I went back to Dr. Lawrence and let him call the home he had mentioned. It was non-sectarian, but it was run by a group of nuns. When I arrived there, carrying my suitcase and exhausted from the long trip, I was taken to a small chapel with a high, arched ceiling.

"Sit here a while and rest." Sister Elizabeth, a gentle woman of fifty, said to me. "We'll prepare your room and take your things up. Perhaps, for a little while, you'll find peace here. So many of our girls do."

It was a queer thing to say, as if she could see into my troubled heart, but I nodded gratefully. After she had left, I sat there staring at the small altar and the dim shadows of the chapel. A soft, restful peace did spread through me as I waited, and this same restfulness was somehow a part of the entire home. The sisters, quiet-spoken and merciful, in their gray robes and stark white headdresses, seemed like angels to me and to the rest of the girls. They soothed our anxieties and took care of us with love and sympathy.

For the first time since Frank's death, I knew a measure of peace and started preparing for the baby's arrival. "Is there any way," I asked Sister Elizabeth once, "that I could come back here afterwards to work and help? Must I join your order?"

"Why no," she said in a surprised voice. "We welcome helpers. But so few of our children return."

"Then could I?" I asked eagerly.

"But why, Carol?" she protested. "Your family—"

"I have no family," I said. "My husband died before he knew about the baby. It's taken so much out of me to come here, to give up my child. I—I've wanted one all my life, more than anything else in the world. Now I have to give it up for it's own sake. Do you know how hard that is, Sister Elizabeth? Do you know how my very soul cried out against it?" My voice faltered, and she touched my arm.

"I know, Carol. Believe me, I know and understand. But coming here—isn't that running away from life?"

"I want to run away!" I said fiercely. "I can't bear to face life without Frank and my baby." I bit my lip, fighting to control my tears.

"We'll see, my child," she said softly. "We have a rule that you must wait six months after you leave here. You see, so many girls come here in trouble and find peace—they forget that true peace can only be found in their own hearts, and they try to hold onto it by staying with us. Do you understand?"

Disappointed, feeling she hadn't really understood me, I said, "Yes, but I'll come back after six months. You'll see."

"I hope so, child," Sister Elizabeth said. "I hope so."

I don't remember much of my baby's birth. It was a boy, as somehow I knew it would be. He had a soft fuzz of dark hair and round cheeks.

"Can I hold him?" I asked the nurse, and she nodded and placed him in my arms. I touched his little fingers, put my cheek to his, and all at once it was as if a sadness greater than I could bear filled my heart and flowed over. How could I give up this child, my own son? Had anything ever been more a part of me? Why, I'd die for this tiny bit of life!

I searched his face with a frantic kind of urgency, eagerly trying to *impress every* feature in my memory. That dark hair—so like Frank's! Would he look like Frank, when he grew up? I would never know!

Feeling the close warmth of his little body, my throat choked up. My child—my son! I loved him with a strength I had never dreamed could exist, and it left me weak and shaken.

For that very reason, I had to let him go! I couldn't take care of him or feed him or give him a home. I had nothing to offer him but my motherhood, and that wasn't enough to make up for all the rest.

Fighting back my tears, I handed my son to the nurse. "Take him away—oh God, take him away!" I gasped. "If there's any love or mercy in you, take him quickly!"

And that was the last I ever saw of my baby. The adoption had been arranged, and I signed the papers that same afternoon

Later I asked Sister Elizabeth, "Will I know who's taken him?" I tried to stop my lips from trembling, but I couldn't.

"I'm afraid that wouldn't be wise, my dear. The parents will never know who you are, nor will you know them."

"But how can I be sure they'll treat him well?" I caught at her hands anxiously. "How can I be sure they'll love him?"

"Now, now, Carol," she said soothingly. "You know they'll love him. People who want a child enough to adopt one love it very deeply. We've checked these people and we'll keep checking them. In a few months we'll have a report for you, and in a year another report. You can follow the baby's growth through us—if you want to. But your life is just beginning, Carol. You're young and pretty. There'll be other men for you, and someday another husband and children."

"No, no!" I turned away from her. "There'll never be another man for me—or another child. When Frank died, something inside me died too. I—I don't want to love again."

She was silent for a long time, then she nodded. "And yet, Carol, we must believe in the resurrection. What has died will live again, even as those who have suffered will find happiness."

I shook my head. "I can't believe that. I can't!"

I left the home two weeks after that, and came back to Boston, feeling as if there were no point in living, no goal. Life was a day-to-day thing, and every waking hour was unbearably lonely. I lived in memories, memories of Frank and our life together, the memory of that one sweet moment when I had held my baby in my arms.

My baby, my, baby! I would wake up at night, my pillow wet with tears, my heart torn within me, and stare into the darkness, remembering—regretting. Why had I given him up? Why? I could have managed, somehow. I should have tried at least. There would have been some way. There must have been!

I tried to forget. I tried to find some meaning in life, some reason for living, but I just couldn't. I had some money, enough for a week or two, and the sisters had found a job for me. Yet nothing seemed to matter. The job was in a shoe plant as an operator. The hours were long and the work hard, but no matter how tired I was, I still had time for my thoughts—and my regrets.

I had never named my baby, though in my mind I called him Frankie. My baby! I had no right to think of him as that. I had surrendered every claim to him.

Those days I cried easily, and yet tears brought no relief. I worked and slept and ate, and my life had no meaning. There were long stretches when I would sit in my room with the shades drawn, staring blankly at nothingness, not even thinking.

I ate only when I vas hungry, and sometimes a whole day would go by without my taking a bite. I grew thin, and my face was pale and strange looking, even to my own eyes. But I just didn't care about anything.

The only thing I felt was a desolate kind of despair, something that was almost a hunger inside me. At night, I would hug my empty arms to my breast and remember that one brief moment when I had my baby, and the memory was almost more than I could bear.

Why had I given him away, I asked myself over and over. What was there to live for now?

I clung to the vague memory of my baby, and I don't know just when—but there came a point when I began to change the. picture, to elaborate and build it up. Now I know why I did it. I had nothing else to hold on to. But at the time, I wasn't aware of my motives.

So I began to retreat into a world of daydreams. Suppose I had kept Frankie a little while, for a week or a month. What would he look like now?

In my mind, I began to build up the picture of a dark-eyed, black-haired baby. In the quiet of my room, I fed him and cuddled him and played with him.

Oh, at first it was make believe and it only hurt me more deeply. But after a while, in a strange sort of way, my pretenses began to satisfy a need. I had my baby—a ghost of a baby, it's true—but one I could love and pour out my motherhood on.

I bought a doll. A little stuffed thing, plaid gingham and wool, and just what a baby would love. I bought it on impulse, and back in my room I knew a moment's uncertainty and pain. What was I doing? Dear Lord, what was I doing?

But it was for Frankie, my dream Frankie, and he clutched it to him and played with it. And all evening I sat there, lost in my world of fantasy.

At first I bought things reluctantly, hesitantly—clothes and toys. But after a while I stopped explaining, even to myself. It hurt no one if I kept these pitiful fragments of a dream—so I clung to them.

But when my moments of reason took over, and I saw what I was doing, I knew a sense of terrible loss. It was easier to stop fighting it and just let my fantasy go ahead.

I don't know if anyone could have helped me then, if anyone could have foreseen and prevented the terrible thing I did. At the time I was alone, so completely alone—and so desperate in my need for something to love and work for—even a make-believe child!

Each day on my way home from work, I would pass the park and I'd see the mothers with their baby carriages. At first I didn't even look at them. I'd bend my head and hurry past. But then, as I sank deeper into my dream world, I began to stop at each carriage and look for a moment at the baby, the way a starving man looks at food.

Only afterwards, the hunger inside me was worse than before. I would come back to my room feeling sick and lost, and I'd look around with burning eyes at the toys and clothes and the empty, meaningless signs of a baby that didn't exist.

Then I'd drop to the floor, my head on the bed, and I'd cry as if my heart would break. I couldn't go on like this. A dream baby wasn't enough. I wanted a real child, a flesh and blood child—my child!

I don't know when I first noticed the dark-haired little baby and the slim, blond woman who wheeled his carriage in the park. I had stopped to look at him one day on my way home from work, and I straightened up to smile uncertainly at his mother. I touched the carriage. "How old is he?"

"Just three months." She moved back the covers to show him to me, and my throat filled up at the sight.

"He's a beautiful baby!" I reached down ,and touched his hand, and then drew my fingers away. With a quick smile, I walked off.

Three months! Why three months ago I had given birth to my own son—and had lost him!

That evening I tried to bring my dream baby back, but somehow I couldn't. I had touched a real three-month-old, and my dream paled into nothingness next to it. I shivered as I thought of that other child. How disinterested the mother had seemed. Why, if it had been my baby—I bit my lip and walked to the window. If I had kept my baby, why I too would be out there, wheeling a baby carriage. Abruptly I turned and flung myself on the bed, my breath coming in great, rasping sobs. How much I had lost—how much I had given up!

After that I began to go out of my way to pass the same spot every day. I'd talk to the mother and admire her baby. The woman's name was Alice Kramer, and she had only been married a little over a year.

"And now I'm stuck with Junior, but good!" she said bitterly.

I looked at her in amazement, and she laughed self-consciously. "Oh, I love the little rascal. It's just—" she leaned over and lifted him, smiling wryly. "Well, a kid ties you down. I never have free time any more."

I watched her hold him, and my arms were almost shaking. "Can—can I take him?" I asked hesitantly.

"Why sure." She handed him to me, and for one dreadful moment

I thought I'd faint. Then I put my cheek to his, and it was like coming alive again.

"Why, you're crying!" she said in surprise.

I bit my lip. "I—I had a baby once," I said softly. "I lost him."

"Oh—I'm sorry."

I held him a moment longer and then reluctantly gave him back. But I couldn't say anything. When I left her, I kept remembering the touch of the baby's cheek, the clutch of his little hand.

After that I would stop each day to talk to Alice Kramer and play with her baby. The child's name was Lee. Alice herself was glad of my company, and more than relieved when I offered to mind Lee while she did a little shopping.

After a while that came to be a regular procedure. Alice would wait for me eagerly, and she actually seemed glad to get rid of her child for a few hours.

"If I could pay for this baby sitting—" she began once.

"Don't be silly," I said. "I enjoy it. And Lee—well, he reminds me of my own. I'm the one who should thank you for letting me watch him."

Soon I began bringing Lee the toys I had bought. When Alice protested I said, "But I didn't buy them for Lee. They're my own baby's toys and—well, they only bring terrible memories. I want Lee to have them."

She was satisfied with that. But then I noticed she was easily satisfied with anything as far as the baby went. She wasn't a very good mother. Lee needed changing every time I was alone with him, and he just basked in the love and attention I gave him. I could see he didn't get enough loving from his parents.

Don't ask me when I began to pretend that Lee was my own little Frankie. It happened gradually, over a period of weeks. It may have started when I offered to baby-sit on Friday nights. I let Alice and her husband pay me, because I didn't want them to become suspicious or think I was queer in my devotion to Lee. I would play with him after they left, and I'd give him his bath and powder him and rock him to sleep, singing soft lullabies.

In those hours, my heart was filled to overflowing. It was so easy to go a step further and pretend he was my baby—my Frankie. I can't excuse what I did, nor can I ever try to justify it. It was more than just thinking of Lee as my own baby. It was Alice's treatment of him too, her obvious neglect—but it was many more things, my own unhappiness, my yearning and heartache.

I used to come to the Kramer apartment at seven on Friday, and Lee would be crying for his bottle while Alice sat in her bedroom, getting dressed for her night out! At the park she would lose her temper and start shouting and once I saw her slap him in a brutal, unnecessary way.

I just stared at her and she grew red. "Oh, Carol, you wouldn't understand. You're such a saint about kids. But he just drives me to distraction sometimes."

I didn't say or do anything, though every part of me longed to pick up little Lee and comfort him. He was crying bitter, heart-choking sobs.

"Well, don't keep looking at me!" Alice snapped. "Oh, Carol, I'm sorry. I guess I'm just not the mother type. If I don't get away from that brat, I'm afraid I'll crack up!"

"Why don't you take a walk?" I asked levelly. "I'll mind him for a while."

"Would you? You're a dear!" She turned and hurried off, her high heels clicking on the pavement.

I bent down and picked up the sobbing child, hatred knotting my stomach. What right did a woman like that have mistreating a baby? She hated the child. She didn't deserve to have him! I loved him more than she did, more than she ever could! Which of us had more right to be this baby's mother?

I didn't think any more then. I acted automatically. Bending down, I gathered the baby into my arms, bedclothes and all. For a second I hugged him to me, weak with the unbearable wonder of his touch. Then I hurried off towards the park entrance. It was late and there was hardly anyone around. I was sure no one had seen me take little Lee.

Outside the park I held the child fiercely. Lee—Frankie, what did it matter? This was my baby, my child! I took a taxi at the corner and rode back to my room, kissing Lee and crooning to him. He whimpered a little as I climbed the stairs, but inside I gave him a string of beads to play with and he began chuckling with pleasure.

I put him on my bed and sat there, the tears stinging my eyes, my whole body yearning toward him. I had a baby, and no one would take him from me—no one! I'd find a way to take care of him.

After a while, the baby began to fret and cry, and I realized he must be hungry. But I had no milk in the house. I'd have to go out to buy some, but I couldn't leave Lee alone.

Suddenly I had an uneasy doubt, a flash of dismay. How could I possibly manage? But I pushed it aside quickly. I'd take Lee with me. I dressed him and then hurried downstairs. For a moment, I wondered about formula. What did Alice use? I thought it was evaporated milk, but I wasn't sure. I kept trying to remember.

I ran my fingers through my hair while Lee kept crying. Then I shook my head. I'd try whole milk. I bought a quart, and at the drugstore I bought some bottles and nipples and a package of diapers.

Little Lee was crying even louder now, and I tried to calm him by rocking him. I almost ran home, and then at the door I drew back in surprise. There was a police car drawn up in front of the building. An officer in uniform was talking to my landlady. A cold chill went through me as I hugged the baby tighter.

So soon? Dear God, had they traced me already? But how? And then I realized what a fool I'd been. Alice knew where I lived. She had my address from baby sitting.

I didn't wait a minute. I turned the corner and almost ran down the block. But what could I do? I had to feed my baby.

Stopping at the first luncheonette, I gave the bottle to the man behind the counter. "Can you put some milk in this? Warm—for my baby. I'm traveling through and he's hungry." I realized I was talking too much and too fast.

"Sure lady." The clerk made cooing sounds at the baby, and then filled the bottle. "It'll just take a minute to warm it."

"Shh, shh, dear," I whispered, rocking him in my arms.

The baby twisted and arched his back, his face red with the strain of crying. I began to grow sick with anxiety. Why didn't the clerk hurry with the milk? Maybe the baby was sick—he didn't sound just hungry.

When he returned I took the bottle, almost snatching it out of his hand, and put the nipple in the baby's mouth. He grabbed it and started to suck furiously, and then after a minute he stopped and started to scream again.

I looked around helplessly. What was I going to do? Then an elderly woman at the counter stood up and came to me. "Let me help you, dear. Are the nipple holes large enough?"

"Large enough?" I stared at her as she shook out some milk, then asked the clerk for a scissors. She cut the hole larger and handed the bottle to him. "Just pour some boiling water over the nipple," she said.

When the clerk handed it back to me, I put the nipple in the baby's mouth and he started to suck furiously. But now the bubbles inside the bottle showed me he was getting milk.

"Is he your baby?" the woman asked pleasantly, and for a moment I looked at her with terror in my eyes.

"Yes, yes—what makes you ask that? Of course he's mine!" I cried hysterically. She stepped back, surprised at my vehemence. "I just wondered."

I sat down on one of the stools, feeling terrified. What had I done? How could I care for my baby? My baby!

But it wasn't mine. Not really. I hugged it to me and hurried out of the store, before there were any more questions. I had some money in my purse, not much, but enough to take a furnished room and buy some clean clothing for Lee.

The landlady who rented me the room looked at me suspiciously. "No baggage?"

"I am going to pick it up later."

She nodded. "Well, it's rent in advance, but I should think you'd have some stuff for the kid."

"My husband is coming into town in a day or so," I said hurriedly. "He—he's got our luggage." I was talking too fast again and my words didn't make sense, but I stumbled on, trying to lull her suspicions.

That night, alone in the room with Lee, or Frankie as I began to call him—was the happiest one of my life. I bathed him and played with him, and sang him to sleep in my arms as I had done before. Only this time no one would take him away, no one would send me home when his real mother took over. I was his real mother!

I spent the night in the easy chair, the baby in my arms, while tears kept running down my cheeks. I didn't want to give up one second of his dear, sweet presence. I wanted to hold him and make up for all the lonely, love-starved months I had yearned for my own child.

That night and the next day I lived only for the moment. I didn't think of what was going to come, of what I would do. Having Lee was enough, and if I was building a hell for myself tomorrow—I didn't care!

But that evening I was shocked back to sickening reality. I had just put the baby to sleep when I happened to look out the window. In the street below was a green and white police car!

I stood there numbly. It couldn't be because of me. They couldn't have traced me this quickly, in just a few days. But if it had been in the paper—they had my description. If the landlady had been suspicious enough to call the police—

I looked around the room wildly. I had to get out of here, not downstairs. I'd take Lee up on the roof.

There was a knock at the door then and my heart froze. I raised my hand to my mouth and stared at the closed door. Oh, Dear *God, show me what* to do, *help me!*

The doorknob rattled and I picked Lee up and kissed him. Then a sudden calm came over me. I walked to the door and opened it—and stared into the solemn face of a police officer.

For a moment neither of us said anything. Then without a word I went back and handed him little Lee. And I put my hands up to my face, my shoulders shaking with harsh, racking sobs.

There's nothing more to tell, not really. They took me to the station house with the baby, and Alice Kramer and her husband were there. It was then, when I saw the terror in her eyes, the misery and almost dead hope—and then the wild relief —it was then I realized how cruel a thing I had done.

This baby wasn't mine, and I had no right to it. If my own tragedy hadn't warped and twisted my mind, I would have realized how much Lee meant to Alice and her husband. What I had seen as neglect and cruelty had been thoughtlessness on Alice Kramer's part. But what right did I have to judge? She loved little Lee, loved him with the same mother love that had twisted me when I gave up my own child. I had never realized that.

The moment I saw her bend down to her baby, crying openly and without shame, I stepped forward—my hand reaching towards her, pleading.

She looked up then and I'll never forget what I saw in her eyes. She caught her baby to her and turned away.

For the first time my own life fell into perspective. I began to understand what I had done. Later, in the days that followed—the days when I was held in prison, and the days of my trial—full realization came, and with it an agony of remorse. Had I gone insane? What had warped and changed me so?

When Frank died I'd retreated from life. I never had the strength and courage to face what had happened. Instead I drew into myself, allowing my tragedy to over whelm me with self-pity, until in the end I could no longer tell right from wrong. I had convinced myself I had a right to take this baby from its mother.

I sat with bowed head during my trial, and when my turn came to take the witness stand, I told my story as honestly as I could, sparing myself in no way.

Afterwards the judge said, "There's no question of your guilt, but this is a court of justice, and justice must be tempered with mercy. There were forces that drove you to do what you did. We would not be doing our duty if we didn't take those forces into consideration."

He paused for a moment and looked clown at his desk. "The jury has found you guilty, and by your own confession there was nothing else they could do. I'm sentencing you to ten months, but I'm suspending that sentence on condition that you submit to psychiatric care and consultation, and that you remain on probation for at least a year."

There were no words I could find to thank the judge. It was as if I had been given a second chance at life. When I left the courtroom that day, I knew that I was leaving all my misery behind me. I would find a new life—a new and healthy life!

It hasn't been easy. I was taken to the State Hospital that same day and thoroughly examined. Then I had a long talk with a young woman doctor, Dr. Elise Brewer. That talk was the first of many with Dr. Brewer. Somehow she got me to go over how I met Frank, our life together, our dreams of a family. Finally, the tests Dr. Brewer gave me proved that while I may have been temporarily insane when I took little Lee, still I had the potentialities to return to a normal way of living.

With guidance and help from this understanding woman psychiatrist, I was able to pick up the twisted threads of my life. I stayed at the State Hospital for two weeks, then I was discharged conditionally. I went back to the nursing home and I worked for Sister Elizabeth for over a year, and during all that time I kept reporting back to the hospital psychiatric clinic and my probation officer.

It was a year of readjustment, a year in which I learned to live again. Now it seems that my life is only beginning. I never thought that I would love another man, but I've met someone who has helped me forget the past and look ahead to a happy future.

I know now that happiness is something you make, not something you find. You work and struggle for it, and if you have faith and courage you find it.

You can't steal it as I stole Lee—nor can it be bought at the expense of others. The torment Alice Kramer and her husband lived through has changed them. I know she'll be a better, more loving mother for it, but it's changed me too. It snapped me out of my dream world into the real world —the only world where I can find true love and happiness.
THE END

FORTUNE TELLER

What pride could he ever take in his mother—a woman who wore outlandish costumes, who pretended to foretell futures, and advise troubled souls about their momentous problems?

Mamie and her husband work for a traveling carnival; he manages one of the rides, and she's just started out as a fortune teller. It's not an ideal time to expect your first child, but it doesn't take too long for Mamie to fall in love with young Kit after he's born. Her husband, though, is a much tougher sell, and her insistence on keeping Kit drives a wedge between them. Eventually, feeling like she has no other option, Mamie agrees to abandon Kit on a rich couple's doorstep.

But that's not even half the story. There's not really a lot of romance here, but the combination of emotional melodrama and gritty crime action makes for something straight out of a 1930s Warner Brothers film. You can almost imagine the soundtrack swelling as Mamie's efforts to rebuild her life and become a fit mother for Kit are suddenly derailed by an unwelcome intrusion from her past.

Before Kit came into this world, I felt no more desire for him than Jim did. We couldn't afford a baby, and weren't situated to give one the proper care. Since our marriage, over a year before, we had been with the Erd & Oldum Carnival. Jim had relatives in the show business. He had been born to the life, and would always follow it. His concession was "The Whip," which he operated for an uncle. I sold tickets for the ride from a little red, white, and blue booth.

The carnival traveled from town to town, usually stopping for a run of one to two weeks. We lived on trains, in hotels, or boarding houses. . . a baby would be a dreadful encumbrance.

As Jim said, "You can't be in the show and the maternity business at the same time."

There was another difficulty. During that first year, I had become acquainted with Madame Le Bon, the buxom, jolly woman who had been reading horoscopes and palms, and telling fortunes for thirty years. She posed as a Persian. She knew all the tricks and all the right answers. She had hosts of followers the country over.

She was old and tired, and had saved money to retire. She offered to sell her name to Jim for a small figure, and to train me to fill her place. Like her, I was olive skinned, dark haired and black eyed. I could be billed as "The Daughter of Madame Le Bon, Greater Seer than Her Famous Mother."

Jim was enthusiastic. "With you on that gag, Mamie, and me on The Whip, we'll be cleaning up."

I objected on the ground that I was not in the least psychic But Jim and Madame Le Bon laughed at me, and I found that being psychic had very little to do with fortune telling. There was technique, of course, but nothing mysterious or really occult. It was another racket, easy to get away with, because people would rather believe than not.

I began to "study" with Madame Le Bon. I learned palms and phrenology. I learned to distinguish human types, and memorized the "patter" to be handed to each type. I found out what was safe to tell, and what people loved most to hear. I learned those glib statements which are so general that they mean anything or nothing, and can be applied to almost any one.

In late spring, about a month after I had started operating independently as "the Daughter of Madame Le Bon," I found that Kit was coming. For weeks I put off telling Jim. I knew he would be furious. His becoming suspicious drove me to admitting it.

"A brat!" he raged. "Just when you're getting started! How can you take the time out? What'll we do with the kid?"

I wasn't enthusiastic either.

Babies had always struck me as noisy, messy nuisances. And I didn't like young oh-ing and ah-ing mothers. But there seemed nothing to do but accept the inevitable.

Jim insisted I must stick to my work until the last possible moment. As we calculated, the carnival would be within a hundred miles of my home at the time of my confinement. I could go there and then rejoin the show as soon as possible.

But I wasn't too confident about being able to go home. It was very doubtful if my father would welcome me, or care about a child of Jim Calvert's.

Father—my only near kin—had objected to Jim. We had met in high school. What might have been merely a passing puppy-love was forced into something more by the attitude of the school principal and my father.

The school was small, and served an orderly, narrow community. The principal allowed no social dancing; at school functions he kept boys and girls separated.

The result was that, instead of having a normal social life, the students were forced into secret affairs. Parents took sides. A few encouraged mixed parties in their homes. Others—the majority, which included my father—supported the principal. And so, when it was learned that Jim Calvert loved me, there was trouble. My senior year was a succession of skirmishes, sly maneuvers and secret rendezvous.

When, after graduation, I ran away, it was not so much because I was in love as because I was defiant. Returning to introduce Jim as my husband, I felt that I had won a righteous victory. It gratified me to hurt and outrage my bigoted father.

He, instead of forgiving me, clung stubbornly to his position. There were a couple of dreadful scenes which ended in his ordering us out of his house, and declaring he never wanted to set eyes on us again.

Father was proud. He had ambitions for me. For me to run away to marry a boy who had barely got through school, who had been a constant trouble-maker and whose future was to be the knockabout existence of a carnival man, was too much at odds with his plans for me.

During our separation, I faithfully sent cards from every town we played. He had never responded with a word. Except as I heard from old friends, I might have thought him dead.

How would he take it if I wrote that I wanted to come home to have Jim's and my baby? Without saying so to Jim, I decided that when the time came, I would simply go, unannounced, and father would have to take me in.

That was what I did. Jim's last words as he put me on the train were, "If you can work it, park the brat with the old man."

I promised I'd try.

I tried to call Father from the station. The operator said the phone had been disconnected. I telephoned his office and talked to one of his partners. Father had withdrawn from the business, and gone only last week to Florida. No, he was not coming back.

My first panicky impulse was to catch a train back to Jim. But that would throw him into a temper, and I was afraid of him. Sitting there on a waiting room bench, I tried to make a decision.

The thought of suicide was persistent, but it came more from self-pity than from real desperation. It was not serious.

I experienced, for the first time in my life, all the terror and perplexity of being alone. And I saved myself from the depression of that experience by remembering that I was not alone. An unexpected surge of compassion for the little one with me made my throat ache and my eyes dampen. For his innocence and helplessness I had a melting sympathy.

He might be a boy. I would name him Christopher, and call him "Kit."

Kit Calvert—what a sweet name!

My decision was made automatically—almost. I would stay there in my home town. I would somehow manage the extra expense. Jim needn't know I was alone.

There proved to be some embarrassment. After I had engaged a room, I called some of my girl friends who came to see me. Where was my husband? Why was I alone? What had I been doing? How did father like Florida? Those were questions not easy to answer.

Then one night very soon, I went to the hospital. At nine

o'clock in the morning, Kit Calvert arrived—eight pounds of perfect babyhood.

I saw him on the second morning. I was shocked. His parboiled look and his pear-shaped head were not what I had expected. There was a period of revulsion. I thought him disgusting. How Jim would sneer at him!

The nurse was angry at the way I talked about my baby.

"But look at him," I insisted, "he's so ugly."

"He's a lovely baby," the nurse insisted. And in a temper, she carried him out.

It was a couple of days before I was able to see that his color was going to be normal, that his little red mouth was a Cupid's perfection, that his button of a nose was delicately cut, that his squinting eyes when he opened them were heavenly blue.

His fist taking my finger took my heart. He won me. I was his mother and I loved him!

With my returning energy, I began to think about him; to hate the prospect of having him grow up to the rough, gypsy sordidness of show life. No home, no quiet, no playmates.

What pride could he ever take in his mother—a woman who wore the scanty sleazy costume and veil of a harem inmate; who pretended, speaking in broken English, to foretell futures and advise pathetically troubled souls about their momentous problems?

Or what pride could he ever take in his father? A coarse-tongue, surly, short-tempered man who had nothing but contempt for all that was fine and gracious?

I burned with shame for both of us. And I resolved, in my heart, that I would bide my time, watch my chance and give my boy something better. That would mean a break with Jim, because Jim would never leave show life. It would involve my finding some other way to make a living.

As I speculated, nothing seemed too drastic, and nothing seemed impossible. The great thing was that my life now possessed purpose.

The first hurdle immediately reared itself. A condition arose that prolonged my stay in the hospital. The doctor ordered a special nurse for three nights. Expense was mounting beyond anything I had anticipated.

Jim must not know. The first letter I had from him told me to "shake out of that high-cost rest cure and get back on the job." Closing, he wrote. "Get your old man to take the brat off our hands."

His attitude vas incomprehensible to me. That he hadn't even a desire to see his baby son seemed inhuman. Yet, a month ago, I had felt much the same way.

The cost of the whole ordeal amounted to three times. what we had figured on, and I had been almost two months out of the show. It was five hundred miles away. Had there been any way financially for me to stay away, I would have done so. But I was down to my last dollar. Jim had to send me railroad fare.

When I reached him, he wanted to know, even before he had looked at Kit, "How much are we in the hole?"

I lied, "Only a couple of hundred. It could be a lot worse."

"How could it?" he snapped.

"Anyhow, Kit's worth it. Look at him, Jim."

There was just a possibility that the rosy-checked little boy would intrigue Jim as he had me.

His father looked at him impersonally. "Why the devil didn't you park him with your dad?"

"I want him myself. And you're going to love him, too, Jim. He's adorable—and good."

"He's wet," Jim growled, and handed him back.

Returned to the carnival, I soon learned that all the work and responsibility of our boy rested on me. I always had to carry him; I had to change him and wash him, quiet him at night and watch over him all day.

I padded the tray of my costume trunk to make a daybed for him in the rear half of my tent on the grounds.

The washing problem, in hotel rooms and on the road, was exhausting. When the bottle period started, there was the problem of keeping things sterilized, and the milk cold.

Kit had no respect for show hours. Where we had been accustomed to sleeping all morning, he was wide awake by six or seven, clamoring for attention.

From what I was taking in at my tent, I was holding out five to ten dollars a week to send on my doctor's bills. I knew it was too good to last.

Jim got hold of one of my outgoing money orders, and demanded an accounting. The way he cursed and reviled and threatened me was enough to foretell murder.

But, as it happened, I was quite serene and for a good reason. I had something on him. Just a few days before, I had learned that he was seeing a great deal of a pretty blonde girl who sold general admissions at the main gate.

"All right," I told Jim when he had finally run out of breath and profanity. "If you can make a row about my paying honest debts, I can make a row about you and Polly Loren."

He gasped. "What are you talking about?"

"You and Polly."

He was quiet a minute and then rose to his own defense. "Me and Polly then," he admitted. "But why not? You never pay any attention to me since the kid came. He has separated us."

I had never, at a crisis, felt more calmly sure of my position. "If I can't love you, Jim, I can't! The way you've acted about Kit has killed any feeling I ever had for you."

"As if you'd always been so holy about him!" Jim said. "What if, some day, I tell him the things you said about him before he was born?"

"You'd never dare do that! Anyhow I've changed. I love him."

"Yes, you love him instead of me. And then you get high and mighty about my having a little fun with Polly."

"I don't mean to be high and mighty, Jim. I just mean to tell you that you'd better let me go on sending the money for the bills."

He glared a while and then gave in. "Have it your own way—only keep your trap shut. And don't be razzing me about not going nuts about the brat. I don't want to. I don't want to be responsible for bringing him into this scurvy life. It's no place for a kid. He'll never have a decent chance. He'll turn out a rotten bum like me. I don't want to be to blame for him, I tell you. So lay off trying to make me fall for him."

Strange maybe—but it was through tears that I watched Jim go.

For the next couple of months, as we moved through Southern towns, and then through the Southwest to California, the relations between Jim and me were little improved.

All the energy I had went into my work and into looking after Kit.

In my future, I saw no Jim. There would be a job in some nice town; there would be a house or an apartment; I would know fine people; Kit would come home from school every day; he would not be ashamed of me; he would have a normal, average chance.

That dream was the real satisfaction of my life. It was always present, back of the aching hectic present, a paradise of escape. Nothing could have been more terrible than the occasional doubt, coming to me usually in the dead of night, that I would never even approach that paradise.

Kit was almost a year old when we opened our first run in a California city. Folks in the show called him the "testimonial baby," because he looked like one of the beautiful infants that advertising artists paint. The color of his eyes hadn't changed. His head was covered with a soft yellow fuzz and he had a cream and pink complexion that was a wonder to everybody.

Jim and I had hitter quarrels about money. But I had insisted on paying my bills. That done, he thought he should be getting more from me. I intended, however, to save, and had opened an account in a Texas bank, in which I expected to make monthly deposits, a foundation for that day when Kit and I would strike out alone.

Then, within a period of a few days, my whole plan and dream was crushed and swept away.

It was our third night in California. I had a customer, a quiet, elegant, elderly man. I was just getting started with him when Kit from his trunk tray in the back of the tent began to cry. I excused myself to go and quiet him.

When I returned I found that my customer was outside complaining to Jim and demanding a refund. Rid of the man, Jim rushed in to me.

So the brat was bawling, and another sucker had gone away sore!

He threw back the separating canvas and stepped up to Kit's trunk. Chubby fists and pink heels waved a greeting. Jim struck the feet down.

"Always in the way!" he yelled. "Always hollering at the wrong time! No rest, no peace, for anybody!"

Kit stared up with blue-eyed wonder at Jim's angry face, and at me in my fortune telling robes. We were indeed an unusual looking mother and father. His look would have melted a stone heart. But not Jim's. He was only more infuriated.

"Listen, brat! We're finding a new home for you. One that's nailed down fast. We'll let your mother here pay for it, she's so anxious to keep money out of my pocket. When you're big enough to be of some use to your old man in the show business, we'll bring you back and make a barker and a bum out of you."

Jim had lost all self-control. In the sick-yellow of the globe in the roof, his eyes had a strange glitter. His upper lip was arched from his teeth. He was hideous.

Kit's movements ceased. He was all incredulous eyes. As though realizing a threat, he let out a scream like nothing I had ever heard from him.

Before I could move, Jim had the helpless, terrified little fellow by the shoulders and was shaking him.

Beating and clawing, I flung myself at Jim and drove him from the tent.

A bundle of quivering, sobbing plumpness, Kit was in my arms. I sat down and we cried together. In the curve of my arm, after one quiet smile, he fell asleep. An occasional sob shook his body and pinched my heart.

Outside, the calliope on the merry-go-round was the high note above the cries of barkers, the mumble and laughter of the crowds. What a place for a baby to have to sleep!

My body and spirit were suddenly keyed up with decision; there had to be a change at once.

I got into my street clothes, picked up my son, and carried him down the gay jostling midway. Jim followed at my heels, pleading and whining. He turned back at the gate.

Once in the hotel, I had every intention of packing and clearing out. But where? There was barely five dollars in my purse. I might appeal to a social agency. But I recoiled from that. My grand resolution fizzled out pathetically. There was no where to go; no money to go with. I was trapped.

Later, Jim came to my door, sounded contrite and anxious, but I wouldn't let him in.

In the morning he came around early. He apologized for touching the baby. He wanted me to be sensible. Couldn't I see the only thing for all of us was to find a home somewhere? I told him bluntly that I couldn't see it. That made him angry again.

My mind went back to my determination to save money and wait for independence. But that afternoon, on arriving at my tent, I learned that Jim had been to Mr. Oldum, the carnival manager, and had made an arrangement that all my admissions should hereafter be collected outside the tent. No money would pass through my hands.

I went at once to Mr. Oldum. He was an iron-hearted man, and Jim had evidently put up a strong case. "The real reason I can't do anything, Mamie," the man, wheezed, "is that Jim owns you. That is, he bought the name you're using from Madame LeBon. The concession is in his name. You'll have to let him run it."

"But my baby, Mr. Oldum—"

"I agree with Jim. Farm him out. Hard on you, but he'll be better for it."

"Then this move on Jim's part," I cried, "is an attempt to force me to do just that."

Mr. Oldum shrugged. He had nothing more to say.

I was too crushed for the time being to carry the fight to Jim. He said nothing about it. He was making an effort to be more kind. I had an idea that he was making inquiries about the possible disposal of unwanted little boys.

He was even nice enough to take Kit and me to the city park several mornings. I was silent and sullen with him. On the last of those mornings he even condescended to carry Kit. He did it impersonally, but still he carried him.

On the way, sure enough, he began to tell me about a nursery home he had heard of in Los Angeles. When we passed through, we would stop to investigate. I made no comment. The conviction was getting a grip on me that I was going to lose my boy. "It was in the cards, in the stars," as I said to the "suckers."

But I was far from imagining what would really happen.

On this last morning in the park we found a shady spot, spread a blanket, and put the baby on it. Jim sat down on a bench with a magazine. I stretched out on the grass, a newspaper over my face. I had never felt more depressed and bitter, yet tensely apprehensive.

I was dozing miserably with my thoughts when I heard a voice. From under the shield of the paper, I could see Kit on his stomach. He was trying unsuccessfully to put his finger down on a big ant. Each time, the ant proceeded a fraction of an inch beyond the point at which he had aimed with his finger.

A man, sitting on his heels, was watching the pursuit and chuckling at each failure. I smiled, too. I was proud of my baby.

Beside the man, her back to me, stood a tall, slender young woman, very trim in tailored gray.

Gingerly the man sat down on the corner of the blanket. He appeared to be about forty, and had the well-fed, well-groomed look of material comfort.

With a humorous frown he studied my son, won his attention and his smile. Experimentally, he offered his finger, his fountain pen. He and Kit were friends. Jim had slipped up. He put his head under the paper next to mine.

"Why is it," be whispered, "that the guys with the time and dough have no kids, while us paupers get showered?"

"You call one baby a shower?"

"I call him a storm."

The man on the blanket was talking in a comradely, confidential way. Kit was listening, his eyes saucer-round; smiling now and then as if he comprehended and agreed.

The young woman said, "Honestly Larry, he's the loveliest child I ever saw."

There was something forlorn in her tone, I thought. Anyhow, I felt a quick, warm sympathy for her. I hadn't seen her face, but she sounded so nice, and as if she wished she had a lovely child like Kit.

The man, satisfied apparently that he had completed an important interview, got up, bade Kit a polite "good-morning sir," took the girl's arm and strolled away, with only a glance back at Jim and me under our newspaper.

Kit waved his tin cup, and crowed eloquent gibberish.

I don't know why, but there was a great lump in my throat.

Jim slipped away. In about half an hour he came back, on the run.

"Listen, Mamie. I tailed that slick guy and his skirt. They blew into that swell dump over there on the corner." He beamed and rubbed his thin, pale hands. "I've an idea, Mamie."

Horrified, I put my hand over his mouth. I didn't dare listen. You read in newspapers about children being abandoned, but you don't do it yourself. You don't relinquish something that is part of your very heart.

Nevertheless, as the Erd & Oldum Carnival was closing three nights later, the Daughter of Madame LeBon was not in her tent.

I might have been seen about ten-thirty, entering the big old-fashioned stone house at the corner of the park, leaving a new wicker basket in the vestibule and then hurrying to the car that waited at the curb.

The master of that house, returning to it, would find a sleeping baby. He would read the note:

Dear Mr. and Mrs. Moylan: Take good care of our little man. We can't. He spoke so highly of you after the meeting in the park the other morning. He'll be a year old Saturday. He takes Grade A certified milk, cream of wheat, mashed vegetables, orange juice and cod liver oil. Love him a lot, please.

To cover up what we had done, I caught a train that night for San Francisco. I was to stay there ten days, and then return. Jim was to tell everybody that I had taken Kit to his grandfather in the South. We had to run the risk of newspaper publicity. Mr. Moylan, reporting to the authorities, might cause a stir that would sooner or later point to us.

But as the show was leaving that night, none in the company would he likely to see the local morning papers.

As it turned out, no stir was made. Jim, investigating, had learned the man's name and that he was an artist of note and independent wealth. We assumed that he was married to the woman with whom we had seen him in the park.

I pass over that ghastly week of idleness I spent in San Francisco alone, with no one to need me or cry for me, with no little hands to wash and stumbling first words to hear. I almost think that grief over Kit's death could have been no more acute. I had to keep up a campaign of argument against myself that Kit would be better off.

Rejoining the troupe, I made up tales about the trip to Florida. The Carnival went on just as before. I told fortunes. Jim ran The Whip. The outer world had not collapsed.

But my inner life was emptiness.

To abandon a child one loves may be an act of cowardice or a valiant sacrifice. I had to believe that in my case I had been valiant— that I had left my sunny, blue-eyed little man on the threshold of a brighter tomorrow.

Before I could have any peace at all, I had to know that the Moylans had accepted him. And so, before leaving California, we made a side trip to the city where we had left him.

Jim wouldn't trust me to go alone. With him as guardian, I spent cautious, anxious hours near the house by the park. Jim thought that police might see and suspect us. My reward was almost more than I could stand.

An elderly woman came out of the house, wheeling a white-clad little boy in a new go-cart. He carried a jointed wooden doll, clutching it tightly about the neck. Pushed along, he sang and chirruped. He did not realize that anything had happened. My heartache was no part of his experience. He was as happy as ever.

Had Jim not been there, I might have revealed myself, such was my longing to seize and cuddle him, to boast to all people who noticed him, "He's mine—this beautiful baby is my Kit!"

"Can't you see, Mamie," Jim urged, "how swell it is? A dame to look after him. Look at the new rags he's wearing. He's in clover. Let's head out of here before we spoil everything for him."

A year passed. The carnival was heading back to California for a part of the winter. Kit must he walking now, talking, feeding himself.

It had been an eternal span of months, a monotony of longing. I felt spiritually dead. Where was the dream that had made life seem so vital a year ago? What did the future hold? I would go on telling the credible lies that were fortunes. I would finish like the original Madame LeBon—old, tired and alone—with a few dollars saved to tide me over to the grave.

Our show went into location on the same vacant lot in that California city. Hungering to see my boy, wondering how I could manage it, aware that Jim was keeping a sharp eye on me, I lived in a state of chronic stage fright.

An unnerving thing happened, which brought me happiness and despair at once. It was our third afternoon in town. I was in my tent, costumed, waiting for a "sucker."

Jim dodged in. "Listen our kid's coming down the midway," he whispered. "He's heading this way."

Jim's fingers dug into my shoulder. "If he comes in here, and you spill anything you shouldn't, it'll be too bad!"

He had hardly more than ducked out when a voice inquired, "Anybody home?"

It was Mr. Moylan. With shaking fingers, I hooked up my veil and called out, "Enter."

A hand raised the tent flap and another urged forward a curly-headed little boy, dressed all in blue. I remember how filled with dismay his eyes could become. He had walked into his first home and he didn't know it.

The woman who followed him said, "Don't be afraid, Jackie darling."

It was the woman I supposed was Mrs. Moylan. I knew her from her carriage and voice though I had not before seen her face. Mr. Moylan followed her.

"We're showing Jackie the sights," he said, "a big day for him." He picked up my boy whose arms circled his neck.

"We thought it would be fun to have his fortune told," Mrs. Moylan explained.

The encounter I could tell was a coincidence. They had no idea who I was.

I asked them to sit down. Mr. Moylan put Kit in the woman's lap. I reached for him, but he shrank away and made a whimpering sound. Mrs. Moylan stiffened and frowned.

"I'd better hold him," she said coolly. That tent was suddenly too small for both of us. And Kit, sitting there on her lap, his eyes so blue and fearful, could not be divided between us.

I could scarcely control myself. With an accuracy that astonished them, I told about Kit's past, how he had been deserted and left to them. And then, my voice rising in spite of me, I made a prophecy.

"I must warn you, little man, that you are destined not to go on in your present way. Some day, before very many years, your own mother will return and take you back; claim you as her own. Verily, I speak it."

Kit turned his face from me and began to cry. Mrs. Moylan stood up, aroused and defiant. Mr. Moylan laughed.

"This is a bit alarming, Madame."

He held up the tent flap for them to go out.

Jim came in, found me standing entranced, my knuckles pressed against the terrific pulses surging in my throat. "What happened?"

"They don't know anything."

"Swell! They had me worried. I thought they might be bringing him back."

"I wish they had been. What a fool I was to let him go! I must have been out of my mind."

"Then you're better off without a mind," Jim said. "The kid's got a fine thing out of it. You wouldn't want to drag him back to this mess?"

"I would!" I insisted. "What's my life worth without him?"

"Quit thinking about yourself! Give the kid the benefit of a good break. You're not fit to take care of him."

"But, Jim, I can't live if I don't have him!"

"You're just talking. At least you can stand it a couple more years." He squinted and smiled and rubbed his thumbs and forefingers together. "This is going to be a pay-streak for all of us. That Moylan guy is lousy with dough."

A horrible premonition darted across my mind. I shied from probing into what Jim meant.

During the remaining week and a half we were in that city, there came back to me with the refreshed vigor of a long rest, my dream of a home made, and a life spent for my son. The chain that held me to that town may have been invisible but it was as binding as handcuffs and iron bars.

I would never again get far away.

I did continue to the end of the California engagements. We were closing in Fresno. From there would follow a two-thousand-mile jump back east.

It was the final night. The last stake had been pulled. Down a freight siding, equipment was going aboard. A locomotive was coupling to our cars.

Jim was asleep in his berth in our compartment. My suitcase was in the aisle outside the door.

When the passage was clear, I slipped to the rear of the train, dropped down on the cinder bed.

From behind a signal-tower girder I watched the red light recede into the night. By the time Jim woke, he would be many miles away.

With an accession of confidence and hope, I turned away from the tracks to begin the recasting of my life. I had a little more than fifty dollars, and the contents of one suitcase. Jim had continued to divert my earnings from me. But I had my purpose and dream. That seemed sufficient for anything.

I spent the night in Fresno, then I boarded a bus for the south. I arrived in Kit's town that same day and the next began my search for a job.

In *only* ten days I was successful. I say *only* ten days, because they seemed ages long, and I never want to repeat them; the blistered, swollen feet, the rebuffs, the wilting courage, the staying awake at night to be lonely and full of despair.

I started in the wrapping room of the Riis department store. I took quarters in the cheapest boarding house and signed up for a stenographic course in the public night school for adults. At first, I couldn't save as much as a dollar a week.

The employment manager, Mr. Peffer, who had hired me, took an interest in my progress—and in me. He pulled for me all the time. At the end of a year, I was on the fifth floor, in the general offices of the store.

Mr. Peffer was a big, stoutish, good-looking man, liked by everybody. He started taking me out occasionally. He seemed to stand rather in awe of me. He wanted to know, "What gives you so much drive? Why don't you ever relax? What are you so intent on?"

Eventually, I told him the straight of almost everything, except that I said I had taken Kit to my father in Florida. It was the desire to prepare a home and bring him back, that gave me "so much drive."

During that year I saw Kit perhaps a dozen times, although I watched for him from the parks days without number.

From Jim, to whom I had written a note saying that we must forget each other and that I was going to settle somewhere in California, I heard nothing. Naturally he would not know where to reach me. What I dreaded was the winter return of the carnival. He would certainly try to find me and might make some trouble over Kit. I had remembered his remark about a "pay-streak" in Mr. Moylan.

Kenneth found out for me that the carnival would not come that year. We celebrated with a grand dinner and a motor ride into the hills. That was the night he said he cared for me.

It was nice to hear. But I told him I had my job cut out, and wanted only that. He made no protest at all. And we went on as we had been before—the best of friends. He was a splendid man.

My second year with the store hurried by. I had a responsible place in the credit department. I was earning sixty-five dollars a week and banking half of it. In another year I would be ready. I would be firmly entrenched in my job; I would have a good sum in the bank. I could take Kit and not have to apologize.

On watch, whenever possible, I saw him more often. I knew something of his routine. And I learned a surprising thing: Mr. Moylan was a bachelor. The girl I had seen with him was his fiancée, Pauline Pryor.

Kit had a governess. There was a houseman, a great tall fellow, who took him often to the park and drove him to an expensive nursery school five mornings a week.

Kit went often to Mr. Moylan's club—the Fortune. Kenneth became a member that year. Through him, I heard other things about my little boy. He was called Jackie. He was a kind of club member, too—a mascot. He had the run of the place. All the men knew and loved him. In the gymnasium he was learning to tumble and box and roller-skate. He called himself "a man's boy."

One evening when I was in the park, the houseman brought him to play. Chasing a hoop, he ran into me and, for a second, my hands caught him to keep him from falling. He begged my pardon like a gentleman and I was able to look straight down into his face. For days after that, every experience I had was heightened and charmed.

Before another year I would have him for my own, to touch and look upon.

That year had almost passed when in a Sunday paper, I noted a disturbing item.

COMING AGAIN, FOLKS! ERD & OLDUM CARNIVAL

I was unnerved with apprehension and foreboding. Jim would undoubtedly be with the show and, in the mere thought of his presence, there was a threat of danger.

My fears were hardly logical, but logic doesn't make the emotions.

I got up from a sleepless night with the conviction that I must do something to protect Kit. At breakfast, I tried to think through a course of action. Should I go to Mr. Moylan and make a clean breast of everything? Or to Kenneth to confide and ask his help? Or engage a lawyer to start legal proceedings?

Above everything in my mind was the frantic clamor of warning that I must obtain my little boy now, or forever give him up. Jim's coming was like a pursuing menace.

As if to find haven, I hurried to the store and into Kenneth Peffer's office. I showed my fright, for he jumped up and seized my arms.

"Mamie, what's wrong?"

"The carnival's coming back! Jim will be here."

It was difficult to give specific cause for my alarm, and he was inclined to laugh at me.

I ended, of course, with the admission that my Kit was not in Florida, that he was there in the city; that he was Jackie Moylan.

Kenneth went pale, though his face seemed to bloat. His lips worked but didn't say anything. He hated and loathed me, I was positive, and that destructive threat that had driven me in panic to his door seemed to be standing over me again.

I sat holding the chair arms, not daring to look at Kenneth. Then he sat down, knee to knee with me, held my hands pressed together between his and had me tell the exact truth of my story as Kit's mother.

"And now," I finished, "I have this awful feeling that I'm face to face with my last chance. I don't know how I know, but I do, that Jim is going to force my hand. I feel as if Kit were out in a big field, playing. He's happy, yes, but alone. There's something stalking him. It'll get him unless I warn him. Kenneth, what shall I do?"

"Darling !" He leaned close, and kissed me. His eyes smiled but his mouth was shut and straight.

Without a word, he turned to his desk, scribbled a note, sealed it in an envelope, and handed it to me.

"Take this to Cliff Danbury, attorney-at-law in the Bank of America Building. You may have the morning off."

He drew me up into the curve of his arm and led me to the door.

"It'll be a battle, my dear," he said. "Larry Moylan loves that child. We may lose." He opened the door and urged me into the corridor. "Good luck!"

Kenneth's moral support helped me more than anything else could have. My heart was drumming and I was shaking when I walked into Clifford Danbury's law office. But that intangible sick terror of an hour ago had left me.

Mr. Danbury was a keen, tense young man. In a few minutes he had the essentials of my story. He hurried me, breathless, toward decision and action.

"I'll have a summons in Moylan's hands before noon tomorrow," he promised. "He'll have to appear in court to explain his possession of this child, and show cause why he should retain him."

"But I don't want any fuss. Isn't there some other quieter way?"

"I believe always in bringing an issue to a head," he countered. "No one is harder to beat in a court of law than a mother. Women seldom hang; mothers are rarely convicted; they almost always win."

He went on to outline his tactics.

"The story we'll use is that your husband drove you into abandoning your child. Life was hell! He threatened you—he threatened the baby. On one occasion he would have killed it but for your interference. What could a mother do? You couldn't afford to buy decent care. You had a horror of public institutions. In your distraction you did what seemed best to you at the time. Now, after years of valiant struggle, you have prepared yourself to receive your baby once more into your arms."

He had become almost flowery. "The beauty of it is that while the Carnival is here, we'll no doubt be able to round up witnesses who can testify as to the impossibility of the situation with your husband." There was an audacity, and even a plausibility, about his argument that made me not hesitant. "We'll swing it," he promised. "It's a cinch!"

He got up and bowed me out. "I'll telephone you in a day or two."

Walking back to report to Kenneth, I felt weak and uncertain.

It was dismaying how easy the first step had been. There must be something false and treacherous behind that ease.

But there was assurance in the way Kenneth took my report. "Danbury's a winner," he said. "When the human element is involved, he can break any judge's, any jury's, heart."

This was on Monday morning. The carnival opened Friday evening.

Friday morning I received a call from Mr. Danbury. The summons had been delivered to Larry Moylan. At two o'clock Monday afternoon he must appear with the child in Judge Lord's court room.

Would I please come to the office that afternoon to assist with details of the story?

I was with Mr. Danbury for two hours. "One very important thing remains," he said. "You must visit the carnival and find two or more old friends who will give support to our contention that your husband's behavior was unendurable—and dangerous. Bring those witnesses to me—tomorrow afternoon or Monday morning at the latest."

Kenneth had dinner with me that evening and then took me for a long, quiet drive into the hills. He couldn't have been sweeter or more anxious for me.

I decided I would visit the carnival grounds the next forenoon. There wouldn't be much doing; Jim would probably be away; there would be a better chance to talk.

Kenneth promised to call for me and drive me to the grounds.

I went to bed about eleven but slept, of course, very little. Kenneth was to call at ten in the morning. The hours after breakfast were that many eternities. All my success depended, I felt, on my finding witnesses among old acquaintances at the carnival. They might not be there. Jim might drop in my path to intimidate or dissuade them.

Then, just at ten, Kenneth telephoned.

"Mamie, I'm at Cliff Danbury's office. He called me over. Something's happened."

Before he said another word, I knew that my foreboding had been sound. Something had happened to Kit. The horror—the shock—of it came ahead of Kenneth's words.

"Jackie Moylan's disappeared. Moylan called Cliff. Seems that Jackie was alone at home with Humphrey, the man servant. Two fellows came to the back door claiming to be gas company employees, inspecting appliances. One of them had Humphrey in the cellar, looking over the furnaces and water-heater. The other must have slipped out with the boy. Anyhow, after they had gone, Humphrey couldn't find Jackie.

"Is that all?"

"No. There was a note on top of the kitchen range. Typed. It tells Moylan to wait for a phone call, between four and six this afternoon. It warns him not to notify the police, or 'Jackie won't he worth salvaging.' Those are the words." I was like a pivot around which the room turned. Luckily I fell into a chair, still holding the phone.

"What of the police?" I asked.

"They haven't been notified."

"What did Mr. Danbury tell Mr. Moylan?"

"Nothing."

"What's going to be done?"

"I don't know. What do you make of it?"

"You don't need to ask," I told him. "I'm going to find Jim."

"I'll be there in five minutes to drive you."

"No, Kenneth; I'd better go alone."

"You'd better not. He might get mean."

"I'm not afraid. I'm not afraid of anything now."

And I wasn't! When the emergency is great enough, you rise clear above fear, because your own life doesn't matter.

Jim was behind this awful thing. Whether to checkmate me, or to bleed Mr. Moylan, whom he had once called "a pay-streak," I didn't know. Kit, in any case, had been "snatched," exactly as premonition had whispered.

In five minutes a taxi was at the curb, and I was directing it to the carnival grounds.

The first familiar face within the gates was Polly, Jim's old flame. She looked so startled and laughed in such a strained way and had such a defiant mouth, that I jumped to the conclusion that the affair was still going strong.

"Imagine seeing you," she exclaimed. "Where's Jim?"

She shrugged.

"He's still on The Whip?"

She nodded. "He's branched out, too. He's made hay. He's organizing his own show before long."

"He told you that?"

"Sure."

Jim, then, was after money from Mr. Moylan. Indirectly he had boasted about it.

"You don't know where he is?" I asked again.

"Haven't seen him this A.M."

"Whom does he pal with now?" I continued. And because she bristled, I added, "I don't mean girl friend—man friend. Who is he?"

"Olin Goetz—a guy you don't know."

"Is he here now?"

"Look around, why don't you?" she answered.

I did. I saw old acquaintances. But no Jim and no Olin Goetz. And no hint to where either might be.

I could wait awhile. Everybody believed Jim would certainly be there when things opened at one o'clock. People were curious about what I had been doing, but I put them off.

About eleven, I decided to pay a visit to the sleeping car. It was a ten-minute walk to the siding. There were only a few people about, none of whom I knew. They couldn't tell me where Jim was.

I started back toward the carnival when Keneth's car drew up, and he beckoned to me. There was a woman with him and I recognized her as Miss Pryor, Mr. Moylan's fiancée.

"They told us you had gone this way, Mamie. Come around and get in."

I did. Miss Pryor was pleasant and shook hands with me, but watched my face every second. There was a barrier between us certainly, but I felt a doubtful cordiality too. She wanted to be friendly; she wanted to be friendly for Kit's sake.

"I came to Mr. Danbury," she explained, because I wanted to

reach you, Mrs. Calvert. Mr. Peffer was kind enough to bring me. I am very close to Jackie. I have thought of myself as taking a mother's place—your place—with him. Mr. Moylan and I are to be married next month." She smiled anxiously. "I have come to you for help."

"Of course I want to get him back," I told her.

She looked at me in silence, and then said, "I believe you."

A fearful thought struck me. "Could anybody believe anything else?"

She nodded. "Mr. Moylan, his friends, his lawyer, are inclined to think you had a hand in the abduction. They think it a part of your maneuver to get Jackie away from us."

"It's outrageous!" Kenneth exclaimed.

"It's natural enough," Miss Pryor said. "They're men, and don't realize how impossible it would be for a real mother to do such a thing. My own idea in wanting to see you, Mrs. Calvert, was to find what kind you are."

I saw how softly deep her brown eyes were. Suddenly I liked her. We were together in the one bond of love for a little boy who was lost.

We were friends.

Kenneth drove me to the carnival grounds and I waited there for Jim or Olin Goetz. Neither came—at one o'clock, or thereafter. Jim had left other men to mind his duties, but they didn't know where he was, or when he might return.

Miss Pryor invited me to her apartment for some lunch. Kenneth let us out there.

After lunch, she telephoned Mr. Moylan, but couldn't reach him.

For an hour or more. I had the solace and the torment of talking to her. I heard everything about "Jackie."

And there began to emerge for me a realization of how far from me my little boy had grown. His world was not my world at all. The future in prospect was something I could never provide. He was having advantages that money alone cannot buy; that culture and background and select associates can give. Travels were planned for him. He would go to Groton School in New England, then to Harvard, as Mr. Moylan had done. Doors I could never peep through would be wide open to his hand. He was mine in blood only.

There was a fatal threat in all this. How could I ever presume to disturb such opportunities?

"Of course, Mr. Moylan will fight to keep him," she said. "But if he wins, you'll not lose Jackie, Mrs. Calvert. Mr. Moylan may retain his custody, but he won't have him for keeps. It will be just the other way round, won't it? He's the one who'll lose Jackie—see him change, grow up, become a man, a stranger—and go away. But you'll have him always—all innocence and warmth and dimples and sunshine. He'll always be a very little boy to you—the little boy you had. Don't you see?"

Then I did see. Kit in my arms, under my own roof with the world locked out, was the whole cry of my soul just then. It had taken years for me to learn what she meant.

About four o'clock Miss Pryor and I left her apartment. She got out of her car and drove me back to the carnival grounds. She was going on to Mr. Moylan's house to be there when the promised telephone call came through.

I was to call her if I learned anything.

I did! Jim had come back when I arrived. I saw him idly barking for customers at The Whip ticket booth, as I approached along the Midway. I knew before I reached him that he was less idle than he appeared. He was watching for me!

What I felt must have been akin to murder, but it gave me anything but a heated madness; it gave me rather a scheming cold-bloodedness.

He saw me coming, but didn't move. "Ticket, lady?"

"Hello Jim! How's tricks?"

"Swell! With you?"

"Not so good."

My swagger, my hardness, puzzled him.

"Heard you were hanging around," he went on. "What you been doing since you oozed out on me?"

"Mostly starving."

"You don't look it."

"I've had a job for a month—in a lousy department store."

He was still more puzzled. He stood up straight and stared down at me.

"Been hanging around the kid, I suppose."

"Not much, Jim. That's what I wanted to do, but they keep him out of sight. And, anyhow—"

"Anyhow—what?"

"I'm not so goofy about him as I was. I've learned things. I've been a fool. I was a fool to quit you, Jim. I've been lonesome."

"Oh, get out!" He called to a man, and handed over the ticket job. He stepped down and joined me. He took my arm.

"You're still swell looking, Mamie. And you've been lonesome?"

"You bet I have, Jim!" I squeezed his arm, and gave him a smile and a soft look.

We sat down on a box out of the way of people.

"Nice to hear show noises again," I said. "Makes me wish I could be back."

"Yeah?" he asked doubtfully.

"Any Madame LeBon with the troupe now?"

"Not since you quit," he laughed. "What you doing, hinting?"

"I might be."

He was wary of me at first, but I was getting on. I began to flirt a little with him. He warmed up to me.

It got to be five o'clock. I wondered who was doing the telephoning to Mr. Moylan.

"They tell me your side-kick is a stranger to me," I said. "What's his name—Goetz?"

"We're not so thick," Jim answered.

"Where is he now? Can't we meet?"

"Oh, he's around," Jim said vaguely and I made a mental deduction. Olin Goetz was doing the telephoning.

After that, I noticed that Jim was uneasy. He promised to think about taking me back. "Come see me tomorrow, Mamie."

I cuddled close, "Why not tonight, Jim?"

"No—o—."

"I'm still your wife."

"I've got to work tonight."

"Not after twelve."

"Come see me tomorrow," he repeated. He looked at his watch and jumped up.

"Hells bells! See the time! I've got an engagement, Mamie, five-thirty."

"Business?"

"Sure! What'd you think?"

He wanted to be nice, and he wanted to hurry. He grinned, and kissed me. I returned it. "You're swell!" he said, and started away. "Come see me tomorrow."

He was gone. Passing The Whip booth, he called, "Be back in an hour."

I followed, down the Midway and to the main entrance. He passed through, stood waiting, looking up and down the street. A coupe came along, slowed down enough for him to climb in. I glimpsed the license. It was an Indiana plate.

Olin Goetz had picked him up to make a report on the phone call. That was my guess.

I found a drug store, and called Mr. Moylan's house to speak to Miss Pryor. She suggested I meet her at her apartment.

She was there ahead of me. She told me that the important call had come to Mr. Moylan.

"It was a man's voice," she said. "He asks twenty thousand dollars in fives, tens and twenties. He instructed Mr. Moylan to drive up the Ridge Route tomorrow, alone—between one and two in the after-noon—and drop the money out ten miles, by speedometer, beyond Deckers. He must keep on, without a stop, to Cedarville. There's to be just one chance—no more! No money—no boy—ever! If all is well at the end of twenty-four hours, no police, no publicity, Jackie will be returned, unharmed."

No one who has not been close to such a demand can guess its strength. It horrifies you; it makes you forget that there can be any goodness or gentleness; it brings up the kind of helpless desperation that condemned men must feel.

It took minutes for me to get my wits back. And then I began to see some things. Jim had not made the call, because he had been with me. He could not see me tonight, because he was to be with Jackie.

Miss Pryor said that the police had not yet been told anything. Mr. Moylan and his friends were debating what to do.

"I feel that I should be with him, too," she said.

I told her then about my visit to Jim. About his appointment; about the coupe with the Indiana license.

"He'll be back at the carnival before long," I said. "I want to be there. If I can, I'm going to stay by him tonight, wherever he goes. I suggest you get hold of Kenneth Peffer, and bring Mr. Moylan. You wait outside the carnival entrance. Be ready to follow us wherever we go. What will happen is your guess, as well as mine. Even if I'm not with him, follow him. Because it may tell us where they're keeping our boy."

This we decided and I hurried back to the grounds.

Jim returned a quarter of an hour behind me.

"You still here?" he asked.

"Peeved?"

"I guess not." But he was uneasy and I had to tease and caress him to make him smile. He was busy, or pretended to be, for some time.

Then he grabbed my arm and took me out to a cafe for dinner. We talked about my coming back as Madame LeBon.

After we had eaten and he saw I intended to accompany him, he wasn't very pleased.

"Do I get to be a nuisance so soon?" I asked.

He laughed and decided to make the best of it.

For a couple of hours I hung about, keeping my eye on him, but pretending not to. He finally came over, sat me down in the shadows of a drink stand and kissed me. I returned his kiss.

"At that," he concluded, "we might get along."

"Of course we could," I said, and kissed him again. "We can get on fine. And no more kids."

"I'll say!" he agreed. "And you won't be bellyachin' for Kit?"

I raised my hand. "I swear it. You were right, Jim—he's a lot better off now, and I realize it. Too bad, though—"

"Too bad—what ?"

"Too bad we'll never cash in on the money he's going to inherit some day."

"You've sure changed!"

"I sure have! And I repeat it's too bad!"

I didn't look at Jim. I didn't dare. I might have betrayed myself.

"You know you said once," I reminded him, "that Mr. Moylan was a pay-streak. Forgotten?"

"No."

He started to edge away. I drew him back. "Going to turn me out tonight?"

"I've got to, tonight, Mamie!"

"Why?"

"Got something special on."

"Secret?"

"Yes."

"Tell me!"

"No!"

"It's a girl."

"No!" he shouted. "It's—" He caught himself, held me away and looked at me. He began to grin. "You'd be surprised, Mamie!"

"Then surprise me—please, Jim." If a woman ever lied with the soul in her eyes, I did then, though I tried to keep a flippant edge on the situation.

"What if I told you—" he began and stopped again.

I began to pout. "I think you're mean. I know it's a girl. Who is it—Polly?"

That was almost a fatal mistake, or the winning thrust—I don't know which. At first he was fighting mad.

"There you go! Jealous ! If you're going to be like that, you can clear out. Polly and I are quits, and that's on the level."

"Then I'm sorry. I was afraid—"

"If I thought I could trust you around the first corner," he interrupted suddenly, "I might—"

"Oh, suit yourself!" I shrugged peevishly. "I was beginning to think you liked me a little again."

"I do, Mamie. But this is ticklish." His eyes went very wide and then became glittering slits. "The fact is," he whispered, "I'm mining that Moylan pay-streak."

My voice barely got above the heart that had jumped up into my throat. "You're kidding! You wouldn't have the nerve."

"Oh, no?"

"Is it going to work?" I glowed with an eagerness he misunderstood.

"Sure! Keep your trap shut and maybe you can tag along." He gave me an affectionate cuff on the cheek. "I said maybe—"

"Maybe I can help," I offered.

"Yeah, maybe—"

Near midnight, I left with Jim. But there was one serious slip-up. He did not take me out by the main gate. Miss Pryor and the others would miss us.

He led me away, instead, by the dark truck entrance at the distant end of the grounds. Crossing a couple of vacant lots, we reached an empty dark street. Only one car was anywhere in sight, the coupe with an Indiana license.

"A man about Jim's build and looks, but younger, was at the wheel."

"My wife, Olin."

He nodded. He was frank. "Can't you ever do anything without dragging in a skirt?"

"Mamie's okay," Jim said.

They put me in the rumble seat alone, and drove away. I couldn't hear anything they said. I kept glancing back, but no car seemed to be following us. Apparently, I was going to have to see the thing through alone.

We were soon leaving the city, and heading upgrade toward the foothills. A thin grove stood up in the vast dome of sky. As we climbed, lights of towns appeared, spread on the flats below. The night air rushing by was cold, and I began to shiver. There was no robe.

A glow overspreading the road ahead proved to come from a gas station and, as we flashed by, I saw the word Deckers. This, then, must be the Ridge route where Mr. Moylan was to drop the ransom money.

Presently we mounted to the very crest of a steep, barren ridge. It was like riding on a knife edge. There were headlights behind, and I could only hope that they might be in pursuit.

Leaving the ridge, we entered a canyon. Mountain walls cut off all lights behind and below.

At a place where the valley opened out somewhat, the car left the paving, pitched down a spur of side-road and stopped in the very bottom of a dry stream bed.

We all got out. Jim had a big thermos jug in his hand. We started, Indian file, up a side canyon where tall brush and sycamores made it very dark.

After fifteen minutes of hard climbing, we came to a kind of terrace from which rose a stone foundation about two feet high. It was covered with planks, dead brush, and rocks.

Olin Goetz lifted aside one of the planks and dropped through out of sight. He turned on a flash light, Jim lowered the thermos jug. -

"Want to go down, Mamie?"

"Of course."

He helped me. I found myself in a stone-walled excavation about ten feet square and five deep. In a corner, on a blanket, a dog collar about his neck and a chain fastened to an iron peg in the ground, lay my boy—asleep

It was knowing that Olin Goetz was watching me with distrust and dislike which kept me from throwing myself down by him. He was on his side, his knees drawn up, his head on his hand.

"Think he's worth twenty grand?" It was Jim's gloating whisper at my side.

I didn't trust myself to say or do anything.

Kit stirred, and threw his arm over his eyes to break the glare of the flashlight. He murmured something and sighed.

"He ain't so hungry he can't sleep," Goetz whispered. "Let's catch a wink."

We all sat down on the dirt floor, Jim next to me. The light was turned off. Nobody said anything.

My feelings are impossible to describe. I was not afraid for myself. I was alive in every nerve; joyously I would have done *anything* to save Kit from that pair of beasts.

One or both of them, I supposed, were armed. I did not believe for an instant that anybody had followed us. Probably we were there to stay until time for the payment of the ransom tomorrow.

I whispered to Jim. "What're you going to do?"

"Wait and see."

"Are we staying here all night?"

"Don't ask so many questions."

Before long Kit began to whimper. I started to get up. Jim shoved me back. "Humphrey, I want a drink—"

The tired little voice cut into my heart. "Jim!" I said aloud.

"Shut up, you!" Olin Goetz snapped.

He turned on his flash. Kit was sitting up, blinking, and was trying to ease the dog collar about his neck. "This hurts," he complained.

I had to dig my fingers into the ground to keep from rushing to him.

Olin Goetz was pouring milk from the thermos jug. He offered a cup. Kit clutched it hard in his two hands and drank gratefully, without a stop. He held forth the empty cup.

"More, please, Mister."

With a big, wistful smile he received another cup and drank it down.

"I couldn't have a graham cracker, could I, Mister?"

"No! Shut up and lie down."

The smile left; the huge blue eyes grew bigger with fear.

Then, glimpsing me, he caught his breath and cried out, "That you, Miss Pryor?"

"Stand up!" Olin Goetz snarled; his foot swung around in a half circle, catching Kit full in the face, sending him down on his back. He let out one anguished little cry.

As if animated by a spring, I was on my feet, flying at the man. His flashlight struck me like a club in the side of the neck. Jim, cursing me, yanked me back on the ground.

"That's what comes of getting a dame mixed up in this!" Olin snarled.

"You didn't have to kick the brat," Jim retorted.

"Why not?" Olin said, and kicked him again in the side. I screamed, "Stop it!" and struggled to be free. Jim held me down, wrenching my arms.

"Sit down, Olin!" he ordered.

He sat down and turned off the light. Jim released me. It was quiet, except for the sounds of our breathing.

"He may be hurt," I whispered to Jim.

"You hurt?" Jim asked aloud.

No answer.

"Jim, I've got to see him. He may be bleeding—"

Jim asked for the light but Olin refused to give it up. "I'll look," he said.

We heard him crawling over to the boy. He put the light on. He was kneeling over him so we couldn't see.

He straightened up, pulled out a dirty handkerchief.

"Hold that over your nose, kid."

I fought to get up, but Jim held me back. "I'll be sore at you in a minute, Mamie."

"A bloody nose'll be good for him," Olin said, and crawled back to his corner in the dark.

There followed a period—I don't know how long—of the most awful apprehension I ever endured. Lying there, hurt, almost under my hand, was the one being in the world who was more to me than my own life. He was so still—not even sobbing. In surges the passion of protest rose up from my chest, up through my throat and against my closed teeth.

Finally I could stand it no longer. I said to Jim, "He may be lying there bleeding to death."

From Olin Goetz came a bellowing of rage. "If you don't make that Jane pipe down, I'm doing it for you!"

"Let me look at the kid," Jim suggested quietly. "Maybe he *is* hurt."

"Sure—maybe he is. What of it?"

Jim said no more. Perhaps he had caught in the other man's voice the note of a defiant fear. *He was afraid of what he might have done!*

Jim was aroused now; maybe the father in him was touched. Anyhow he got up. "Give me your light, Olin."

"I will not!"

"You heard me!"

The light came on, in Jim's hand.

Kit lay on his back. His nose was broken, his face was bloody and there was a long bruise across his cheek, just under his brow. His eyes were closed and his forehead was as white as paper.

My vision whirled and went black. I grabbed Jim.

Together we knelt over the limp little body. I put my fingers under the collar to loosen its tension. His neck was warm. Jim's ear was at his chest.

"He has a pulse," he said.

He opened the padlock on the collar, and threw aside the chain. We had to use milk to wash and bathe Kit's face. He began to breathe better, and his heartbeat became stronger, but he would not wake up.

When we had the bleeding stopped, I sat on the ground, with his head in my lap, the pale, broken little face beneath my eyes.

Olin Goetz, surly and still frightened, sat in the corner and watched.

Jim cursed him occasionally, and Olin finally yelled back, "What of it? He'd be less trouble for us if he was croaked!"

"Sure!" Jim admitted. "But we ought to play the game. No croaking unless there's no money."

My blood went cold. Jim Calvert could murder his own son! All he cared about was to "play the game," to punish Mr. Moylan if the twenty grand was not delivered?

He saw the questioning expression. "Forget it, Mamie. We'll get the dough all right."

Kit did not stir. Jim remarked that the light was burning dim. He turned it off.

I heard the sound, I think, before the men did. I thought they must be deaf.

Then Olin gasped under his breath, "Somebody's coming!"

There was the noise of both of them scrambling to their feet. They were quiet then, listening.

The sound that came was distinctly that of footsteps crunching along in gravel. "We've gotta beat it!" Jim said. "The jig's up."

"Not much! We can carry the kid out."

"They're too close."

"Quitter!" Olin snapped. He was groping toward us. "Let me have him. I'll pass him up to you, Jim."

Against my breast I drew Kit. The man's hands encountered my back. "Shove over! Out of the way!"

"You can't!"

"Oh, no?"

"No."

Fists began pounding my head.

"They're right on us!" This from Jim.

"I'm going to scream!" I warned. A curse was Olin Goetz's farewell. Within the space of sky where a plank had been moved, I saw him scramble out and vanish.

Then a shout: "Hey, look! There's somebody!"

Running feet hurried overhead. Voices shouted commands to halt and threats to shoot.

The sound of the chase faded away rapidly up the valley. Then, from the distance, came the crack of pistol shots.

I drew Kit close and heard his shallow breathing. I touched his hands and found them cold. His sleep was so deep! Would it never let him go? Would he never again hold tight to his milk cup, and stretch it out for more? Might those brown locks never again fly in the wind as he ran at play? Oh, it couldn't be! He was too young, too little.

I prayed. With eyes wide open and lips motionless, I talked to God, to whom I had never spoken before.

"He's been here such a little while—my little boy— You can't want him back yet, can you? Let his spirit stay here. He has friends with whom he hopes and plays. Why break their hearts? Why stop all his fun with his kites and drums and things? Dear, dear God, suffer this little child to stay with us. Forbid him not! Do this for me, and I'll do whatever as his mother I should. I promise—I do promise—"

Two deputy sheriffs found us there, a few minutes later. All that I learned, or, all that I could absorb on my way back to the city, was that officials had been told of the abduction and, among other things, about the coupe with an Indiana license. A touring squad of county officers had found it, parked off the road, and had gone scouting.

Mr. Moylan, Miss Pryor, Kenneth and many other people were waiting at the emergency hospital as we drove up. Word had run on, ahead of us.

Kit was still unconscious, and was put immediately into the hands of physicians. And only after the promise of life had come from behind the white, closed doors, was I able to attend to anything else.

My troubles seemed hardly to have begun. Police stood at my elbow, ready to take me off to Detective Headquarters as an accomplice in the abduction.

Olin Goetz, it seemed, had been shot down, and had sworn that I had been a party in the crime. Jim was still being hunted in the mountains.

Miss Pryor and Kenneth came with me and supported my story. Nevertheless I was detained until morning, questioned for another two hours and finally, toward noon, released.

Only then did Mr. Moylan show the least kindness. Over the question of my guilt, he and Miss Pryor had come close to a parting. But once I had satisfied the police he softened, his gratitude and praise were unlimited.

He invited Kenneth and me, before a visit to the hospital, to have lunch with him and Miss Pryor. We went to his house on the park. So spacious and homelike it made your heart ache. I saw Kit's room, his playthings, his library.

And then I remembered! "This is Monday, isn't it?"

There was embarrassment and sudden constraint. "Don't worry—I'm not going to court."

"I'm afraid," Mr. Moylan said, "that you've earned him without recourse to law."

"Not if you still want him. I have so little to give—as against all this, and all of you."

It was difficult to talk about because the spirit of enmity was dead among us. We determined to let our decision rest.

At the hospital, we found that Kit had been conscious most of the morning. He was about to nap again, but the nurse said Mr. Moylan might go in for a moment.

He came back very sober. His eyes seemed to be afraid of me. He motioned and I followed.

We stepped through a door and around a screen.

There he lay—brown head on a white pillow, pink arms lax on the spread. His face was bandaged, but his eyes held their bright gallant blue.

"Your mother, Jackie."

He held up a stout little hand. "'Lo!" I took it, held it hard.

"Won't she have a seat?" he asked, so mannerly and manly.

I was too choked to speak. He was cool and studious. He kept a tight grip on my fingers.

"I guess you're a pretty nice lady."

"Thank you."

"I don't like women so much—except Miss Pryor. She's going to be my next mother. She's nice."

"You're right."

"But you're nice, too. You've got nerve, haven't you? You're no sissy. That's something."

We were silent. Mr. Moylan had stepped out.

"I'd like to kiss your forehead, Kit—Jackie."

He frowned. "Well, we're not so much for kissing, but go ahead."

I planted one kiss. With his self-possession he made me feel shy and awkward. "I want to thank you for--for things," he said earnestly.

"Oh, you're very welcome."

"I hope you'll come and see me sometimes. Larry says you can."

"I'd love to."

"You'll like it at our house."

"Do you like it?"

"Oh, lots!" His eyes snapped, and he repeated, "Yes, lots!"

He turned his head half away, and his eyes began to droop. He sighed again and again. The lids wouldn't stay open. The lovely young head, deep in the pillow, sank down in sleep.

He had made and announced the decision, and I was content.

Three or four times a month I go to see the Moylans or they come to see us —the Kenneth Peffers.

Jim Calvert? He has never been found.

Jackie (only I remember his other name) goes east to school this fall. We let him start with no shudderings of fear, because he has no fear. His strength and self-possession, his charm and personality will carry him. THE END

TAKE MY DAUGHTER—PLEASE!

This proclamation led to my ultimate shame—courtesy of my very own mother!

Meg's only been married a few months, and she and her husband need to live with her mom for the summer to save some money. Mom doesn't see it that way, though, and when Meg's ex-boyfriend shows up, she speaks her mind...

It's hard to tell whether this setup is being played for laughs or indignant outrage, or maybe a little of both. And what the heck is up with the weird epilogue? Even for a story that laughs at closure as "a Dr. Phil word," that's some left-field ending—quite possibly two paragraphs longer than it needed to be. Or maybe a lot shorter?

"**H**ow lovely!" I heard my mother saying. "Just a moment."

Feet padded across the carpet. The bedroom door opened. She peered around it.

"Meg! It's Dennis Quinn!" she hissed. "He's here to see you!"

"Tell him I'm sick. Tell him I can't come out," I whispered, and then buried my head under the covers. Along with acute discomfort, I felt, deep down, a little, secret thrill just knowing he hadn't forgotten me.

Most of my friends from my high school days had come to my wedding back in May, but Dennis was out of town at the time. Although it might've been romantic to have an old beau in attendance, brimming with unrequited love, it could well have become *too* dramatic, what with Dennis's feelings to consider, spilling over into some kind of inappropriate behavior.

At any rate the ceremony was beautiful, out of doors in the garden where white lilacs formed an arch over our heads. "You're so lucky, Meg," my bridesmaids murmured.

"You have everything—a handsome husband with a job in high tech and you teaching in the fall. Your life is perfect!"

I acknowledged their admiration while smiling for the camera. There was no need for them to know that I'd abandoned my cherished dreams of moving to New York or Los Angeles to pursue an acting career. I'd faced up to my lack of talent and accepted the fact that my best bet was a job teaching theatre arts in a school system.

And there was no need to tell them that Randy was dull compared to mercurial Dennis, and that on the morning of our nuptials I stared at myself in the mirror and admitted that I was making a "safe" choice.

So I thought.

Who could have predicted that Randy's job would dissolve—and not a month after our marriage! To save money we had to sublet the apartment for the summer and come back and live with my mother. We were stuck there until September, when my teaching position would help us along. As it was, we told all our friends that we were "home for the summer holidays, just taking it easy." There were no other jobs to speak of in our respective fields in the small town where I grew up, so we'd decided to rest up and enjoy ourselves as best we could.

Of course I never imagined that Dennis Quinn would have enough money or vacation time saved up to come home to see his folks that summer, but there he was—

Standing outside on my mother's front porch!

Beside me, Randy breathed evenly. Perhaps Dennis had come over to drop off a wedding present and he would leave in a moment or two. The footsteps and voices had faded; perhaps Mother was serving him coffee in the kitchen or showing him the garden out back, where she spent hours on end.

Then there was movement again out on the veranda, just outside our bedroom window. Glassware clinked, liquid was poured, and wicker chairs creaked. Mother was serving Dennis lemonade out on the veranda, where only a wall and an open window separated him from Randy and me, lying together just as naked as the days we were born!

"So, Dennis," I heard Mother say, "tell me about Shakespeare in the Park."

Evidently Dennis had an acting job for the summer. His voice was all-too distinct as he told her about this gig, and about doing a national commercial, as well. At one time he'd spent more time waiting on tables than acting. Back when we were young and naive, performing together in a high school production of My *Fair Lady*, we imagined that we'd both become huge stars and go on to collaborative careers on the big screen, like Tom Cruise and Nicole Kidman back when they were married. But then we were accepted at different universities and over time, I had the sense to give up on my fantasies and settle for a teaching certificate.

Outside, out on the veranda, my mother interrupted Dennis mid-sentence: "Son, we've known each other for many years so I'm going to speak frankly."

Dennis sounded a bit taken aback. "Well, uh, sure, Mrs. Cannon. You go right ahead, ma'am."

"Now I *know* that you're not here because you wish Meg a happy marriage. You've come here today because you're still in love with her, Dennis Quinn!"

"Oh, now, Mrs. Cannon, I wouldn't say that. What I mean to say is that a lot of water has, well—it's passed under the bridge, Mrs. Cannon, and, well . . . I mean, time has passed and--"

"Only a few months have passed since you last made a fool of yourself outside Meg's apartment. That was just back in March, Dennis Quinn. She was trying to study at the time, as I recall."

Dennis mumbled something about my doorbell being out of order then.

"That's not what I heard," Mother countered firmly. "As I heard it told, it sounded to *me* like something straight out of A *Streetcar Named Desire*, with Stanley bawling: 'Stella! Stella!' or from *Wuthering*

Heights, with Heathcliff crying, 'I cannot live without my heart! I cannot live without my soul!' You knew that Meg had Randy living with her then, didn't you? You most certainly did, Dennis Quinn! In fact I happen to know for a certainty that one of your mutual friends *told* you that Meg and Randy were engaged—and that you tried to break them up!"

Dennis mumbled something I couldn't hear.

"Oh, you most certainly have a flair for the dramatic, Dennis Quinn, but it was more than that. No, if you ask me, to my mind—you *still* fancy her!"

Dennis faltered. "I—I don't know what to say, Mrs. Cannon. . . ."

"This wedding present you've brought with you today—this clock showing the masks of comedy and tragedy—it's a dead giveaway, Dennis Quinn! You're trying to remind her of you!"

"Honestly, Mrs. Cannon—I didn't come here to make trouble," Dennis insisted. "I just wanted to achieve . . to achieve closure!"

"That's a Dr. Phil word, Son, and I don't buy it for a moment—not for one cotton-picking instant! You're still hot for my daughter! Admit it!"

Dennis didn't speak.

I froze.

Beside me, Randy stirred and then slowly, languidly propped himself up on one elbow.

How long had he been awake? How much had he heard?

I reached for the radio to turn on some music and try to drown out the marching band volume of my mother's shrill voice, but my husband stayed my hand.

"Don't you be embarrassed, Dennis," my mother continued. "It's not too late."

In bed, naked, Randy and I gaped at each other in absolute silence.

"Mrs. Cannon!" Dennis exclaimed. "But I always thought you *disliked* me and thought that my prospects weren't good enough for Meg."

"And all of that is true, my dear boy, but I'm an old woman and

I'm entitled to change my mind anytime and any way I see fit. Randy Bobeck has turned out to be nothing but a lazy, good-for-nothing layabout and Meg has taken right to his low-class ways! Right now, for instance, the two of them are camped out in my front bedroom like vagrant squatters! They're living off me for the summer and in the meantime I've lost all my privacy and independence! Compared with those two, your life is downright *fruitful*, Dennis Quinn! At the very *least* you're following your dream and supporting yourself and I, for one, am proud of you! Now if you can only persuade Meg to take up with you again, *please--by all means*—feel free to carry her away on your white horse and do what you will with her! No matter what occurs, you have my blessing!"

"But, Mrs. Cannon—she's married!"

"So? These days, half of all marriages end in divorce!"

At that, Randy and I sprang out of bed, each of us grabbing a sheet. Draped in them we strode out of the bedroom and out onto the veranda.

"My, my! A toga party!" Mother exclaimed. "Did I wake you?"

"Mother, how *could* you!" I began, and then burst into tears.

"Why, Meg—whatever's the matter?" she asked primly.

"How *dare* you show such disrespect for Meg and me!" Randy hollered.

"We're *not* getting a divorce, Mother!" I blubbered. "No matter what you say!"

Randy drew himself up to his full height. "In fact, we'll impose on you no longer, Mother Cannon. We're leaving!"

"I'll be off, too," Dennis interjected quickly. "Good-bye." He was off the porch so fast that he was a blur. Seconds later his car sailed down the street and out of sight.

We packed our car in record time and were on the road by one o'clock that afternoon. Later, as we sat in the McDonald's on the 401, Randy and I looked at each other and realized that it was he and I against the world. It was a new feeling, a challenging and compelling emotion. I reached across the table for his hand and he clasped mine every bit as firmly.

We didn't see my mother again till Christmastime. I didn't much want to go to visit her even then, but Randy insisted that Christmastime is the season for putting animosities aside.

And so we slept on the pullout couch in the living room, as Mother had put up her quilting frames in the front bedroom and turned my old room into a study. Out in the garage, I noted the brand-new Bombardier snowmobile. When we suggested a Boxing Day movie she begged off because she'd already promised her widower friend that she'd pick him up and take him ice fishing. THE END

BACKSTABBING MOM: HER WEB OF LIES RUINED MY MARRIAGE

Even the thought of my husband's betrayal couldn't compare to the way my heart shattered when I learned my own mother had deliberately set out to destroy my life...

Meg's mother didn't get very far in her efforts to sabotage her daughter's relationship, but she didn't really try very hard, either. Amanda's mom, though? This woman is ready to do whatever it takes to get rid of her daughter's husband, and her motives are completely transparent. "We'll be back to the way we were," she tells Amanda. "Just you and me, precious. No complications. No bothersome man around." It's sort of amazing that Amanda would fall for this trick, until you realize how thoroughly her mom's been manipulating her emotions ever since she was a child.

The story takes a somewhat unusual turn in order to take Amanda's husband off the playing field while she hashes things out with her mother, but without that plot twist we wouldn't get to meet the magically understanding one-night stand, one of the most unbelievable—and yet, in an odd way, most endearing—supporting characters in our entire anthology. He's something of an old-fashioned stock character in pulp romance, but this time around he comes with a modern, psychological spin.

"**I** saw them again, Amanda. He was sitting there, big as life, with that same girl!"

Mother's voice rang with righteous indignation as I listened, disbelieving. *Surely, she's mistaken,* I thought hopefully. "It has to be someone who looks like Chester." I wasn't aware I'd voiced that hope until Mother spoke again.

"No, I'm sure it was Chester. I couldn't mistake my own son-in-law, now could I?"

"Oh, Mother, I just can't believe it. He wouldn't do that to me." I couldn't keep the disappointment out of my voice. Chester and I had been married less than a year, and this was the second time Mother had seen him with that girl. "Please excuse me. I just can't talk about it now. I just can't!" I burst into tears and headed for the bedroom. Still talking, she followed me.

"I don't know what he has to do before you realize he's no good, Amanda." Mother seemed unaware of the pain her words inflicted. "Far be it for me to say I told you so but you will remember I was against this marriage from the start." She shook her head, frowning at me. I threw myself down on the bed, wishing she would just leave me alone.

"For one thing," she persisted determinedly, "you are both far too young and he doesn't even have a decent job. Can't even support you! And wanting you to go to work! So he could have more time to cheat, no doubt! You should have filed for divorce the first time I told you about him and that hussy!"

"But Chester said you were mistaken. That he hadn't been with any girl," I protested tearfully. He'd wanted to confront Mother and I'd begged him not to.

"I believe you, darling," I had insisted. "That's all that matters. If you say anything to her, it might bring on an attack. You know she has a weak heart."

"You really do believe me, Amanda?" My husband's brown eyes stared solemnly into mine. "I love you. I don't need or want anyone else." He touched my face tenderly.

"You're like an angel, with your silky hair and innocent eyes. I'll never cheat on you." He kissed me passionately, erasing any doubts Mother had aroused.

And now, here it was again—the suspicion and confusion as to who was telling the truth. I wanted desperately to believe Chester, but then, why would my own mother lie to me about something as important as my relationship with my husband?

Although she'd made it obvious from the get-go that she disapproved of our marriage, she'd insisted we live with her until we found, or could afford, our own place. I thought it was a good sign, feeling once Mother really got to know Chester, she'd learn to love—or at least like—him a lot. Until now, I'd thought it was working out.

Chester, Chester, I cried silently. *How can you hurt me like this? I believed you when you said you loved me—that I was the only one in your life. Has it all been lies?*

I thought of how Chester and I'd met on a blind date and fallen in love almost immediately. I hadn't dated much, mostly because Mother didn't like being left alone. My father died soon after my birth, and it had just been her and me since. She'd had a couple of heart attacks and felt vulnerable. Anyway, there weren't many places I went to that she wasn't with me. Chester was the first boy who came between us; the only one I fought to be alone with.

Mother didn't like it and wouldn't even try to understand. But Chester was very understanding and even sympathetic to Mother. "You're pretty darn lucky," he used to tell me, "the way she cares About you. I wish I'd had a mother like yours." His had left when he was very young, and his father and grandmother had raised him. Although he'd had a good childhood, he still felt the loss.

I knew he was awfully hurt when Mother treated him so coldly. He was hoping, as I was, that she'd learn to care for him. He tried hard to please her, but she was always finding fault with everything he did.

It was hard on all of us, living together in her house. I knew Chester felt like an intruder, and we both resented our lack of privacy. Almost every time we went to our room to be alone together, she'd find something for one of us to do; something that had to be done right then. It was very frustrating, but neither of us felt we could say anything. She was doing us a favor by letting us live there. She wouldn't take rent money, which helped us at the time. But it did make us feel as if we had to be at her beck and call.

I said something to her one day, about finding a place of our own.

That brought on an attack that lasted two days. "How would I manage, Amanda? What would I do if you left me? I depend on you so. Besides, what would you use for money?" she complained, her voice sounding weak and helpless.

I didn't bring it up again, but Chester did, and she gave him the same argument, only more so. So, rather than take the risk of making her ill, and admitting to ourselves we really couldn't afford it, we gave up the idea. Now I wondered if we'd given in too easily. Surely, we could have managed somehow. Other people did. Then maybe Chester would be with me now, instead of with that girl.

"Oh, Mother," I moaned. "What am I going to do?"

"There, there, dear. Don't cry." She sat down on the bed beside me and brushed the hair back from my tear-stained face. "Everything will be all right. Mother will take care of everything. Thank goodness you haven't started having babies. Divorce will be so much easier." She smiled. "Then we'll be back to the way we were. Just you and me, precious. No complications. No bothersome man around." She patted my cheek as I stared at her in horror.

Divorce? Divorce Chester? But I loved him. Sure, I was hurt and mad now, but I wanted to remain his wife. I just knew he could explain and make things right again. No. I didn't want a divorce. I told Mother so in no uncertain terms.

"Darling, you don't know what you want. But you certainly don't want a man who cheats on you. And so soon after your marriage! Who knows?" she hinted. "This may have been going on all along." She got up and began to move around the room, eyeing Chester's things distastefully. "Really, it's good that you found out so soon, before he had a chance to wreck your whole life—both our lives. What hurts you, hurts me. After all," she added bitterly, "he's betrayed my trust, too."

"But, Mother, don't you think we should give Chester a chance to explain?" I pleaded desperately.

"What for? What could he say except lies? I saw him, didn't I?" She shook her head angrily. "Believe me, Amanda, it was no innocent meeting. The way they were looking at each other . . . Well, there was no mistaking what was going on!" She went to the closet, pulled out Chester's suitcase, and began stuffing clothes into it.

"Mother! What are you doing? Are you out of your mind?" I leaped off the bed and grabbed the suitcase, pulling it out of her hands.

"Well, there's no use dragging this out. If you let him in, he'll just butter you up with his lies, the way he did last time. After all," she raised her eyebrows, "he's got a good thing going here with free room and board. He won't want to give that up without a struggle."

"But, Mother, Chester loves me. I know he does."

"Love! Love! That's what they all say." She jerked the suitcase away from me and laid it on the bed. "Now come on. Help me get this packed and we'll set it out on the porch."

"No, Mother! No! I won't let you do this!" I protested frantically. "If I pack Chester's things, I pack mine too!" She stared at me as if I'd lost my mind. "I mean it, Mother," I said, realizing with some surprise that I did.

"Amanda, you're behaving like a stupid child!" She took my hand and pulled me down on the bed, sitting next to me. "I didn't want to tell you this. Didn't want to hurt you any more than you are already . . . but I guess I'll have to."

"What are you talking about?" I yelled in frustration.

"Well, there've been several phone calls from some girl—no doubt the one I've seen him with. Anyway, she wouldn't believe me when I told her Chester was married. She said something about a baby. I hung up on her."

"No! No! I don't believe you!" I screamed in pain. "Chester would never let that happen! You're lying, Mother. Why? Why do you want to hurt me?"

"I have no reason to lie. I'd never hurt you, Amanda. Why, you're my baby. You're all I've got in the world." Her voice sounded weak and she looked as if she were about to cry. Suddenly, she slumped back on the bed, clutching at her chest. "Amanda," she moaned. "Help me."

"Mother! Mother! What is it? Is it your heart?" My defiance vanished and I was once again the guilt-ridden child I'd always been in the face of Mother's attacks. "Your pills? Where are your pills?"

"Apron pocket . . ." she whispered, her breath coming in short gasps. "Hurry, dear. Hurry. Oh, the pain . . ."

"Don't try to talk, Mother," I cautioned as I searched for the capsule in her pocket. Finding it, I placed it between her teeth, then pushing Chester's suitcase to the floor, I put her legs up on the bed and arranged a pillow under her head. Guilt and sympathy enveloped me as I stared down at her white face. How could I have been so selfish?

It was a bad time for Chester to come home. "What's going on, Amanda? What's wrong with your mother?" he asked, approaching the bed.

"Get out!" I screamed, jumping up. Fear for Mother had completely overridden my earlier defiance and defense of my husband. I felt only hate and bitterness toward him now. Hysterically, I began crying and hitting him with my fists. "Get out! If it weren't for you, this wouldn't have happened! Go on! Go back to your girlfriend! We don't need you!"

Chester looked at me as if I'd gone mad, then pushed me into a chair and went over to the bed. Mother was breathing hard, her hand still clutching her chest.

"I'll call 911," Chester said and headed for the door.

"No! Call Dr. Balister. He's the only one who can help me," Mother called out. "I don't want strangers."

"But, Mother, he may not be able to come. You need immediate help," I protested, going over to take her hand.

"I'll call him. No use arguing with her," Chester said, leaving the room.

"Don't let him sweet talk you, Amanda. Don't let him talk you out of a divorce," she warned in a weak voice.

"Hush, Mother. Don't try to talk."

Chester was back within minutes. "Dr. Balister said to keep her calm. He'll be here shortly." Chester leaned over Mother and patted her shoulder. "Just take it easy. You'll be okay."

Mother stared at him bitterly. He turned to me, a look of utter confusion on his face. "What is it, Amanda? What am I supposed to have done? Why are you both so angry at me?"

"Get out!" I muttered through clenched teeth. "Go back to your girlfriend. The one you vowed you didn't have." I shook my head disgustedly. "To think I was actually going to leave my mother for a . . . a cheat and a liar!"

"I don't know what you're talking about, Amanda. I've told you the truth. There is no one but you." He touched my face. "For God's sake, darling. I love you. You must believe me."

I looked into his eyes, felt his hand on my skin, and Lord, I wanted to believe him.

"Amanda . . . Amanda." Mother's voice was barely a whisper, but it was enough to rekindle my resolve.

"Don't darling me! I believed you once. I won't be such a fool again." I turned to Mother and placed my hand on her brow. "It's all right, Mother. I'm right here. I won't leave you."

Chester stared at me, shaking his head. "I can see this is not the place or time to try to reason with you. I'll wait in the other room till the doctor gets here."

"Don't bother!" I yelled as he went out the door. Turning to face my mother, I said, "Oh, Mother!" I couldn't hold back the tears.

She reached up and covered my hand with hers. "There, there, dear. Everything's going to be all right now." She sighed deeply, but her breathing seemed to be under control and her voice sounded stronger.

The doorbell rang and I got up hurriedly and wiped at my face. "That must be Dr. Balister," I reasoned.

"Bring him in, Amanda, then leave us alone," Mother called as I left the room.

Chester had already let him in and directed him down the hall to my room. "Oh, Dr. Balister," I began.

He interrupted me, saying, "Don't worry, Amanda. She'll be fine." He entered the bedroom and closed the door behind him.

Chester was waiting for me in the living room. I turned to leave at the sight of him, but he rushed over and grabbed my arm.

"Look! We have to talk. I'm entitled to know what this is all about. We need to discuss it."

"You mean like we did last time?" I shook my head. "No thanks! Just leave. Okay? We really have nothing more to say to each other." I pulled away from him and ran into the bathroom, locking the door behind me.

"Amanda! Amanda! We have to talk!" He pounded on the door. I turned the faucets on full blast so he wouldn't be able to hear my sobs. Finally, he went away.

The doctor left soon after helping Mother into her own room. "She'll be all right, Amanda. Just an emotional reaction. Guess you two had a fight, huh?"

"Well, yes, Dr. Balister. It was about Chester. She just doesn't like him and well, I'm torn between them. I love them both, you know?" I could feel my eyes welling up with tears.

"Of course you do. Only natural." He patted me on the shoulder. "You know, your mother only wants what's best for you. You've been her whole life since your father left. I'm afraid she became a very bitter woman when he deserted her. Never liked men after that." He grinned wryly. "Only puts up with me cause I'm a doctor."

"Father deserted us? But I thought . . ." I stared at him in confusion.

"Yes, it's true, and it's time you knew the truth. Your mother felt it would be too traumatic for you to know you'd been deserted, and because your father was dead to her, she wanted him to be dead to you. too." He shook his head. "I never did agree with her, but it was her decision and I had no right to interfere." He patted my shoulder gently.

"But, Mother's heart condition . . . how can I leave her?" All kinds of thoughts were running through my head. I felt dazed; betrayed by my mother as well as my husband. But at least, I calculated, my mother had done it out of love for me.

"That's what I wanted you to know. She doesn't have a serious heart problem, Amanda. Those pills she takes are just placebos. I'm afraid she dramatizes to gain your sympathy and support and to encourage any guilty feelings you have. She wants you all to herself." He shook his head and started for the door. "I've known your mother for a long time, Amanda. She's a good woman and means well. She'll be mad as hell when she finds out I told you anything. But, I see what she's doing, and it's not right."

"Thank you, Dr. Balister. I don't know what to say." I managed a cynical laugh. "You've definitely given me some insight."

"Yes, well, your mother's resting now. I gave her a mild sedative. You might want to lie down awhile yourself. You look like you could use a nap."

We said our good-byes and I went to my room to think. All these years Mother had led me to believe that my father was dead.

She must hate him with a passion, I thought. *Why had he left?* I wondered, resolving to ask her when she woke up. Now that I was aware that I really had nothing to fear as far as causing a heart attack, I suddenly thought of a lot of questions I wanted to ask.

I still had the problem of settling whether or not she was lying about Chester. A *good woman* and *means well,* the doctor had said. Did "means well" entail contriving a vicious story intended to separate me from my husband? Lord, my head was spinning. *Well,* I decided, *I'll find out when she wakes up.* I closed my eyes and escaped into a fitful sleep.

I was awakened by a kiss on the cheek. Half asleep, I imagined it was Chester. "Wake up, dear. Time for dinner." Mother. I turned my head to hide my disappointment. She looked bright-eyed and fit as a fiddle. *No wonder,* I thought resentfully. *She was never sick in the first place.*

"C'mon now. Get up!" she ordered gaily. "I feel like eating out tonight. It will be like old times. Maybe we can even take in a show."

"Sure, Mother." I agreed, deciding to wait until morning to confront her about my father. "Uh," I hesitated. "Did Chester call?"

"Why, no, Amanda. You didn't really suppose he would, did you? I think you made your feelings pretty plain." She shook her head, adding, "And about time, too."

I began to get angry again. *To hell with him,* I thought bitterly. *If that's the way he wants it, fine. I'll be damned if I come crawling. Who needs him, anyway?*

Mother was right. We'd be better off without him. Now that I had it straight in my mind, I wished I could get my heart to stop hurting. Maybe a night out was just what I needed. Maybe during dinner, Mother would say something to indicate whether or not she was lying about Chester. Of course, she had denied it earlier, but maybe . . . Oh, who was I kidding—I wanted to believe in Chester. I wanted to believe he really loved me.

The thing was, I *knew* Mother loved me. Therefore, I had to believe she wouldn't lie about something so important.

We had a good time over dinner, but I didn't learn anything new. The fact was, every time I mentioned Chester's name, Mother insisted on changing the subject.

"Let's not spoil the evening, Amanda. What's done, is done. You'll get over it. I did." I looked at her curiously. Was she going to confess her deceit? "I mean, when your father died, I thought I'd never survive." She shrugged her shoulders and smiled. "But here I am."

When the evening finally ended, and we were on our way home, Mother seemed happier than I'd seen her in a long time. I tried to match her mood, but all I could think of was going to bed alone in the big bed I'd shared with Chester. I thought of our nights of love and I wondered bitterly if that girl was now enjoying the attention that had given me so much happiness.

Later, after Mother went to her room and left me alone with my misery, I cried—pushing my face deep into the pillow so she wouldn't hear me. The ache of longing finally gave way to a bitter determination to get even with Chester. I fell asleep vowing that somehow, some way, I'd make him pay.

Mother woke me early the next morning with the news that we were taking an impromptu trip. "I've been on the phone all morning, Amanda. It's all set. We're going to Mexico for three days. Isn't that wonderful!"

I guess she could tell by my expression; I was not too happy with her announcement.

"It's just what you need, sweetie. I know how hard this is for you.

Even though he's not worth it, I know it hurts." She smiled warmly. "Trust me, baby. This little vacation will do us both good."

I hesitated. I didn't want to admit that I'd rather stay home in case Chester should call. It was so confusing the way my mind kept changing. I hated him for his lies and deceit, and yet I wanted to see him I was weak and would probably give in to him again. Yes, I thought, *it's best to go away for a while.*

The little town we visited was in the middle of a three-day festival. It was overflowing with people dressed in colorful costumes. Mother insisted we join in the festivities, even buying outfits for each of us.

The costume I chose was as unlike me as anything I could imagine. But I felt that since I hadn't been doing so well as I was, a drastic change was in order. With the vivid green material clinging to my body and the dangerously low-cut blouse, I felt as wicked as I looked.

I brushed my hair until it shone and painted my lips scarlet. *Chester should see me now,* I thought, and hated myself for even thinking of him.

"You're not going out in public like that, Amanda?" Mother exclaimed in horrified tones.

"You bet I am! Whee!" I whirled around the room, laughing gaily. "Don't I look wicked?"

"Well," Mother managed a weak laugh. "I can't honestly say I approve, but if you're happy. Well, that's why we came. Right?"

"Right!" I agreed. "And since you're not ready, I think I'll go down and wait for you in the lobby." I paused, considering, then decided, why not? "In fact, Mother, I'll be in the cocktail lounge. I think a drink is just what I need."

"Amanda!" Mother's mouth flew open. "You wouldn't."

"Mother, you keep forgetting. I'm not a baby anymore. Don't worry," I assured her. "I'll behave myself."

I thought defiantly, *What's the use of looking wicked, if you don't act wicked?* Besides, I needed something—someone to take my mind off Chester.

The lounge was packed and I had to squeeze by several people in order to find a place at the bar. "Excuse me," I apologized, more nervous than I was willing to admit.

"My pleasure," a low, male voice returned. "Here, let me help you." The tall, broad-shouldered young man elbowed his way up to the bar and pulled out an empty stool. I slid upon it and turned to thank him. An older man, obviously intoxicated, leaned over my shoulder and asked with a leering smile, "Buy you a drink, honey?"

The way he looked at me made me feel dirty. I shook my head, wishing I hadn't been quite so daring as to come here by myself, dressed like I was. My courage was departing fast. I contemplated retreat.

"The young lady is with me." The voice at my side was firm.

The unwanted company turned hurriedly away. "Thank you," I whispered gratefully, turning to look at my Sir Galahad. It was the same handsome young man who'd secured the seat for me.

"Again, my pleasure," he said, gazing down at me with a look that made me blush. "Now, may I buy you a drink?"

I smiled and nodded. Somehow it seemed okay. As he tried to get the bartender's attention, I stole another glance at him. He certainly was attractive. His dark, curly hair and warm brown eyes had broken many a girl's heart, I supposed. A surprising thrill raced through me as the crowd pushed us closer together.

"Sorry," he apologized with a smile. "What a mob! Now I know how a sardine feels." We laughed together and he asked, "What would you like to drink?"

"Oh, a Tom Collins, I think," I said, trying to remember what Chester always ordered for me.

We had our drinks in a matter of minutes and I took a long, hard swallow of mine.

"Now, tell me about yourself," he murmured. "You're too beautiful to be here alone. Waiting for someone in particular?" He glanced down at my left hand and I was suddenly glad I'd left my wedding ring at home.

"Yes, and no," I replied teasingly. The outfit I was wearing seemed to be affecting my personality. Or maybe it was the Tom Collins.

It was several drinks later that I remembered Mother. By then,

I wasn't really interested in seeing her. Pierce and I had introduced ourselves, and his charm combined with the alcohol and the prevailing carefree atmosphere—not to mention my own commitment to getting even with Chester—had me feeling pretty reckless.

When Pierce suggested we go someplace where we could dance, I agreed. I made no objection when he put his arm around me and walked me out the door. I thought I saw Mother sitting in the lobby, looking very agitated, and I hid behind Pierce until we were out of her range of vision.

The cocktail lounge was small and intimate with a postage stamp-sized dance floor and a trio of musicians playing music. Pierce and I sat close together in a secluded booth. Even though my head was spinning, I didn't protest when he ordered me another drink. *Why not?* I thought. *Why not have a little fun?*

Chester was probably doing the same thing. At the thought of him, my heart began to ache. To ease the pain, I moved closer to Pierce.

The warmth of his body excited me and I trembled. He must have felt the current, too, for his eyes got a funny look and he took my arm and said in a husky voice. "Let's dance, angel face."

"Oops!" I giggled, stumbling as I got to my feet. "S'cuse me."

"You're all right, angel. I'll take care of you. Just lean on me."

I snuggled close to him, feeling cozy and secure in the strength of his embrace. We danced, barely moving, his lips brushing my cheek. Closing my eyes, it was easy to pretend it was Chester's body that pressed provocatively against mine; Chester's lips on my cheek.

"Let's get out of here," Pierce whispered.

Somewhere in the back of my mind, a small voice was saying, *No. Stop while you can,* but another, stronger voice reminded me Chester had started this. He had cheated first and now I had my chance to get even. *Besides,* I told myself, *I'm not going all the way. Just a few kisses. That's all.*

I hadn't reckoned on my body's natural hunger or Pierce's undeniable expertise. He wasn't a teenage boy and I wasn't an innocent young girl. My body had known passion and fulfillment and it was not to be denied now. I hadn't realized I could feel such desire for a man I didn't love. I'd mistakenly believed love and desire went hand in hand. How wrong I was! I was certainly not in love with Pierce. Yet my body responded with a passion that amazed me.

After it was over, I wanted to die. The desire had been satisfied and the drinks had worn off. I had full awareness of how far my so-called need for revenge had taken me.

Self-disgust filled my soul as I thought of Chester and how I had defiled the beauty of our love. I knew now, no matter what he'd done, I still loved him and wanted to be with him. I hadn't been fair, expecting him to live in Mother's house, catering to her every whim. I hadn't acted like a wife. I'd acted like I was still Mother's little girl. No wonder he'd found someone else.

I couldn't control the sobs that shook my body as waves of shame flooded over me.

"Amanda, honey. What is it?" Pierce's voice was full of concern. "What's the matter?" I couldn't do anything except shake my head as the tears streamed down my face.

"Look, Amanda, if you're crying because of what happened, don't. It was beautiful. You're a wonderful girl." He handed me a tissue. "Believe me, Amanda, I never wanted to upset you. I thought you wanted me as much as I wanted you. I thought it was a mutual attraction."

"Oh, it was, Pierce! It was! It's just that I had no right to let it happen. I'm married, Pierce!" I burst into fresh tears.

Pierce pulled me over and I leaned my head on his chest. "I'm listening if you feel like talking," he said quietly.

I poured out the whole story. I mean, all of it. As I talked it out I began to believe Mother had lied to me, or at least made things seem worse than they were.

"Obviously, she's made you her whole life, Amanda. She isn't going to give you up, no matter what she has to do to keep you, including breaking up your marriage." Pierce shook his head. "Some people are like that. They don't believe love can be shared. Your mother got a bum rap and she held onto it instead of letting it go and making a life for herself." He held me away from him and dried my tears.

"If I were you, angel face, I'd hightail it right back to that husband of yours and find a place of my own. Even if it's just a cubbyhole."

"And what do I tell him about . . . you know . . . us?"

"You don't tell him. It would only hurt him and it wouldn't solve anything," Pierce advised gently. "You've learned things do happen, no matter how much you may love one another. You're a little wiser and a lot more understanding, I'm sure. Even if your mother is telling the truth, I think Chester deserves another chance, don't you?"

"Yes. Oh, yes." I smiled happily until Mother's face popped into my head. "Oh, dear. What am I going to tell Mother?"

"Just tell her you cut the apron strings and she's on her own now. You're an adult. Maybe if you act like one, she will, too. It's worth a try." He smiled. "Now, get dressed and I'll take you back to your room." At my door, he leaned down and kissed me softly on the cheek. "Good luck, Amanda."

"Oh, Pierce, I don't know what to say. You've been so helpful. If this had to happen, I am so glad it happened with you." I put out my hand and he took it gently. "I'll probably never see you again, but I'll never forget you."

Well, it wasn't as simple as Pierce made it sound. It's not easy acting like a grown-up around a person who only thinks of you as a child. Mother and I had a real nasty fight, but I stood my ground. She had her usual fainting spell and "heart attack," but I didn't give in. I gave her her pills and offered to send for the hotel doctor. She took the pills but refused the doctor.

I didn't say anything to her about my father. It was so long ago and she'd obviously been hurt very badly, so I saw no point in confronting her with the truth. And I had no desire for information about the father who'd deserted me. Maybe later, I'd want to know, but not now.

However, Chester was a different matter. I kept after Mother and finally she admitted she'd exaggerated the whole thing, and even that there had been no phone calls, except from Chester. He'd even called that afternoon while I was sleeping and Mother had told him to come over the next day. That's why she'd arranged the sudden trip to Mexico.

"You're all I have, Amanda," she sobbed. "I've sacrificed my whole life for you!"

"I'm sorry, Mother. You're not laying that trip on me anymore. I appreciate the fact that you raised me by yourself, but I don't feel I owe you my life. What you did was wrong. Horribly wrong. Do you realize how much pain you caused me and Chester?! I don't know if I can forgive you. I'm sorry," I told her sadly.

I was sorry. Sorrier than she'd ever realize. Not only had I lost the respect I'd once felt for her, but because of her lies and my stupidity, I might have lost my husband.

Well, I wouldn't give him up without a fight. Not this time, I wouldn't. Remembering his words the night I'd first accused him unjustly, *I don't want or need anyone else*, I went to him.

I told him everything except about the night with Pierce. I felt like a hypocrite when he held me in his arms and renewed his vows of love, but Pierce's advice seemed wise and I followed it. God knows, I didn't want to hurt Chester any more than I already had.

"You married a child, darling," I admitted shamefacedly. "But I come to you as a woman now, if you still want me."

"If I want you? Good God, Amanda! I've never wanted anyone else!"

Chester and I moved to another city, some distance from my mother. I haven't yet asked about my father-if he's still alive and what happened between him and Mother. I think maybe I'm afraid of the answers. There's still that little girl in me who's afraid to hear the truth.

We don't see much of Mother and when we do, it isn't the greatest. Chester thinks it will be easier for her to love and accept the parents of her grandchildren, so we've been devoting a lot of time toward that project. THE END

DAY AND NIGHT MY MOTHER BEGS: 'HONEY, FIND A HUSBAND!'

Rosalie is 24 years old, working full-time in a local factory and taking night classes to earn her college degree. She's also living at home with her mother, who's putting the pressure on her to get married. There is a guy in one of her classes, except, as Rosalie confesses, "I liked Damien just fine, but no way was I in love with him." Will she be able to make her mother understand that she doesn't have to attach herself to the first man who comes along?

Although her mother plays a prominent role at first, ultimately this is a story about Rosalie's need to learn that "I have a responsibility to myself... I'm the only one I really have to answer to, and my own obligation is to myself, to protect myself." Only then, she realizes, will she be able to have a successful relationship with an equally well-adjusted man—and that's something that needs to happen on her schedule, not her mother's.

Mama waddled into the kitchen, and our whole third-floor apartment shook. She looked tired after a day at the sewing machine in our living room. Mama was an excellent seamstress, but she didn't make enough money for us to live on. I'd been working at the window factory full-time since I was sixteen.

"Rosalie," she said, "are you seeing Damien tonight?"

"I don't know, Mama," I said, swallowing the last bite of the hasty supper I'd thrown together after I'd gotten home from work. I grabbed my books and papers for my evening class and got up from the table.

It seemed like I'd been going to night school forever. First to get my general equivalency diploma, since I'd dropped out of high school in order to work. Now I was working toward my college degree in journalism.

I didn't want to have the "when-are-you-going-to-find-a-nice-young-man-and-get-married" conversation with Mama again. I already knew Mama worried about my future. But how many times had I told her that college was the key to my future, not marriage?

"Damien sounds like such a nice boy, Mama mused, easing her tired bulk into a chair. "When are you going to say yes, Rosalie? When are you going to get married? You're not getting any younger, you know."

I kissed her cheek as I headed out the back door. "I'll cross that bridge if Damien ever proposes, Mama," I called out to her as I hurried down the back stairs to the alley.

Damien will never propose, I thought, feeling safe, because for one thing, Damien was the shyest man I'd ever met. For another, we weren't even "dating." Oh, sure, Damien was a sweet guy, but I had no intention of ever saying yes to him, ever. Or saying yes to any other guy, for that matter. I wanted to get my degree so I could get a real job. I didn't intend to work at the factory forever. And like Mama herself always said, I wasn't getting any younger.

I caught the bus and had just enough time to sit and catch my breath before I got off at the university. I loved taking classes, and the atmosphere on campus filled me with such hope. Everything would be perfect if I hadn't made the mistake of telling Mama about Damien, I thought.

I'd met him in my creative writing class in September. Of all the students, Damien obviously had the most talent. When our professor, Dr. Masten, read our work, Damien's was full of beauty and yearning. Mine was cut and dried like a newspaper article, the way I wanted it.

Then I happened to run into Damien at the Student Union one evening, and we got to talking. We'd been meeting there ever since for coffee and conversation, but you'd think we'd been having a passionate love affair the way Mama carried on when I told her about it.

"So? What did you two talk about?" she always asked excitedly whenever I came home from hanging out with Damien.

I'd thought it safe to tell her about someone I wasn't interested in. Wrong again.

With me not married at the ripe, old age of twenty-four, any man was fair game for Mama. The fact that Damien and I talked about assignments and literature didn't discourage Mama. As far as she was concerned, I'd "found a man."

"Invite him for supper," Mama told me. "I'll make something wonderful and tell him you made it!"

Sure, I wanted to be married someday, but I hadn't even had my own life yet. Working at the factory was not my idea of a life. I'm not saying everybody who worked there was wasting their time It's just that I had all these dreams, you know? And nobody there had anything else they wanted to do, except maybe get drunk or get laid on the weekends. Sure, I'd had plenty of opportunities to do both. I was probably one of the last virgins in the entire world. But I was holding out for love.

As I rushed into the classroom, I saw Damien in his usual seat in the far corner, waiting for me. I'd explained to him that I didn't like sitting so far back, so I waved to him and took my usual place in the front row. A few moments later, he slipped into the chair next to mine.

"Hi," I said. "Did you do the assignment?"

Damien shook his head and looked away. He was always so deathly serious.

He wore his hair very long; it was naturally curly and made him look like a real intellectual. His clothes were always rumpled. He lived alone over his brother's auto-body shop, and I don't know how he stood it there. He'd invited me to visit once, and I'd gone because I'd been curious about how a guy like Damien lived. Big mistake.

Damien had had a perfumed candle burning in a votive on the only table in the place, along with a smoking stick of incense. The freshly made hide-a-bed couch had been like an open invitation to sex. Damien was shy, but he was also very horny. Intellectual or not, men were men.

But his apartment had smelled like motor oil and old tires. Somebody had been pounding out some dents downstairs in the shop, cussing and playing classic rock really loud. I couldn't imagine writing the beautiful stuff that Damien wrote in such a place, and I'd never gone back, even though he'd invited me often.

"Want to go for coffee after class?" Damien asked me as the professor walked in. All the other students got quiet.

I didn't want to spend another evening with Damien—not really. Having coffee with Damien meant that nobody else would sit with us. But I always felt so energized after class, I knew I'd be dying to talk to somebody, even Damien.

"I guess," I said, "but I can't stay long. My mother worries when I'm out late."

Two hours later I was so full of ideas and energy, I talked all the way to the Student Union with Damien walking alongside me, silent as usual.

It had started to snow. With the old-fashioned street lamps glowing along the campus pathways, it was an inspiring sight.

I guess I was aware of how Damien watched me, with this kind of soft awe in his eyes, but I pretended not to notice. I didn't want to encourage Damien; if having coffee with him was leading him on, I sure didn't mean to do it. I just didn't know how to turn him down so I could go sit with others from class.

Damien selected his usual corner table, as far from other people as he could possibly get. I decided not to protest. The Union was half empty at that time of night, anyway, and I did have a lot I wanted to talk about.

We sat, and I talked until my coffee got cold. Damien was actually very easy to talk to, because he seemed to hang on my every word without adding anything of his own. Damien always acted like he thought everything that I said was wonderful. That was a great feeling for me because, deep down, I really wasn't so sure of myself yet.

Finally, I stopped talking long enough to take a deep breath, and I said to him, "So, what do you think?"

Damien just looked at me. I had to wonder if he'd heard a single word I'd said. It was maddening: I was thinking Grand Thoughts; Damien was probably wondering how he could get into my pants.

"You make me crazy when you stare at me like that," I blurted out finally "What are you thinking, Damien? Quick! Empty your head! Don't hold back!"

"You're so full of life," Damien said at once, surprising me by actually doing what I'd asked. "The way your eyes light up . . . the way your lips move . . . I love you. Rosalie."

He said it softly, as if he said that kind of thing every day. But I knew he'd probably never said it before. I believe those words were the most difficult Damien had ever said.

"Well, I I. . . thank you, Damien. You—you're a real sweet guy."

I felt scared suddenly. I didn't want to hurt Damien, but I just didn't have time to get serious. And besides, I wanted to fall madly in love. I wanted to be swept off my feet by some dynamic, hard-hitting reporter with a winning smile who would, so to speak, shove a microphone in my face and yell something like, "Marry me right now on camera, Rosalie! Film at five!"

I looked at Damien and, honestly, he looked like a lost, very hairy puppy. He had beautiful, soulful brown eyes. But he also looked like he could be crushed if a big bug stepped on him. He seemed so sensitive, and I wondered for a moment if I was being fair to him. *I should take him more seriously*, I thought. *He's probably a very nice guy. And I could do worse*. I thought.

Then I shook myself. I didn't want to go soft on Damien. I didn't want to go soft on any man.

"Everything I write," Damien said, his voice quavering like he was scared sick, "is about you, Rosalie. When I look at you—"

I must've gotten this oh-no look on my face, because Damien stopped speaking and looked away.

This is not how I want things to go, I thought. *First the degree. Then an exciting newspaper job. Then the dynamic prime-time reporter sweeping me off my feet--into a kitchen filled with dirty dishes, crying babies, and mountains of laundry.*

Oh, no! Not for me!

I was certain I'd crushed Damien's delicate little heart, but then he seemed to draw new strength from somewhere deep inside. He looked at me very seriously for a moment. Then he dug deep down into his backpack—a backpack, by the way, that looked as if he kept it buried in a dumpster most of the time—and pulled out a small, cube-shaped box wrapped in rumpled gold foil paper with a tiny, matching gold-foil, star-shaped bow on top. The whole thing looked a little squashed.

Oh, no, I thought. *Oh, no!*

Damien placed the box on the table on top of all my notes. All the while I'd been gushing about class, Damien had been working up the courage to present me with this, I realized.

"Oh, Damien," I whispered. "Wh-what have you done?"

Honestly, the way he looked at me, I thought if I did or said the wrong thing, he'd do something drastic. Never write again. Become a drunk. Jump off a bridge. Who knew?

His heart is in his eyes. I thought. *But this isn't, fair! I don't want to be the keeper of your feelings, Damien! I don't want to be engaged!*

"Please," Damien said softly. "Just open it."

What on earth am I going to do? I wondered as I gently peeled open the wrapping paper. The gift looked like it'd been opened before. *He probably wrapped it himself,* I thought.

I lifted the lid. There was a dark blue velvet, hinged jewelry box inside. I shook it out and opened it—and stared at a tiny diamond engagement ring nestled on the plush cushion inside.

"Oh—oh, Damien," I said with a sigh, choking back the lump in my throat, "it's—it's very pretty. Very sweet."

"Do you want to?" Damien asked *me* gently.

"Want to what?" I said like a moron. "Does—does this mean what I think it means?"

"It can mean whatever you want it to."

The way he ducked his head, I thought to myself *Jeez, he's acting like a ten-year-old.* But I wasn't going to talk in riddles with him. I decided.

"To me, an engagement ring means two people are engaged to be married," I said.

"Yeah," he said, nodding. "Me, too." He looked at me with those big, brown eyes.

I wanted to feel happy. I tried to feel flattered. But what I really felt—and I felt guilty for feeling it—was annoyed. Damien was laying something heavy on me that was completely unexpected, and completely unwelcome. And yet, I suddenly felt obligated to him, as if now, I had to rearrange my life around what *he* wanted. That made me mad.

Luckily, I didn't let my feelings show.

"Damien, the thing is—to me, two people who get engaged should know each other a long time and . . . and . ." I didn't know how to say, two people should be madly in love, not mildly in like.

Because I liked Damien just fine, but *no way* was I in love with him. No way could I imagine spending the rest of my life with him—not even to please Mama.

Why does this always happen to me? I wondered. Why was I always in situations where people expected things of me—like Mama, or people at work, or friends, or Damien? I didn't know how to tell them that I couldn't deliver.

I took a deep breath. If I said the wrong thing, I'd ruin Damien's life; I was sure of it. *It's time for tactful honesty and gentle truth,* I told myself.

What came out of my mouth was a cowardly effort to avoid both.

"I . . . I think you should meet my mother first," I said.

The moment the words were out of my mouth, I was sorry. I'd been thinking *He'll realize how momentous being engaged is. He'll meet Mama and get a bellyful of her expectations, and he'll back off.*

But Damien brightened. Then he smiled. He sat up straighter, and I thought, *Wow! Look at what I can do for him!* It gave me this amazing feeling of power and self-worth to think I could make someone look so happy.

"When?" he asked breathlessly. "When can I meet your mother?"

I squirmed. "Sunday?"

Oh, no, I thought. I was getting in deeper by the minute!

Damien got up. He looked like he couldn't think of what to do next. He stuffed all his papers into his already stuffed backpack. I had to wonder what he had in there. Everything he'd ever written in his life, probably.

Then he looked down at me, his face beaming. I felt like a worm. *Now I really am leading him on,* I thought. I could tell he thought I really was seriously considering his proposal; I could see it in his eyes.

He came over to me and bent to kiss my cheek. I felt awkward; almost like I wanted to turn away. But somehow, his lips found mine, and he kissed me quickly.

No fireworks.

I felt like such a coward. But I didn't move. I couldn't be responsible for ruining a sensitive man's life. And Mama would be so deliriously happy. *What's the harm?* I thought. In time, I'd find some way to tell Damien I didn't really love him.

Damien left the Union looking like he'd won the lottery. I looked down at the ring box in my hand and thought, *How did I ever get into this mess?*

And how do I get out of it?

When I got home that night, I didn't tell Mama that I'd invited Damien to dinner on Sunday. I couldn't. She'd be in such a tizzy, I wouldn't be able to think straight watching her get ready. Oh, well, I guess it was natural for a seamstress who'd sewn bridal gowns all day for twenty-five years to think marriage was the answer to any woman's dreams.

Except mine.

I lay awake for hours that night, trying to figure out how I'd gone from mildly "in like," to virtual engagement with Mr. Damien Larchmont.

He'd dropped one of his poems earlier on his way out of the Student Union. A girl had brought it over to me as I'd sat staring at my cold coffee after he left. Now the poem was tucked into my notebook. I was afraid to look at it, afraid to see Damien's raw feelings for me written on paper.

I overslept the next morning. Mama was already at the sewing machine as I kissed her cheek and dashed for the door. I was going to miss the bus; I was sure of it.

"Did you see Damien last night?" Mama called out to me. "When are you going to invite him over for dinner?"

I paused on the landing. "Sunday," I called back to her. Then I dashed down the stairs; I didn't want to explain. There wasn't time.

For a little while, I was able to forget about Damien that day. There was this guy Andy, at work. I'd been avoiding him forever. too. But he was at the door that day as I dashed in through the employee entrance at the factory. Andy was one of those let's-get-drunk-and-get-to-know-each-other-in-bed types.

He always had a naughty smile for me. As it was, I could have reported him for sexual harassment for all the things he'd said to me over the years, but he was really just a harmless jerk. He was married and had half a dozen kids. That morning, though, he wiggled his tongue at me, and I decided not to put up with him anymore. I went off on him.

"Back off, Andy!" I snapped as I hurried to my station on the line. "You're a jerk! I wouldn't do you if I were dead!"

Andy only snickered at me with his buddies.

I brooded all day. How come I could speak my mind to a creep like Andy, but I couldn't tell a nice guy like Damien the truth?

Then, when I got home that night, Mama was all questions.

"You invited him here for dinner on Sunday, Rosalie? For heaven's sake, why didn't you wake me last night? Tell me *everything!*"

"There's nothing to tell, Mama," I said with a groan. "We were just talking, and I decided to invite him. Damien's so skinny, anyway; he looks like he could stand a good meal."

Mama scowled disapproval at me. "Rosalie, why would you keep this from me? You know how much I worry!"

Mama opened her hand, and nestled there in her plump little palm was the blue velvet jewelry box with the little engagement ring inside of it. In my haste to get ready for work that morning, I had taken it out of my purse and left it in plain sight on my dresser!

"Mama—it doesn't mean anything," I hastened to explain. "Damien's just . . .well, you'll understand what I mean when you meet him. I—I don't love him, Mama. That's why I have this ring—because I didn't know how to give it back to him without hurting him." I looked at her, pleadingly. "How do I tell the truth without ruining his life, Mama?"

Even Mama didn't know what to say about that. She looked so disappointed, I could hardly bear it.

"I want to make a beautiful wedding gown for you, Rosalie," she said finally in a soft, wistful voice. "I've had the money set aside for years, ever since you had to go to work to help make ends meet around here. Sometimes it was just a dollar a week, but...I want to see you walk down the aisle, my darling—more than anything in the world..."

She started to cry.

I threw my arms around her.

I started crying, too.

"I will, Mama. Someday, I'll marry a wonderful guy and walk down the aisle in the most beautiful dress you've ever made!"

Mama drew away from me for a moment and looked up at me with tears shimmering in her beautiful, dark eyes. "Is he a nice boy?" she asked softly. "This Damien—is he a good boy?"

"He seems to be," I said, letting her go. "But you know, I have a strange feeling about him. I mean, I've never even held his hand, much less kissed him, Mama. So where did he ever get the idea that I would marry him? Doesn't it seem a little sudden to you—a little odd? You don't want me to make a mistake, do you. Mama? After all, you've said yourself a thousand times that you should've known better than to marry Daddy."

Mama shook her head. "I know, Rosalie, I know. He drank so much," she said, shaking her head sadly.

She wiped her eyes and looked away, probably remembering the terrible time before Daddy's heart attack. Years of drinking had left him too weak to recover. I never could decide which was worse: being poor because Daddy wasted so much money on booze, or being poor because he was dead and gone.

I saw Damien in class that week and gave him my home address.

He kept looking at me expectantly, like I was supposed to say or do something special, or like he wanted to ask me something. What he wanted or needed, I had no idea.

I had the jewelry box in my purse. I itched to give it back to him and call off dinner on Sunday. But it seemed easier to just go along torturing myself than to tell the truth and crush Damien.

That Sunday, Damien showed up at our home looking no different than he usually did. Long hair curling past his shoulders. Rumpled clothes. Dirty backpack.

"Mama, I'd like you to meet Damien Larchmont. Damien, this is my mother, Rose Genovese."

Mama was more than a little shocked at the sight of him. Damien could hardly look her in the face.

Damien sat on the couch, looking around our living room. There was the sewing machine set up under the window so that Mama could look out on the seasons changing as she worked year after year. There was the clothes rack brimming with gowns in garment bags. There was the bookcase filled to the top with folded fabric and sewing supplies.

Mama whispered to me in the kitchen: "I was imagining a clean-cut boy."

I chuckled. "I know, Mama, but this is the Nineties."

Mama loved all those romantic movies from the Forties and Fifties. She'd probably been imagining Pat Boone or Tab Hunter. I admit I loved those movies, too, but I liked Elvis much better.

We didn't have a dining room, just the table in the kitchen. As I was setting three places, I kept thinking about my creative writing class. I hadn't had time to finish my latest assignment. Thinking about Damien and what to do about him was taking up all my time and energy. I knew it was wrong of me to lead him on, letting him think I was introducing him to Mama because we were engaged, when in fact I was hoping somehow to discourage him!

Watching Mama put the finishing touches on a meal fit for Thanksgiving, I thought about how happy it would make her to see me walk down the aisle. But wouldn't it be even *more* wonderful to see me walking down the aisle to accept my diploma? Wouldn't it be wonderful to see me get my dream job?

I could always change colleges if I didn't like the one I was going to. And I could always get a different job. But marriage? To me, marriage was for life. Being engaged should feel natural, and wonderful, and right. Getting married wasn't just an excuse for wearing a pretty white dress.

We ate dinner in our crowded little kitchen. Mama made every effort to draw Damien into conversation, but he looked uneasy and uncomfortable the whole time. *Maybe I won't have to let him down easy*, I thought, with rising hope. Maybe he'd ask for the ring back and disappear from my life that very day.

No such luck.

"Walk with me to the bus stop, Rosalie?" Damien asked when Mama asked if he could stay a while to talk. "I have to be getting back," he told her.

"I'll get my coat," I said.

I put the jewelry box in my pocket and went down to the corner with him. We stood there, waiting for the bus, not saying anything. My heart was pounding. I didn't know how—or where—to begin.

Should I just stand there on the sidewalk with the snow coming down and hand the box back to him? Should I wait until his bus was pulling up to the curb so there wouldn't be any time for him to protest? Should I wait until next week, or the week after, or the week after that?

The semester would end eventually. And I had work to do. I couldn't be in torment all the time, trying to work at the factory all day and study all night—worrying about Damien, too.

"Damien," I said finally. I was sure I could hear the bus coming.

"Thanks for inviting me today," Damien said, as if he sensed what I was going to say and wanted to stall me. "I can see what a hardworking person your mother is. Now I understand why you work so hard, too. You want so desperately to get away from her and your miserable life there—"

"Now, wait a minute!" I blurted out, glaring at him. That was about the last thing on my mind, and certainly the last thing I'd ever expected him to say.

"I love my mother!" I said rather loudly. "I don't wish I could get away from her! I get along with her just fine, Damien, and I don't have a miserable life! I've got a good job, and I'm doing very well in school—I'm going to be a reporter someday soon!"

He stared at me with those big brown eyes.

Oh, no, I thought. *I've gone and used that tone on him that tone that other guys have told me makes me sound hard-bitten and ambitious. So? What's wrong with being ambitious?* I usually said right back.

"Damien—" I said before he could think of something more to say that would make me feel angry, guilty, and obligated.

I pulled the blue velvet box from my coat pocket and forced myself to watch his face go white.

"Damien, I'm not ready for this," I said, as gently as I knew how.

"But---"

"I thought that by inviting you over today, you'd see just what you saw—that Mama and I work very hard—that we have plans and dreams and. . . ."

It was coming out all wrong. *I sound selfish,* I thought.

I pressed the blue velvet box into his hands. "Before you give a ring, Damien, you should—we should—" I shook my head. "—It was too soon, Damien." *No, that's not right, either,* I thought. *That still gives him room for hope.* I wanted him to understand very clearly that we were only ever going to be friends.

"I don't want to be engaged, Damien," I said finally. "It's been nice, talking with you after class each week, but. . .

The bus was only two blocks away; Damien looked so unhappy. He was shaking his head. Suddenly, he stepped closer and touched my cheek with his fingertips; he was trembling. I felt so awful for him.

"Rosalie, please . . ."

I got a creepy feeling then, kind of like what was happening wasn't even real. Damien looked so distraught. And I kept thinking: *He doesn't even know me. How can he feel this strongly for me?*

And that's when I got a little scared. I thought: *What if he's nuts or something?* I stepped back. The bus arrived at the curb and the door opened.

Something came over me then. Anger, I guess. It just didn't seem fair that I should be embroiled like this in some weird kind of relationship with a guy I hardly knew. After all, what had I really done to deserve all this—any of it?

"Get on the bus, Damien," I said suddenly, as if he were a child. "I can't see you anymore."

And I turned away.

No, no, no, I kept thinking. *This is turning out all wrong. I'm hurting him.* It was easier to hurt myself than hurt people I cared about. And I did care about Damien, a little.

But I didn't look back. Something inside was telling me this thing with Damien was all wrong. *If I shut off that little voice inside,* I thought, *I'll have to silence it for the rest of my life.*

I started down the sidewalk so fast, I slipped a couple of times on the ice. I heard the bus pull away. I felt so guilty, I almost couldn't stand it. I felt like I'd just killed Damien.

I even cried a little. I didn't like thinking I was a selfish person, but I just couldn't sacrifice what I wanted to please someone else. And I had a right to the life I wanted; that was the one thing I was sure of.

When I got back to the apartment, Mama was already washing the dishes.

"I'll do that, Mama," I said, a little more harshly than I should have. When she turned to look at me, Mama looked very sad.

"I'm so sorry, Marna," I said, feeling like I'd really betrayed her somehow. "I- I gave the ring back. I want very much to make you happy, but I think Damien is a bit weird. I just can't—" I burst into tears. "—I feel so terrible, Mama!"

She took me into her arms and let me cry. After a moment, she asked me, "Did you love him a little?"

I drew away and met her gaze. "No, Mama. But I feel so—so *scared!* I feel like when. . ."

Oh, I hated to bring up bad times from the past. But I could see that Mama just didn't understand. She didn't always realize just how intense my desire to better myself was.

"Mama, I feel like I did those times when Daddy would be out drinking, and I'd think, he's going to get in a fight, or get hit by a bus, or. . ."

Mama put her arms around me. "I know," she said. "I used to think if I told him how I hated the booze, I'd kill him. Kill him with words. Then, when he died, I was sure it was my fault anyway."

"But it wasn't," I said.

"No, but I thought it was." Mama straightened and looked at me proudly.

"You did the right thing today, Rosalie, I want you to know this. This Damien wasn't the one for you, and I'm sorry I made you think you have to marry the first man who comes along just to please me. I want you to be happy, Rosalie. Really happy. If you can wait, I can wait," she said with a wonderful smile.

The next week I really dreaded going to class. Because I wanted to enjoy it, I was angry to think that Damien had spoiled it for me. When I arrived, however, he wasn't there. I worried, of course. *It's all my fault,* I thought. *He dropped out on account of me.*

When he wasn't in class the following week, I knew I was going to have to do something or go crazy. So on Saturday, I went over to his brother's garage.

"Is Damien home?" I asked the greasy mechanic banging away in the shop.

"Gone," he yelled over his shoulder.

"When do you think he'll be back? He wasn't in class last week. I wondered if he was sick... or something."

The mechanic straightened up. He looked me over. Then he wiped his face with a shop towel and came up to the door where I stood.

"Listen, you look like a nice girl, so I'll give it to you straight. Damien's not all there, you know what I mean? To be honest with you, I let him live upstairs because I can use the rent money. He sees his doctor once or twice a week, and he behaves himself, but I don't like to think he's inviting girls over. He's been in and out of the hospital since he was fifteen, understand? He's a nice enough guy, but do yourself a favor: Don't get mixed up with him."

I looked at the mechanic, and honestly, I didn't know what to think.

"You're trying to tell me your brother's crazy?" I said finally.

He gave me a strange look. "Brother? Damien's no brother of mine. His parents pay his rent—I don't even know what he does all day. Heck, I didn't even know he was taking classes at the university until he told me about you." He gave me another look. "You really studying to be a lawyer?"

"Huh?" I said.

He shrugged. "Okay, so you're not going to be a lawyer. Damien makes things up," he said. Then he laughed. "For the first year he lived upstairs, I thought he really was a writer—I mean, the guy told me he was famous." He shrugged again.

"Hey, what do I know? I don't read much." I stammered out some kind of thank you and wandered back to the bus stop in a daze. I was surprised, upset, scared—and angry. I'd been worrying myself sick over some poor guy who—

Who what?

Was Damien really the nutcase I'd sensed he was?

I didn't know what to think. So I went home. I didn't tell Mama anything about what the mechanic had told me. After all, maybe the mechanic had lied to me. How was I to know?

Then I saw that rumpled gold foil lying on my dresser—the wrapping that had held the engagement ring. I looked it over and thought, *Yeah, it does look kind of old.* What if Damien had given that ring to other girls like me, softhearted girls who'd tried to be nice to him?

Because that's when I really admitted to myself that Damien really was just a very strange young man. I was sorely tempted to go to the dean to inquire about him, but I didn't really think I had any right to do that.

When I went to class that week, I was startled to see Damien in his usual seat in the back. I felt scared, suddenly. I'd thought it was over between us. What if it started up again?

I didn't wave to him. I just looked over at him once or twice, wondering. Damien didn't join me like he had in the past. In fact, he didn't even seem to know I was there. The professor read a few of the better assignments that had been turned in earlier, and of course, Damien's was first. *He has such talent,* I thought.

After class, I argued with myself about whether or not to talk to Damien. I had worried about him so much, I really did feel like I'd become his friend, in a way.

But Damien went off with another girl! A real mousy-looking girl with bad skin. I was blown away!

I sat at my desk a long time, trying to sort out my feelings. Finally, the professor saw me still sitting there and came over to me and asked, "Is there something you wanted to talk about, Rosalie?"

I looked up at him, blushing. "No," I said. "I—I was just trying to figure something out."

He went back to his lectern and started gathering up his papers. "Oh," he said, holding up a thick manuscript, "would you mind giving this to Damien when you see him? I've seen the two of you together at the Union. Damien wrote this, and he asked me to read it. It's quite good, of course, but . . . Perhaps you could tell him to submit more current work to this class. I don't have time to evaluate work he wrote in high school."

"Sure," I said, not understanding what he meant.

As I went outside, I took the manuscript out of my bag and looked it over. The handwriting looked like Damien's; the paper was yellowed, but the quality of the writing seemed up to his usual standards.

Feeling a little strange, I pulled out the poem I remembered was in my notebook, the one Damien had dropped and the girl had given to me a few weeks before in the Union. The paper was the same yellowed color, and just as dog-eared as the manuscript.

Did it mean he'd written all this stuff over seven years ago? Just how many girls had he met over the years and used these poems on?

Suddenly, it all just sort of dawned on me. Damien's sad eyes and soft sighs were all an act! I was willing to bet he invited every girl he met over to his place in the hopes of having sex with them. He'd probably even offered that same, lousy engagement ring over and over and over—that was why the wrapping paper looked so rumpled. After each girl gave the ring back, Damien just wrapped it up again and found himself a new love.

Damien had never really loved me, I realized. He'd just wanted to love—and be loved—by *somebody*.

How sad, I thought.

How completely pathetic.

I hurried over to the Student Union, unsure of what I would do if Damien were there. He was, sitting in a far corner with that mousy girl with the bad skin. She was reading him something—one of her own poems, probably.

I didn't exactly feel used, and I didn't exactly feel tricked. I just felt kind of stupid for worrying so much about a nutty guy who'd tried everything he could think of to have a relationship with me—with anybody, really.

I felt sorry for Damien, but that didn't mean I had to be responsible for him for the rest of my life.

Damien noticed me then. His eyes were cold.

I met his gaze and went over to where they sat and said a casual, cautious hello. "Are you all right, Damien?" I asked him. "You missed two classes."

He looked at me with a kind of blank expression. Where was all that desperate love he'd felt for me two weeks before?

"I'm okay," he said finally in a coolly glum voice.

I reached into my bag and pulled out the manuscript our professor had given me, handing it to him. "Dr. Masten asked me to give this to you." I reached back into my bag and handed him the poem, too. "You dropped this a couple weeks ago; I forgot I had it. You know, you're a really good writer, Damien. I hope you keep up with it."

"Thanks," he said, as he tucked the papers into his backpack.

I wanted to say more. I had a million questions. I wanted to ask when he'd written the stuff. Maybe he'd never even written any of it at all, I realized. Maybe he'd found all of it in the trash, along with that filthy backpack.

I looked at him for a long time, wondering. The girl looked worried, like I was going to take Damien away from her. Damien had turned his back to her, and he had that soft look of awe on his face as he stared at me. I was tempted to warn her, but who was I to intervene? Maybe they were meant for each other.

I waved good-bye and walked away, back into my own life.

I guess I'll always have a soft spot in my heart for long-haired guys who look like lost puppies, or anybody who needs something from me, like Mama. But I have a responsibility to myself, too. I'm the only one I really have to answer to, and my only obligation is to myself, to protect myself. I realize that now more than ever. Just because a guy says he loves me doesn't mean I owe him my life.

When the term ended, I took my A in creative writing and moved on. I've never seen Damien since.

But I think about him sometimes. And I wonder…THE END

Ron Hogan co-founded Lady Jane's Salon, a monthly reading series dedicated to romance fiction, and has been its primary host since 2009. He's also produced literary events throughout New York City, and was one of the first people to launch a book-related website, Beatrice.com. In addition to digging through the TruLoveStories archives for great stories, he publishes a digital magazine (also called Beatrice!) of interviews with some of today's best writers.